Warlord

KEITH MCARDLE

Copyright © Keith McArdle 2019

The right of Keith McArdle to be identified as the author of this work has been asserted by him in accordance with the Copyright Amendment (Moral Rights) Act 2000.

This work is copyright. Apart from any use as permitted under the Copyright Act 1968, no part may be reproduced, copied, scanned, stored in a retrieval system, recorded, or transmitted, in any form or by any means, without the prior written permission of the author.

This is a work of fiction. Names, characters, places and incidents are products of the author's imagination or are used fictitiously. Any resemblance to actual events or persons living or dead, is entirely coincidental.

Map designed by Simone McArdle of Art By Simi.

Cover design by Pen Astridge of The Mighty Pen.

Edited by Tim Marquitz of Dominion Editorial.

All rights reserved.

ISBN-13: 978-0-9925657-6-3

A catalogue record for this book is available from the National Library of Australia

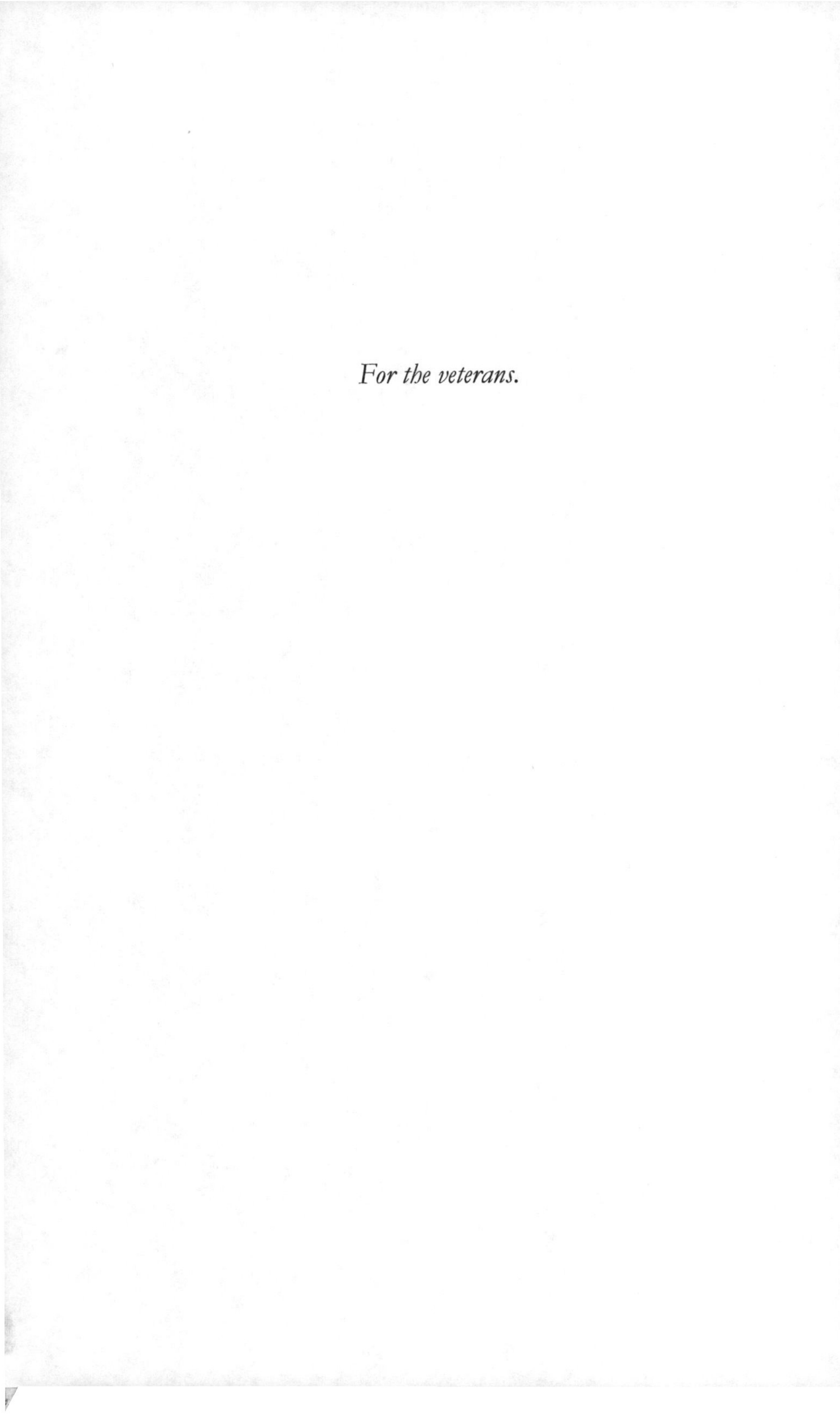

For the veterans.

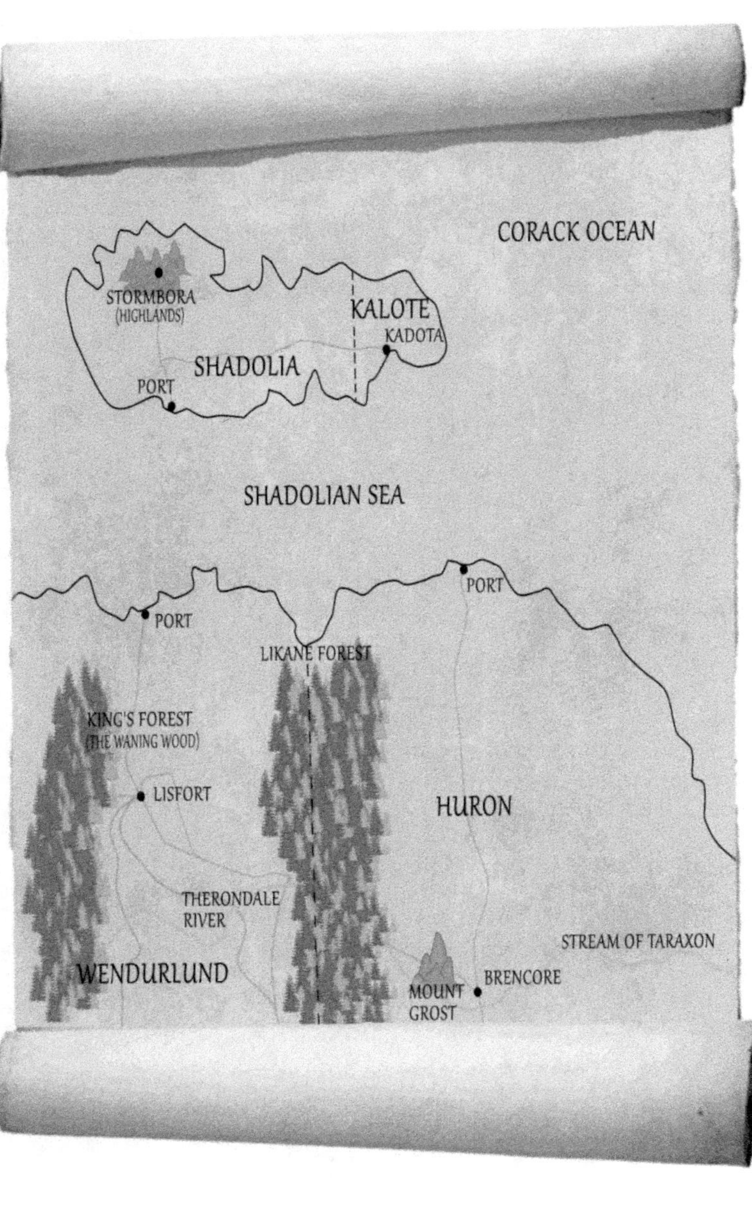

CORACK OCEAN
STORMBORA
(HIGHLANDS)
KALOTE
KADOTA
SHADOLIA
PORT
SHADOLIAN SEA
PORT
PORT
LIKANE FOREST
KING'S FOREST
(THE WANING WOOD)
HURON
LISFORT
THERONDALE
RIVER
STREAM OF TARAXON
WENDURLUND
BRENCORE
MOUNT
GROST

Part I

Evading Death

I

Thick vines wrapped around wide trunks, climbing up their host until they reached the dense canopy in search of the sunlight they desperately craved. Some trees with which Baras was unfamiliar were in bloom, bright yellow flowers, interspersed with red, a stark contrast against the green mash of the Huronian forest.

"Sir!"

The voice broke his reverie. He returned his attention to the single file of mounted King's Own warriors arrayed before him. The formation snaked through the woodland, moving at a fast trot towards their distant homeland. With their prince rescued from the enemy and securely positioned in the centre, their mission was complete. He caught movement in his peripheral vision, and a soldier slowed his horse from a gallop to match Baras's steady trot.

"What is it?"

"Sir, enemy follow up."

Gods, I'm a bugler, not a commander. Damn Rone for leaving me in charge. Guilt swept him immediately as his thoughts turned to Rone, who'd ridden back towards tens of thousands of enemies simply to retrieve the body of one of his soldiers.

Baras nodded. "Numbers?"

"At least a couple of hundred. Huronian cavalry, sir."

He suppressed a curse. "Ride to the head of the formation, bring it to a halt. Summon Dreas to me."

"Aye, sir!"

The man's horse snorted and obliged its rider's command, accelerating into a headlong gallop.

Baras felt a tap on his shoulder and flinched. *I'd*

forgotten about the assassin!

"This is my stop," the assassin spoke into his ear.

He twisted in the saddle and focused on the highlander. The man held his stare, that one blue eye skewering Baras's soul.

"What do you mean, highlander?"

"My horse is tethered a few hundred paces that way." He gestured to the right of the column. "You didn't think I walked all this way, did you?"

"If you wait, we'll be coming to a halt."

"I'll be fine, Baras." The highlander vaulted from the horse and landed with a lithe agility that belied his powerful stature. The assassin smiled. Then he disappeared behind a stand of close-cropped trees.

Baras faced front again. *Bloody madman.*

The formation slowed and came to a stop, aside from two mounted warriors galloping along its length. They skidded to a halt beside Baras.

Baras pointed at the first. "Return to your post, lad."

"Aye, sir."

As the dull thuds of the departing horse drifted into silence, Baras appraised Dreas, the third most senior soldier.

"We have an enemy follow up."

The man continued to glare at him as if willing the bugler to tell him something more interesting.

"We will ambush them."

The corners of Dreas's mouth creased upward slightly.

"I'll take fifty soldiers and setup an immediate ambush here. I want you to take another fifty and push back the way we came. You'll be the cut off party."

Dreas touched his forehead with an index finger. "I

can do that, sir."

Baras was about to speak again, but movement through the nearby forest to their flank stayed his tongue. Dreas leaned forward in his saddle with lack of speed and pulled free his musket.

Soldiers close by brought the butts of muskets or blunderbusses into their shoulder, stared down iron sights, and waited.

The highland assassin, mounted on a black mare, walked into view.

Baras held up his hand. "Hold your fire."

"Lucky boy," Dreas muttered, sheathing his musket.

The horse was astonishing. She was tall and powerful, her silver mane and tail such a glaring difference to her dark fur.

"Nice horse."

The assassin reined in beside him, Baras's war horse sniffing the nose of the highlander's mount. "I suggest I take the prince and make a break for Lisfort while we still can."

"I had the same thought, highlander."

"Vyder."

Baras committed the name to memory and threw a glance in the direction of the emaciated royal mounted nearby. "Agreed, Vyder."

"Then let us get it done. Time is no longer an option we have."

"Keep him fed, keep him safe, and get him home. We shall fight a rear guard."

"We go now. We go *right now!*" the voice of the Kalote woman cut through the forest.

The bugler noticed the woman with smoke coloured skin glaring at him through narrowed eyes.

"Aye, get you gone. Ride fast. Tell the king of what approaches his keep."

"We shall do that, Baras. Fight well." The assassin nudged his horse past, and then he was gone, the mount of the Kalote woman cantering beside him.

* * *

Baras positioned his men off the rudimentary track they had been traversing. The fifty mounted King's Own warriors were spread out in extended line, hidden behind thick shrubs, or mighty trees, their horses waiting in silent patience as if anticipating what was about to take place.

He'd ordered his warriors to engage with blunderbuss. Shards of ice speared his spine. The thunder of galloping hooves and occasional shouts or laughter pervaded the woodland in which he and the men of the King's Own waited. The incessant *thudding* grew in volume until the gentle whisper of wind teasing the forest canopy was drowned out. Birds took to wing, shrieking their warnings to one another.

Pushing his mount forward a step, Baras leaned in his saddle beyond the thick, tall shrub so as to see the track with better clarity. The Huronian cavalry burst into view. They were urging their mounts on hard, the horses winded, coats sleek with sweat. *They can't hold that pace for long.* He allowed the first few to pass his position. When twenty or thirty had streaked past in fast order, Baras lifted the bugle to his lips and blew the command.

Fire.

The blunderbusses spoke in deafening unison. *Boom!*

Men and animals both screamed in pain and fear.

Soldiers were bucked from their saddles, horses fell to the ground to lie beside their human counterparts, blood oozing from mortal wounds.

The bugle screeched again. *Move right!*

Baras swung his horse to the right and cantered parallel to the killing ground. He reined the animal to a stop, the bugle's cold kiss touching his lips.

Halt! Face left! Fire!

A moment later, the blunderbusses roared back to life, casting thick, grey smoke to drift across the woodlands. More confused cavalrymen bore the brunt of the onslaught, falling lifeless from their horses. The screaming and shouting increased in both volume and urgency until the remaining cavalry turned and retreated along their axis of advance.

The bugle's call cut through the noise. *Charge!*

"OBRAGARDA!" the word, erupting from fifty King's Own throats, echoed around the forest, and the warriors urged their horses into a gallop, spears clasped in their hands where moments before blunderbusses had been brandished.

Baras may not have carried flintlock weapons, but he could wield a spear along with the finest of the warriors. The smooth, wood was cold comfort in his hand, sharp spearhead flashing in the light as he held the weapon out before him. When his horse had reached full gallop, he was amongst the retreating enemy soldiers. One of them cast a look over his shoulder, eyes bulging. Baras's spear slammed home just right of the man's spine.

The haft was almost ripped clear of his fingers, but Baras kept tight grip. He stood in the stirrups, twisted the spear, and jerked it free. The enemy soldier slumped forward in his saddle, screeching, although his cries of agony were drowned out by those of his comrades as the small force of King's Own battered through their ranks.

The King's Own could fight on any ground or in any weather, on horseback or foot. But cavalry was only ever agile enough to engage an enemy on an open plain. A fact Baras's soldiers were exploiting with devastating effect. The bugler urged his mount into a gallop once more, brought the spear to bear, and plunged the blood-soaked tip into the back of another soldier. The weapon slid in deep.

Bright blood exploded from the wound, and the man straightened in his saddle. Clenching his teeth, Baras pulled the weapon free and watched the enemy fall from the saddle. The cavalryman slammed onto the ground with a sickening *thud*, the body rolled several times before the trunk of a tree arrested its momentum. Baras swept past the corpse, surrounded by his comrades, heavy on the heels of their fleeing prey.

Sheathing the spear into the leather holster forward of his right knee, Baras lifted the bugle to his mouth and blew a command.

Disperse right.

The tiny King's Own formation obliged, thundering off the track, horses dodging trees or leaping clean over bushes.

About turn! Blunderbuss.

The horses regained their breath, some snorting, other stamping hooves upon the leaf litter. The twenty or thirty enemy soldiers Baras had allowed to gallop past prior to triggering the ambush came into view along the track. They were hesitant, trotting after their retreating counterparts. The eyes of the man leading the group were the size of saucers, his focus glued to the forest immediately before him.

Baras's lips nestled around the bugle.

Fire!

The throats of fifty blunderbusses spewed death upon the enemy. *Boom!*

Charge!

"OBRAGARDA!"

The warriors of the King's Own were amongst the enemy like a bolt of lightning, hitting them with the same force. One Huronian cavalryman was lucky enough to gallop clear before Baras called off his soldiers. He lifted the bugle to his mouth.

Enemy withdrawing to you!

The instrument's piercing voice echoed to silence and remained unanswered. Beyond the gentle ringing in his ears, Baras listened to the soft breeze gliding through the canopy high above. The high-pitched din echoing through his skull would disperse over the following hours. *Always happens after I'm near muskets or blunderbusses firing.* He shoved a finger into his ear and twisted it backward and forward with little effect.

A single, distant blunderbuss echoed through the forest. Fleeting moments passed before a group of blunderbusses echoed the bellow of the first, *boom*. The screams of dying men started again. Dreas's cut off party would make short work of the survivors. Another volley of blunderbusses sang their lethal chorus, followed by The King's Own war cry. The single word sliced the forest, and the muffled clash of steel on steel rose above the soft, high-pitched noise bouncing around Baras's skull.

* * *

Ahitika pushed the chest-high fern out of her way

in one slow, fluid movement. She placed a moccasin enshrouded foot forward and stepped past the plant, allowing the fronds to return to their original position behind her. Even though night's blanket covered the woodland, the small, grey ball remained still and silent perhaps ten paces in front of her. The rabbit was scratching amongst the leaf litter with gentle practise, searching for fresh shoots. The warrior stood still, brought up the arrow-nocked bow, and drew back the string. The cord touched the flesh of her cheek, the aroma of animal fat drifted to her. She rubbed it into the bowstring to keep it supple and strong.

She exhaled and released the arrow. *Hiss, thud.* Ahitika strode forward and knelt beside the dead rabbit. She touched the fur of the animal, smeared blood upon her forehead, and then leaned back to look at the stars interspersed between the forest's canopy.

"Thank you for giving your life this night, so that we might live."

She butchered the rabbit with expert skill, skinned it, then buried what she did not take with her. She strolled back to the camp, the smell of the smoke drifting to her long before she spotted the dull, orange glow amongst the tree trunks.

Ahitika advanced into the clearing and held up the rabbit to the two men sat staring into the fire.

"That didn't take long," the highlander spoke.

She squatted beside the scrawny one named Henry. "Hungry?"

The malnourished man brushed hair out of his face, his eyes meeting her questioning stare. "No, I don't feel hungry."

"You eat."

"Ahitika, I don't think I–"

"You *eat*! Long journey, fast journey. Not much rest."

Vyder leaned forward, picked up a twig, and flicked it into the fire. "She's right you know, Henry. You have to keep up your strength."

The suggestion attracted no response.

She skewered the rabbit onto a stick, held it out over the fire with one hand, and tapped her chest with the other. "I cook." She pointed at the living skeleton. "Then you eat."

When the food was ready, they ate in silence. She enjoyed the taste but cast furtive glances at the skinny one, ensuring he continued to chew on the meal. Although the bones of his chest, shoulders, and back were visible beneath his skin, it was clear to Ahitika he had once been powerful. *And might be again.* She watched his face, the flames reflected in those ocean blue eyes. *Handsome too.* She looked away, tore a chunk of meat off the bone with her teeth, and grinned.

She ate her fill and held the remnants out to Henry. "You eat rest of this."

He shook his head, long, matted hair hiding his face. "I can't. I'm full."

She held the small portion of meat closer to his face. "You eat now."

Vyder's soft chuckle mingled with the crackle of the fire. "You're not going to have a win, Henry."

The prince flicked dirty hair out of his vision and fixed his gaze upon the Kalote warrior. Even in the dull light thrown by the flames, she enjoyed those piercing, blue eyes. His brow softened, slight wrinkles adorning the corners of his eyes, hinting at the smile beneath the thick beard hiding his mouth.

"Thank you."

He took the proffered food.

Definitely handsome. But more so if he didn't smell like a corpse.

She dropped her hand onto her thigh. "Welcome."

The fire drew her attention, flames dancing beneath and upon the wood like living creatures, occasionally spitting embers into the darkness, where the tiny orbs of light drifted in random patterns before blinking out to be consumed by night's shroud.

"You stink," she muttered.

"You know," his words muffled as he chewed on the cooked meat, "where I'm from, you'd have your head removed for talking to me like that."

She prodded the fire with a stick, enjoying the army of sparks exploding skyward. "Where I from, men wash."

A deep rumble echoed over the clearing, and she realised it was coming from Henry. She paused and looked at him. His shoulders were shuddering, and she realised he was laughing. She relaxed and grinned.

"If we stop near stream in future, you wash stench from skin. Yes?"

"Aye, Ahitika."

"And hair." She gestured at him, withdrawing her razor-sharp blade with deft skill. "If we have time, we cut."

He finished his meal. "Right you are."

* * *

Rone lay amongst waist high grass, still and silent. A half-moon cast limited light upon the open plain across which he and his soldiers had charged half a day before. The Huronian Army had marched onward and would be camped elsewhere for the night. *But for these bastards.* He clenched his teeth as anger warmed him. Kneeling up in a slow, deliberate movement, the dark blobs surrounding the corpse of his soldier came into view. They were laughing and chattering amongst themselves, although Rone could not understand their language.

The King's Own officer climbed into a crouch and placed a leg in front of him, allowing his boot to touch the ground heel first. Rotating his foot forward, he ensured there was no branch, twig, or rock in the way to either cause unnecessary noise or push him off balance. When his boot came to rest flat upon the ground in silence, he brought his other foot forward in a similar manner.

He took another pace forward, a third and fourth. Time ebbed past in painful lethargy, but with disciplined persistence, Rone came to a halt several paces behind the closest enemy soldier. The scene was clearer now. The Huronian soldiers, three in number, were facing away from Rone. They crouched over the corpse of his fallen comrade. One of them giggled as he tugged on the boots of the dead man. Another delved into pockets, but he came away empty handed.

He's probably already been looted long before now.

The boot finally ripped free, and the soldier fell backwards onto the ground, his prize clasped in both hands. His laughter bellowed out over the plain. He shouted something in his foreign tongue before sitting up and turning his attention to the second boot.

Rone dropped his hand to his belt and drew a blade without haste, the weapon sliding free of its deer hide sheath in silence. His eyes never left the back of the Huronian tugging upon the boot of his dead comrade.

One of them shouted a string of words, the noise giving Rone his opportunity. The King's Own officer lunged forward and swept one hand around the closest man to clamp upon his forehead. He pulled the man's head back. With his other hand, he plunged the knife into the neck of his enemy under his ear and pushed the razor-sharp blade forward, the weapon bursting through the front of the Huronian's throat, severing both the windpipe and voice box.

A soft hiss of warm air exploded from the terrible wound at the man's throat as he tried to scream, probably in pain or fear, or both. He fell onto his back, both hands clamped to his throat, coughing, gurgling, and choking upon the blood filling his lungs. The pair of Huronian soldiers paused in their chatter, the strange noises of their comrade drawing their attention.

The hilt of the knife was slick with warm, fresh blood. Leaping over the dying man, Rone barged into another soldier, slamming the man to the ground. He straddled him, slashed open his throat, and was on his feet a moment later, running clear of the third Huronian. The remaining man shouted a sentence. Although Rone did not understand the words, the fear was evident in the voice of his enemy. The soldier stood, the dead King's Own warrior lying behind him, long forgotten. He drew his sword and roared another few words in the Huronian language. Rone remained still and silent, lying on his guts, mere paces from his adversary.

With a final, weak spasm of one leg, the first man stopped moving. The second had rolled onto his side and attempted to push himself onto all fours but dropped flat on his face, where all movement slowed and eventually ceased. Rone remained like a statue hidden amongst the tall grass, his focus boring into the final

Huronian who stood close by. The limited light provided by the moon was enough to see the man's chest expanding and contracting in rapid repetition.

He turned away, boots crunching upon the dry grass beneath. He now stood side on to Rone. The terrified soldier was breathing through his mouth, the soft whisper ebbing and flowing, in time with the movement of his chest. He muttered something in Huronian, but Rone was not oblivious to the quiver that accompanied the words.

The soldier moved again, presenting his back to Rone. The King's Own officer exploded to his feet, teeth bared. Before his opponent turned toward the sudden movement behind him, Rone, both hands on the knife, drove the weapon into the soldier's neck with all the strength he could muster. The blade cut through the bones of his spine at the base of his skull, and the Huronian soldier dropped to the ground without a sound. The knife's hilt was ripped free of Rone's grasp before he could withdraw the weapon.

Placing a boot between the shoulder blades of the dead soldier, Rone leaned down and levered the knife clear. The blade finally came free, and he cleaned the metal on the shirt of his deceased adversary. Sheathing the weapon, he stepped over the corpse and knelt beside the body of the King's Own soldier, which the trio had been looting mere moments before. Rone placed a hand upon the cold, dead skin of his forehead.

"Stand down warrior. Rest you in peace," he muttered. Shifting his hand down the dead face, his fingertips told him the man's eyes were still open. He brushed the eyelids closed and held them in place, ensuring they would remain shut when he removed his touch.

Grasping a forearm, he pulled the dead King's Own warrior into a sitting position. He squatted and lifted the corpse onto his shoulders. Rone screwed shut his eyes, jaw clenched. He grunted as the mighty muscles of his legs bulged, protesting against the extra weight, but he stood in one slow, strained movement, and stumbled a step as he lost his balance. Shooting a leg out to stop himself from travelling any further in the wrong direction, he began walking. Shrugging the dead body into a more comfortable position over his shoulders, he cursed. While the corpse may have shifted position slightly, it was no more comfortable.

"Time to go home, lad. Your duty is at an end." The words steeled Rone's resolve, reminding him of why he'd come all this way. His lips clamped together, and he refused to complain any further.

Rone quickened his pace, his determined focus placed several feet in front of him, in an attempt to watch for trip hazards or obstacles in his path. Although the top of the grass brushing past his thigh was easy to see, the light of the dim moon was not powerful enough to pierce deeper. He just had to hope luck was on his side.

He shrugged the body again and persevered, ignoring the ache in his shoulders, the pain in his lower back, and the burning in his legs. Sweat beaded on his forehead, his breathing deepened and increased in speed. Still, he did not slow. The dull *thump-thump* of his boots upon the ground provided his ears a pace to maintain. He sniffed, wiped his brow, and strode onward.

"We shall bury you beside your brothers," he whispered to the corpse lying across his shoulders. "You'll be in the finest company." Rone frowned, eyes narrowing. The dark smear of the tree line was faintly visible, in which was tethered his warhorse. "The finest company in the world."

Vyder sat, leaning against a tree, chewing idly upon a piece of grass. He relaxed, slumber's heavy blanket not far away, although his body ached. It'd been another long day in the saddle, but they'd made good progress. Storm stood nearby, almost invisible in the darkness. His legs were ramrod straight, joints locked in place, head hung low. The powerful animal was dozing. On the far side of Vyder's mount was the King's Own horse. Soft rustling suggested the animal was still awake, searching for pick amongst the forest floor.

His head touched the trunk and the world disappeared behind closed eye lids. Aching muscles relaxed, weary bones rested and a voice called.

"Vyder?"

It was a woman's voice. A familiar voice. He groaned and attempted to reply, but no words came. He was cold. So very cold.

"Vyder!"

The gentle voice was louder. Clearer.

"Vyder, come to me my love."

Verone! He shouted the name in his mind, intending for the word to breech his lips, but silence remained in control.

"Come to me."

He reached out and his fingers touched her hand.

Not yet. Gorgoroth's voice boomed to life in his mind.

His eyes snapped open and the oppressive freezing wind departed, warmth flooding his body. Vyder took a

25

deep breath, fresh cool air filling his lungs. Sadness and fury filled him. Vyder stood and stretched. They were outnumbered and in the middle of nowhere. Perhaps if they were overwhelmed and killed, it would quicken his journey into Verone's arms. Guilt filled him as soon as the thought entered his head.

"Get Henry home first," he muttered.

He touched the dark, charcoal disk beneath his shirt. The pendant was attached to a piece of string around his neck. If they found themselves in dire need and survival looked uncertain, all he need do was strike a spark to the disk and call Agoth's name. The fire spirit would be summoned to them in a matter of moments. Or at least, that's what Agoth had said when they'd last spoken.

It's all you need do, little brother.

Henry had cooked their evening meal, consisting of the boiled roots of a legume Ahitika called Kofat, sprinkled with various herbs and topped off with roast pigeon. As had become her custom, the Kalote woman ensured Henry ate his fill. When he refused to eat more than he was familiar, she forced him to consume another few mouthfuls.

"Help stretch belly," were her words each night.

He spat out a small chunk of grass, placed the thin stalk between his lips again, and recommenced chewing. He rested his head against the trunk, the slight ache in his neck immediately vanishing. The bright orange dance of the campfire drew his attention, and his focus slid to the pair sitting in front of the small blaze. They sat far enough away from each other to remain aloof, but close enough to suggest they were attracted to one another.

One corner of Vyder's mouth creased upward. The Kalote woman had her legs crossed and drawn up to her chest, her arms hugging them. She was talking in soft tones to Henry, the son of the Wendurlund king. The young, skinny man sat, legs stretched out before him, staring into the flames, his face painted with a flickering light, shadows dancing upon his skin. He nodded every now and then and smiled at others. Occasionally, his long, lank hair flicked from his cheeks when he turned to look at her.

A rapid beat filled the encampment. The pair by the fire, however, remained deep in conversation, oblivious to the noise. He stopped chewing, brow creasing. Vyder pulled the grass from his mouth, flicked it away, and reached for his knife. His mouth opened, ready to shout a warning to Henry and Ahitika.

Can you hear her heartbeat? Gorgoroth's silent voice filled his mind, causing him to pause. His tight grip upon the knife hilt relaxed, and he slammed the weapon back into its sheath.

"Aye," he muttered.

Vyder felt one arm descend into numbness, and the limb raised, an index finger pointed towards a section of the forest's star riddled canopy.

There she is.

His vision narrowed to slits, but his eyesight did not improve.

An owl.

"You might have just said that," he whispered.

The silent chuckle pervaded his thoughts.

Shall we fly?

Vyder relaxed again. His hand dropped from the knife sheathed by his side. Heaviness swept him, dragging him down into sleep's kiss, then his stomach lurched into his throat, and he ascended towards the stars. His arms, of their own volition, stretched out either side of him. The cool night air slid over his wings. His eyelids broke apart and, aided by the owl's sharp vision, the forest floor far below came into sharp focus.

They twisted and turned to avoid trees, branches, and vines. With a flick of their wings, they changed direction with sudden power, and Vyder found himself concentrating at a section of the forest floor near a thick bush. He squinted, and the mouse scavenging through the leaf litter came into sharper focus. The tiny creature used its front paws to bring a nut to its mouth.

Are you controlling the bird, Vyder?

No. Not yet, at least.

The wings snapped closed against their body, and they plummeted straight toward their target. Vyder's stomach lurched again. Cool air blasted his ears. The surrounding forest blurred past in dark hues of grey, dark brown, and black. The mouse paused, stopped chewing, and listened. It pushed itself up onto its hind legs and sniffed the air. They ripped beyond the trunk of a tree with no more than a finger's breadth of room, and the mouse was now only moments from becoming dinner.

The animal dropped to all fours and scampered beneath the bush, disappearing from view. Their wings opened, arresting their speed, and they turned away. Powerful muscles drove the wings, and they ascended towards the forest canopy again. Each flap brought a whisper of sound. Vyder felt himself twist so that the right wing pointed towards the ground, and the left at the night sky.

Now I have control.

They dodged through gaps between the boughs of mighty birches, oaks, and pines, to rise above the forest so that only the open night surrounded them. They flew at speed, light from a half-moon casting a dull silver blanket upon the seemingly impenetrable forest canopy sliding below. Vyder smiled, a sense of freedom pervading him. They flew for what seemed like an age, although Vyder could not be sure of the exact amount of time.

We are here.

We are where, exactly?

Here, human, that is all you need to know.

They descended towards the forest, piercing the canopy, the sprawling floor of the forest coming back into view. Spreading their wings, legs reaching out, they landed upon a branch. Doubt edged into his entrails, the ice touch spreading across him.

What's going on Gorgoroth?

We're checking on the horse warriors.

Directly beneath them, arrayed out in a circle hidden in the depths of darkness, slept the King's Own soldiers. They were positioned far away from any track, path, or road. Horses stood over or slept beside their masters. One man on each compass point of the circle sat fifty paces from their comrades, facing out, a musket clutched in his grip.

So, they survived. The smile in the nature spirit's voice was evident.

You really are drawn to them aren't you, Gorgoroth?

They intrigue me. I've not come across any humans quite like them before.

Leaping clear of the branch, they plummeted to the ground, and with a snap of their wings, landed upon a branch much closer to the soldiers. The warrior sitting guard closest to them leaned back and looked straight at them, his glare boring into them. Vyder was not oblivious to the fact the soldier's index finger had shifted onto the trigger of his musket. Stretching his back, the man returned his concentration to the forest around him, index finger moving clear to rest upon the trigger guard.

Stretching their wings wide, they stepped from the branch and were airborne again, the defensive circle of the King's Own sliding by beneath them. A towering Ghost Oak loomed out of the darkness, easily visible in contrast to the black forest around it.

Look at her, Vyder.

They ascended towards the oak's upper branches, a twisted mass of huge boughs and dense foliage blotting out the star strewn sky. The Ghost Oak dominated its area of forest, like some general of old rallying troops to his banner.

She must be two hundred years old. Maybe more.

Moments slid by into nearly an hour by Vyder's guess. The moon ascended into the night sky, eventually reaching her zenith.

And here they are.

Vyder felt the nature spirit shift the bird's head down so they were staring at the leaf-littered forest floor beneath them. Scattered throughout the forest in every direction were the sleeping forms of Huronian soldiers. A few of the large campfires around which some slept had long ago burned out, but others still held a slight glow, wisps of smoke drifting up towards Vyder. Onward they flew, banking with gentle ease around trees, and still the Huronian Army littered the forest.

Can Wendurlund withstand this, Vyder?

Doubt crept into his chest like an assassin, a cold stab of fear piercing his heart.

More Huronian soldiers appeared from the forest, sliding by beneath them to be replaced by an endless mass of inanimate human forms, deep within sleep's embrace. No matter where they looked, enemy warriors slept.

I don't know.

Ascending, they broke through the canopy and out into the open night. As before, freedom leaked around them, saturating and pleasing simultaneously. Gliding above the carpet of forest below, Vyder could see for miles in every direction. To their north, the wide band of the Likane Forest stretched to the horizon, as it did southward. But to the east, and their direction of travel, the forest ended in the near distance to be replace by open plains. In the far distance, Mount Grost stretched into the night sky. The dark behemoth blotting out a section of stars and almost reaching the pale white orb, casting its soft light upon the world.

When the Likane Forest began to grow thin, they dropped towards earth, pierced the sparse canopy, and landed upon a branch not so far from the ground. They raised their head to the sky and sniffed. Vyder detected the sickly-sweet aroma of death, mingled with the stale sweat of both man and horse.

There is one more warrior to check upon.

Movement caught their focus, and through the trees, a man sitting astride a mighty horse appeared from behind a thick tree trunk. Lying across the saddle in front of the rider was slung the dead body of a second man. The powerful horse drew closer, and Vyder was able to see the various weapons holstered in the leather sheath in front of his right knee, and realisation descended upon him.

It is the King's Own officer.

The warrior was slumped in the saddle, his head dropping slowly, eyes closing before his head popped back up and eyelids snapped open. Taking a deep breath, he muttered something, but soon his head dropped again, eyelids drawing closed once more. Vyder felt their beak open and a sharp, ear-piercing shriek blasted from them, echoing around the forest. The officer sat ramrod straight in his saddle, brought the warhorse to a halt, and rubbed his eyes.

Scanning the forest, his eyes eventually locked onto them. He chuckled then, shook his head, and yawned. Dismounting, he pulled clear his deceased comrade and gently laid him upon the ground before unsaddling the horse and rubbing it down with a soft cloth.

"Time to rest, my lad," the officer's words drifted to them perched upon the branch above.

Best we return to our body.

Casting one more glance at the warrior about to stretch out upon the ground in preparation of sleep's embrace, they flew away. They travelled back towards their starting point, re-negotiating over the Huronian Army in all its silent might, past the small King's Own unit. As the moon descended towards the horizon, they landed in the boughs of a tree overlooking their campfire. Only glowing coals remained alive in the guts of what had once been a blaze. The Kalote woman lay on her side, legs drawn up to her chest, one hand beneath her head. Nearby slept Henry. The royal lay on his back, hands behind his head.

Vyder realised the prince was not asleep. A glint of dull moonlight glimmered in his eyes. The young man sat up without speed and stared at them. On the far side of the remnants of the fire sat Vyder's inanimate body.

It is strange seeing my body from the outside. I look...dead.

Gorgoroth's laugh boomed in his mind, but the nature spirit chose not to reply.

Stretching, they burst into the air, wings beating, lifting them higher. It took the better part of an hour for Gorgoroth to ensure the owl had enjoyed its fill of food and water.

If we were to leave it without ensuring it is sustained, the bird would be too exhausted to hunt or drink. It would be a slow, painful death for her. When we leave her, she will return to her home, a hollow in a log or trunk somewhere nearby, to sleep the day away.

Makes sense, Vyder agreed.

I may allow you to take control of one of my children one day, brother. You must not forget this. Ensure the animal is adequately fed and watered before you leave them. Do you understand?

Of course, and if I don't, you'll be there to nag me. I mean remind me.

Laughter echoed through Vyder's mind.

* * *

A flurry of sound brought Henry awake with a lurch. His chest expanded and cool air rushed into his lungs. He blinked the sleep from his eyes, the sound which woke him from slumber still pervading his memory. His sleep addled brain analysed the noise, and he finally realised it was the flapping wings of a bird.

It's close, as well! It was right above me.

Henry relaxed and stared up at the pitch forest above him. Patches of night sky, riddled with tiny stars were visible through small gaps of the forest canopy. But his focus was drawn to something to his left and much closer than the distant canopy. The hairs on the back of his neck rose of their own volition, fear, cold as melting ice, trickled down his spine. His mouth dropped open, and he sat up slowly. It was an owl, perched on a branch not much higher than his standing height. The bird was staring at him. But it wasn't its stare which caused him fear, it was the eyes. One of them was a bright, glowing blue.

And it pierced his soul.

<h1 style="text-align:center">II</h1>

It had been a long day. They'd been riding hard for most of it, starting before the bright orb of Yanahee's Fire rose over the horizon to drive away the cool night air. Their horses maintained a brisk walk, interspersed with bouts of trotting where the path and the stamina of the animals allowed. But now they were sat on the banks of the river, relaxing. Ahitika leaned back on her elbows and looking out upon the mighty river, the current drifting by with a soft burble. Close to the bank, small eddies danced in the water, twirling and moving in random patterns. Further out, a log bobbed, carried along by the powerhouse that was the Stream of Taraxon.

The Therondale River, she corrected herself. Henry and the people of Wendurlund knew it as such, and she thought it sounded more powerful and demanding of respect than a simple stream.

Henry sat beside her. "There's a good current here."

She frowned, unsure of his meaning. Ahitika was improving with her understanding of the Wendurlund language, but Henry sometimes still spoke words she found difficult to understand.

He pointed, his finger following the direction in which the water moved. "Strong water," he said.

Her frown disappeared, and she smiled. She'd spent all her life learning about Huron that she'd never stopped to consider the mighty empire of Wendurlund to the west. Huron had, at one time, at least, been home to her people, after all. The people of Kalote had been driven north across the Shadolian Sea by the Huronian settlers, hundreds of generations before.

She clenched her teeth, jaw bulging, and lips narrowing into a tight line. Her ancestors had fought, and fought hard, to protect their land, their homes, and their hunting grounds. But they'd been outnumbered, and soon, the Huronian Army had waded into the fray, destroying entire tribes.

Flee and survive to fight, or live on as slaves or worse, disappear from the world forever. She scratched the skin of her cheek, her thoughts focused upon her ancestors and the decision they would eventually make to ensure the survival of their people. She touched the long, thin beads of her breastplate, created from animal bone and imbued with the power of the Great Spirit by medicine men. In the end, it was a simple choice. *Live on your knees, or die on your feet.* She flicked her head, a long strand of dark hair flying out of her vision. But the land known as Huron still sang to the people of Kalote, beckoning them home.

She dropped a hand and touched the scalps attached to her belt, soft hair tickling her skin. All Huronian scalps, cut from warriors who'd offered her a strong fight. *Another three scalps and my initiation is at an end. I will be a Kalote warrior.* She leaned back on her elbow, ignoring the skin of her hand that demanded to be scratched. *But only Huronian scalps.*

As far as she was aware, there were more than forty other Kalote initiates strewn throughout Huron eager for the same right. In any given year, more than one hundred Kalote initiates would travel into Huronian lands to prove their right to become a warrior. *Three more scalps.* She returned her attention to the log, carried by the river, making its slow journey into Wendurlund, until it disappeared behind a thick stand of trees.

A splash of water drew her attention. Henry waded into the river, and when he was chest deep, he undressed, casting sodden clothes upon the bank before ducking below the surface. When he reappeared, spluttering, long hair clinging to his face, she cupped her hands around her mouth.

"You frighten I see you with no clothes?"

He held out his hands and grinned. "I'm a gentleman, Ahitika."

She pointed at the bundle of wet clothes sitting upon the pebbles near the water. "You still need to leave river. You walk out naked." She smiled and tapped the skin under one eye, "I see you then."

He chuckled, shrugged, and ducked below the surface again. When he appeared, he washed the dirt from his skin. The bones of his rib cage, shoulders, and arms were clear beneath a thin layer of skin and muscle. He turned away from her and scrubbed his hair.

He was definitely a powerful man at one time. She brushed a lock of hair behind an ear, acutely aware of the naked man stood in the river before her. Bony as he was, the muscles of his shoulders and back suggested he'd been well built prior to being starved near to death.

Henry ducked his head below the surface, reappeared, and washed under his arms. Ahitika stood and lifted the breastplate over her head and placed it upon the pebbles with care. Her shirt followed and, within moments, she stepped out of her trousers. The cool air felt good upon her naked frame. She walked to the river, the water refreshing against her legs. Henry turned toward her and paused, watching her. His mouth dropped open.

Ahitika grinned and dove beneath the surface, the water's chill invigorating. She swam beneath the river, strands of weed reaching up from the bottom to tickle her legs. A small school of fish, startled by her proximity to them, broke rank and darted away in all directions. Her shadow passed over a crab wandering along the bottom. The creature scuttled to a large rock and disappeared beneath it. Then the form of Henry appeared, becoming clearer the closer she swam.

Well endowed, too. Air bubbles exploded from her mouth as she laughed. She rose towards the blurry orb of Yanahee's Fire above her. Ahitika broke the river's surface and drew in a breath of fresh air. Flicking her head, strands of long dark hair flew from her face to slap against her back. She bounced along the slippery river bed, returning Henry's stare, coming to a halt when she was mere inches from him, her breasts pushing against the skin of his chest.

"I not gentleman," she whispered through a smirk.

The lump in his throat rose, then fell and his cheeks flushed. "I can see that."

She clamped a firm grip of his hips and squeezed, her smirk widening into a grin. When she felt his erection pressing against her belly, she pushed away from him and ducked below the surface again. Swimming away, Ahitika dove to the river bed, fresh air clutched within her lungs. The smooth stones slid against her skin, weeds tickling her, and a brush of movement against her leg suggested a fish, misjudging her proximity, had darted away to safety. She angled upward and erupted clear of the water.

* * *

Henry watched her depart. For too long, he'd been starved, frightened, angry, filled with self-loathing, terror, and fury that he'd forgotten what it was to be human, to be a man. Passion, heat, and lust swept his weak, slim, bony body. It was then, as he watched the dangerous, violent, but beautiful woman swim away from him, that he knew he wanted to live.

Ahitika's head broke the surface, she pushed hair away from her face, tucking the soaking locks behind her ears and stood. She walked towards the river's bank, glistening beads of water sliding down her flanks and dripping from her breasts. She looked at him, held his stare and smiled.

Gods above. His knees felt weak, more so than if he'd been locked away in a Huronian prison for months on end. *That's not true.* At least he could walk more than a few steps now without losing his breath. He watched her progress with keen interest until her full, naked form was clear of the river. She glanced over her shoulder at him and smirked. He shuddered. He watched her dress, oblivious to a clump of free-floating weeds gliding against his arm, ignoring the tapping on his legs as fish swam between his calves. When she was dressed, she finally lifted the Kalote breastplate over her head and dropped it in place. Only then did he exhale. She touched the breastplate. She closed her eyes, and her lips moved, although he couldn't hear her words.

Henry's purpose returned to him, and he finished washing himself, scrubbing clean his dirty skin and hair. Although he owned no soap or clean smelling liquid the aristocracy liked to spray upon themselves, he was content that he smelled less foul than he did before he waded out into the might of the Therondale River.

"Are you coming?" her voice reached him.

He spluttered and blinked water from his eyes, sweeping dank hair away from his vision. Focus returned, and the beautiful Kalote warrior stood upon the river's bank, a hand on her hip.

"Uh," he sniffed and coughed, "give me a minute." He felt his cheeks flush again.

She chuckled, turned from him, and walked away.

When the memory of her naked form no longer encouraged his body, he walked towards the bank. Although he still thought of her soft breasts and hard nipples pressing against his chest.

He knelt in the shallows and washed his clothes, scrubbing the filth from them. He rinsed them one by one, rung them by hand, and then beat them against a dry rock to exude as much water from them as possible. Then he dressed, the damp fabric cool against his skin. Buckling on his belt, the weight of the blade at his side tugged at his hips. He grasped the hilt to avoid the sword entangling in his legs as he walked and headed away from the river. Already, the smell of wood smoke was drifting through the forest.

Pushing through the waist-high undergrowth, he caught the orange flicker between trunks and headed towards it. Advancing into the clearing, he paused to watch Vyder kneeling before the fledgling fire, his eyes squinted against the smoke. He used a stick to encourage life into the small flames.

The *crunch* and *crack* of movement through the forest in the distance foretold Ahitika was in search of more firewood. He stopped beside the fire, stepping to one side as the soft wind changed direction, sending the thin plume of smoke drifting toward him.

"Have you finished your strength exercises?" Vyder didn't look up.

"Not yet."

The assassin jerked a thumb over his shoulder. "Get to it, young prince."

Henry spotted a thick, horizontal branch jutting

from a tree at a perfect height. He approached the branch, reached up, and curled his fingers around the branch. He wasn't yet strong enough to lift his chest to touch the wood. But Vyder had shown him how to strengthen the large muscles of his upper back. He jumped up so his chest touched the branch and held himself in position for a moment, before lowering himself slowly to the ground under control. When his boots touched the forest floor, he leapt up a second time and repeated the exercise. He repeated the exercise, each repetition becoming more difficult than the last.

His back was on fire, muscles protesting against the assault under which they found themselves. Henry dropped back to the ground and released his grip upon the branch, sucking in great gulps of fresh air, beads of sweat sliding down his cheeks.

Probably should have done this before I went to wash.

He planted hands on his hips and waited until the rhythm of his chest slowed. He wiped his brow, and when the burn retreated from the muscles of his back, he dropped to the ground. He stretched himself out so that the only points of his body in direct contact with the forest floor were his palms and balls of his feet, then he lowered himself down, maintaining a straight back until his chest touched the leaf litter. Pushing himself up into his original position, he repeated the process. He grunted as the muscles at the back of his upper arm and across his chest began to burn. On the fifth repetition, he collapsed. Leaves crunched under boots as someone approached. There was a whisper of movement and a *crack* of a knee joint. He opened his eyes. Vyder was knelt over him.

The highlander tapped him on the arm. "Get up."

Henry pushed himself to his feet and drew in a

deep breath. Vyder rose beside him and pointed at the nearby horizontal branch. "Again."

"But I've done that one. I'm–"

"Do it *again*."

***

Rone steered the destrier north away from the road. Being the same path down which the might of the Huronian Army had recently passed, it was not worth the risk to follow in their footsteps. Any professional army worth their salt would have a guard watching and protecting its rear. It'd be a long, slow slog, but to the north, there was another path through the Likane Forest towards Wendurlund.

Failing that, I'll cut my own way through the forest. He nudged the war horse forward through giant clumps of grass, pushing past tall, thick bushes, and negotiating around massive trees, the trunks of which dwarfed both horse and rider. Rone looked at the canopy high above him, which seemed to become denser with each passing moment. The sky faded until it was almost completely hidden from view by a mash of greens and browns. Daylight was defeated by the forest's density. Afternoon light became more like that of dusk and night, no doubt, would provide no visibility whatsoever.

The further he travelled north, the less likely it seemed human kind had come this way in decades. *Perhaps even generations.* The steed picked his way through the forest, down into small, dry creek beds, up moderate inclines and around obstacles. Through seldom gaps in the canopy, Rone was able to spot slivers of the sun, ensuring he was maintaining a northerly direction. By mid-morning the next day, he'd be on the path leading towards Wendurlund if it lay where he expected it to be. He'd been shown the path on his first scouting mission into Huron almost ten years ago.

Someone shouted in front of him, followed immediately by the laughter of several voices. Rone pulled on the reins and remained frozen in the saddle, his eyes raking the forest. The destrier's ears flicked forward with keen interest. *There!* A group of ten Huronian soldiers were wading through chest-high grass in the direction of Wendurlund. Possibly a wayward section of the Huronian Army's rear guard, or deserters, or just a group who'd become separated from their unit for some reason. Either way, if he sat atop the horse for any longer, one of them was bound to spot him.

Rone dismounted, ensuring he remained silent when his boots touched the ground. He untied the corpse of his comrade and pulled the body from the warhorse. He gritted his teeth, his face becoming a silent snarl, muscles burning under the weight. He laid the dead soldier upon the ground as noiseless as possible. He backed the destrier several paces and tugged down on the reins. The powerful animal ignored him. He tugged on the reins again, clicking his tongue against the soft pallet of his mouth in a gentle sound. The horse knelt, dropped to the ground, and then lay on its side with a soft snort.

Grasping the butt stock of the musket, he drew the weapon from its holster and knelt down behind the warhorse, laying the cold barrel upon the animal's flank. Pulling the butt into his shoulder, his cheek touched the cool wood of the stock, and his master eye stared down the metal sight at the group of enemies in the near distance.

Laughter peeled amongst the forest once more,

several of them chatting in their foreign tongue. A tall man stopped, turned towards Rone, untied his breeches, and pissed amongst the grass. He shouted something over his shoulder, more laughter answering his words. Rone lined the sights up with the centre of the man's chest and remained silent, his index finger teasing the musket's trigger.

The chest of the enemy expanded, and a staccato of coughs erupted from his mouth. He hawked, spat, and wiped his mouth with the back of a hand. The flow of piss stopped, and he re-tied his breeches, his eyes sweeping the forest before him with indifference. The noise of his comrades, blundering through the forest were fading in the distance. The soldier sniffed and started to turn before he froze. He looked back at the forest near Rone as if he'd unconsciously detected something abnormal. Rone's heart quickened, and he took up pressure on the trigger, the sights still hovering over the chest of the enemy.

The eyes of the tall man drifted at the patch of woodland directly behind the King's Own officer, then descended until they rested upon Rone. The man's brow creased, then his eyes bulged, lines in his forehead deepening. His eyebrows shot towards his messy fringe. His lips parted, and his mouth opened wide. As the first shouted word left him, Rone's musket roared to life, and the enemy soldier disappeared behind a cloud of burned gunpowder.

The officer dropped the musket, unholstered his blunderbuss, slung it across his back and ripped free the spear. He was on his feet and running. Distant shouting echoed between the thick forest. The sound of confusion breached the gap of any language. Boots thudded towards Rone. The dead soldier's comrades were returning to check on him.

He threw a glance over his shoulder at his destrier. "Hold!" The animal rolled onto its stomach, and with a powerful blur of movement was on his feet. Ears pointing forward, he watched his master depart. If he needed assistance, the warhorse would be by his side fast, fighting alongside him.

Rone dodged a tree, jumped over the enemy corpse, leapt, and grabbed hold of a thick branch above his head. The spear almost caused his grip to slip, but he tightened his clutch of the branch. Hauling himself up, he stood and padded towards the huge tree trunk from which the horizontal branch had sprouted. He crouched, waiting and watching. He was located above the newly dead soldier. His destrier still stood in place, watching him with keen interest. Boot falls grew in volume, as did the shouting, and the group of enemies appeared behind a juvenile Ghost Oak, running toward him.

They formed a circle around their deceased friend, some of them breathless. One of them took a step away, hand covering his mouth. Another crouched and touched the hole in his comrade's chest where the musket ball had ripped the life from him. A third pointed at the destrier and shouted. The crouching one stood with one slow, smooth movement and muttered, "Deesak glodta." Rone knew what those words meant, at least. It was another Huronian name for the King's Own.

Death riders.

Rone's mouth widened into a grin. The soldier who'd so recently spoken, and obviously the leader, blurted a command, sweeping his arm around at the forest surrounding them. The others, their eyes wide, took a step back, but were hesitant to move away from their group in search of their enemy.

A dull *thud* echoed around the woodland as the destrier stamped a hoof upon the ground, his eyes boring into the group of soldiers. They offered no threat, yet. But when they did, the warhorse would be amongst them before they could react. One soldier unclamped his hand from his mouth, bent over, and vomited at his feet. Hissed words from his comrades followed, and they moved away from him. One of them stepped back several paces, so that he was standing directly beneath Rone. He noticed the soldier carried a large haversack over one shoulder. It was filled with berries and roots. *A foraging party, looking for food for the main army. There're probably hundreds of these patrols dotted around the forest.* He cursed. *Not as untouched by humans as I'd thought.*

He clamped the spear with both hands, pointing the metal tip downward, and waited. The leader shouted a string of words, his soldiers flinched at the obvious command and walked away in different directions in search of their adversary. His heart sank toward his boots.

They won't leave until they've found and killed me. He clenched his jaw and snarled. Only two options remained. *Fight or die.*

He jumped from the branch, the weapon clenched in a vice grip, the ground racing to meet him. The spear smashed through the back of the man's neck and slid on to cut down through his chest and into his guts. The weapon was ripped from Rone's hands as the soldier fell face first onto the dirt, dead. No way he was getting the spear out of the body, it was embedded too deep.

The group of departing enemy warriors paused and turned towards the *thump* behind them. Rone unslung the blunderbuss, brought the weapon to bear and roared, fury filled hatred lining his face, veins pushing against the skin of his neck. He pulled the trigger, and the blunderbuss added its voice to the bellow. He was immediately immersed in a thick cloud of gunpowder. Throwing the weapon into the air, he caught the warm barrel and reversed the blunderbuss, ready to use the wooden butt stock as a club, then sprinted forward through the acrid, grey mist.

When he broke clear of the cloud, soldiers were dead or dying at his feet. Four remained standing, one clutching his shoulder, blood streaming between his fingers.

"Obragarda!"

Rone brought the blunderbuss down in a savage sweep, the thick wooden stock smashing into the man's head, knocking him from his feet. The second followed in a similar fashion. But the other two, swords now in hand, charged at Rone. He blocked the sword of the first with the blunderbuss, but the second stepped to one side and brought the blade down towards Rone's neck, the razor-sharp steel whistling through the air. Then he disappeared in a thundering blur of brown, the destrier knocking him to the ground and striking hooves upon his face until his skull burst.

Rone stepped into his enemy and slammed the stock of the blunderbuss into the Huronian's face. Blood exploded from his ruined nose, and he dropped to the ground, unconscious. Rone reloaded the blunderbuss with practised speed, slung the weapon, and jogged back to his deceased comrade. Stooping, he retrieved his musket, and with the same smooth skill, readied it to fire.

Gesturing at his destrier, he clicked his tongue, and the animal walked to him with brisk strides, stopping to nuzzle his hand. He sheathed the blunderbuss and musket, then flicked the reins, once more asking the horse to drop to the ground. The warhorse did so. Rone dragged his dead soldier to the horse and with a grunt, lifted the corpse onto the horse. Tying the deceased man in place to avoid him slipping off, the officer straddled the lying horse, placed one foot in a stirrup, and with the other, tapped the destrier's flank.

"Up." He tapped his boot against the animal's side once more. "Up you get."

The horse complied, and with a loud snort, pushed himself to his feet. Rone settled into the saddle and placed his free boot into the remaining stirrup and guided his mount to the north. Only one enemy soldier, lying face down, blood leaking into the leaf litter around him, still moved. Well, at least his left leg still moved, but it was difficult to know whether it was death spasms or if the man was still alive. Either way, he was no threat.

Rone cast his eye upon the soldier in whom his spear was embedded. He felt foolish for the slight pang of sadness that passed through him at the thought of leaving his trusty spear behind after all these years. He'd been issued the weapon on the day he'd been selected as a successful candidate for the King's Own. It had seen so many deployments. The weapon had been by his side so often that it felt like a part of him.

"Goodbye, old friend," he whispered and urged the warhorse into a canter. Distant shouting pervaded the forest. Many voices added their urgency.

Time to leave. The destrier picked his way between trees. The yelling increased, and the noise of boots drifted to him. *A main patrol. No way in the Gods I can fight them off.* Rone realised he'd taken on a small foraging party, which had probably separated from the main patrol as the hours endured. He pushed the horse faster, allowing the beast to pick his way through the forest but ensuring they always moved north. It wouldn't have been the musket shot which drew the attention of the main patrol, or the shouting, screaming or dying. It was the deafening roar of the blunderbuss that alerted them.

He patted the blunderbuss. *You saved my life, but by fuck, can you make some noise.* He smiled, turned in the saddle, and looked over his shoulder. But the forest was clear, and the sound of enemy movement had faded to near silence.

* * *

Sunlight danced across the leaf littered ground, strong winds battering the forest's canopy. Great boughs and small branches swaying and rocking in time to the rhythm provided by the assault. Light twinkled upon the surface of the babbling Therondale River to their left. But the sky remained bright blue and clear of any clouds.

We are in Wendurlund.

"And how do you know that?" muttered Vyder.

His arms grew numb, and they stretched out horizontal either side of him.

The forest, she welcomes us home. Well, she welcomes me *home.*

The silent chuckle rattled around Vyder's mind.

He turned in the saddle and stared at the pair sat on the King's Own destrier behind. "We grow closer to Lisfort with each passing day." The animal's ears flicked forward at his voice, its attention drawn to Vyder. "I believe we have now passed into the land of Wendurlund." He focused upon Henry, mounted in front of the Kalote warrior. "You are almost home young prince."

Henry's brow furrowed. "Should we not then increase our pace?"

"Not yet, lad. Soon, we will be beyond the Likane Forest, and only flat plains remain between us and home. It is then we must press hard for Lisfort. Hiding in a forest is easy. If the Huronian Army catch us in the open, they will destroy us in moments."

"Or recapture me."

"No, Henry." Vyder turned to face front. "They *will* kill you this time. This thing is done. War is inevitable, and your worth to them is now nothing."

A thin veil of protection remained to them in the form of the tiny King's Own patrol providing a rearguard action. But skilled as they were, outnumbered and outgunned, Rone's soldiers could only do so much to hold off the enemy torrent.

So, what you're saying is I get to kill more little humans?

Vyder heard the smile in Gorgoroth's voice.

"It'd seem so," he whispered under his breath. "Just make sure they are deserving of death's touch."

All humans are deserving of death.

Vyder drew in a long breath and rolled his eyes. "Gorgoroth –"

I jest, Vyder, I've learned so much about you monkeys since I've been alongside you. I once thought you all a blight upon the earth. A virus to be eradicated. But it seems not.

"Good, because if the Huronian Army is victorious, do you think your precious little Waning Wood will stand a chance against their flame?"

They wouldn't dare!

"They wouldn't think twice, Gorgoroth. I'm sure their version of ancient myths and stories of that section of forest are even worse than those whispered into the ears of Wendurlund's children."

Then we shall stop them!

"All thirty thousand of them?"

Wendurlund has an army do they not?

"I don't know, you and your *children* were the last to attack them. Do they?"

Silence pervaded Vyder's mind.

"Gorgoroth?"

If my knowledge then was what I know now, I would never have summoned my children against Lisfort.

"Not what I asked."

We did some damage, I admit. Exact numbers are bereft of me, but it would be in the thousands.

Vyder's mouth retracted into a tight line, and it was his turn to remain silent.

* * *

Henry sat astride the King's Own warhorse, aware of Ahitika's body pressing against his back. The breastplate she wore dug into his skin, but he didn't mind. He knew how much it meant to her. He often caught her touching it and whispering something to the wind. A smile stretched his lips. He'd much prefer feel her breasts pushing against him. A rapid tap on his shoulder broke his thoughts, and the pressure of Ahitika's body against him increased.

"Crazier than I thought," she hissed into his ear. She pointed at the highlander.

He focused upon Vyder sat upon his horse. The animal walked in front of them, patches of late afternoon sunlight able to pierce the forest's canopy glistening against its coat. The highlander muttered to himself, occasionally gesturing with his hands. Sometimes, Henry was able to make out a few stern words, but mostly his voice was a burble.

I have to agree.

It became increasingly evident the highlander was arguing with himself. "Crazier than I realised, as well." Henry swung in the saddle and stared into Ahitika's eyes, her face mere inches from his own. "But–" his eyes were drawn to her lips. He licked his own and felt the skin of his face grow hot. He looked away from her soft lips and focused upon a nearby log instead. In his peripheral vision, he noticed a slight smile tease one corner of her mouth.

"But?" she asked, her voice almost inaudible.

"But as long as he gets us," he returned his attention to her face, her dark brown eyes boring into him, and he stammered. His voice trailed away. He cleared his throat and her lop sided smile grew wider. "What I mean is, as long as he gets us home, that's all that," he took a deep breath. "That's all that matters." He exhaled in a rush and turned from her, his erection pressing against his breeches. He swallowed and shifted in his seat.

The pressure of Ahitika's body against him reduced, and he knew she'd leaned back in the saddle. He heard her quiet chuckle. "Indeed," she replied.

Gods, she drives me to insanity. Another breath of fresh air filled his lungs, and he let it out slow, regaining control of his body.

"Not what I asked," Vyder's voice drifted to him.

He stared at the highlander in front of them. Henry's eyelids drew closer together, and he cocked his head, but Vyder fell silent. *What in the hell was he saying? And who was he speaking to?*

The pressure increased against him again, and Ahitika's voice whispered into his ear. "He made of two people, highlander okay, other one crazy. Other one I don't think person. Other one I *know* not person."

He swung in the saddle and stared into her face again. Ignoring the increasing discomfort in his breaches, he held her eyes. "You don't think the second one is a person?" His brow furrowed.

"Person." It was her turn to stammer. "Uh." She licked her lips, her eyes drifting to the sky. "Not sure of Wendurlund word."

"Human?" a chill drifted down his spine.

"That the word I mean! Other one not human."

Gods. The hair on the nape of his neck stood on end. "What is he…it, if not a human?"

"I know not, Henry. Not to be angered though. Very violent." She snapped her fingers. "Change from calm to killing like that."

He faced front again, and his guts lurched into his throat. Vyder was looking back at them over his shoulder, that piercing blue eye scorching through him like a seared spear.

"Could be demon," Ahitika whispered. Her fingers brushed against him, and he knew she'd clutched a hold of her breastplate. "But handy in fight."

The highlander coughed. "Soon, we'll be out in the open." He looked away. "We'll stop shortly for one last night to rest," he called over one shoulder. "Then the next destination will be Lisfort. We'll only be halting to briefly feed and water the horses after tonight."

Sections of sky visible between small areas of thick forest canopy was streaked with hues of light pink, the bright blue of daylight fleeing before the gloaming's onslaught. But on they walked, following the path paralleling the Therondale River. The river's soft burble, accompanied by the intermittent twitter of birds and buzz of insects the only noise pervading the mounted trio. When the sun's light failed and night's power splashed their surrounds in gun metal grey, they halted.

The horses were led to the river and allowed to drink their fill. Once done, they were tied with a loose rein so they could feed upon what pick was available. Henry lowered himself to the ground and sat. He suppressed a groan and leaned against a tree, stretching his legs. The dull forest disappeared as his eye lids closed. A slap on his arm, and his eyes snapped open.

Ahitika knelt beside him. "We need firewood, lazy. You help."

One thing he liked about the Kalote warrior, was she spoke her mind and did not molly coddle him. He may have been through a less than desirable experience, but she treated him the same as any other, and he respected her for it.

"You'll be okay by yourself."

She slapped him harder. "You up, now."

"Alright, alright." He gathered his legs beneath him and stood, arresting another groan before it broke free of his lips.

Inside an hour, the small campfire flickered, casting warmth upon them and setting shadows dancing from the nearby forest. A pot sat upon the coals on the outside of the blaze. Steam drifted from the mouth of the pot, water occasionally spilling over the edge sliding towards the glowing coals where the water hissed in protest. Ahitika had hunted another rabbit, cut it up, and added the meat to the water. Mixed with various roots, the meal promised to be a tasty stew. Henry caught a waft of the meal, and his stomach tightened, growling.

"Have you exercised yet, young prince?" the highlander's voice was quiet.

He tore his gaze away from the flames and fixed them instead upon Vyder. "Not yet, no."

"There's time before dinner, lad." He jerked a thumb over his shoulder. "There are plenty of branches to choose from."

I'm too sore, I'm too tired. He hesitated, but before the thoughts had faded to silence, anger swept through him, warming him. *Get your sorry arse up!*

Henry stood, stretched his legs, ignoring the twinge in the muscle of a thigh as a cramp threatened, and walked away from the camp. The flickering orange light illuminating the forest around him with intermittent persistence was enough for him to spot a thick, horizontal branch above his head. He leapt and pulled his body upward until the wood slammed into his chest. He held his position for a moment, and then lowered himself until the ground touched his boots. He repeated the process again. On the third repetition, the heat of the campfire seemed to have entered the muscles of his back and shoulders. When his chest touched the branch for the seventh time, sweat beaded his forehead and his breathing came in short, rapid rasps. He dropped to the ground and released his grip of the branch.

When his breathing slowed, he lay on the ground, palms flat upon the carpet of long-ago fallen leaves, twigs and dead bark, then pushed himself up until his arms were ramrod straight. He lowered his body, until his face was close to the earth and then pushed himself upward once more, the muscles of his chest and arms protesting and weakening with each repetition. On the fifth occasion, his arms failed, and he slammed onto the ground, face buried in leaf litter. Boots crunched towards him, stopped followed by the familiar *crack* of that knee bending.

Vyder tapped him on an arm. "You are getting stronger, lad. Not strong enough yet. Not by a long shot, but if you keep doing this every day, your strength will increase at a rapid rate."

Henry sat up, his breathing still coming in rapid gasps. He brushed a dry leaf stuck to his lip and appraised the highlander knelt beside him. "I feel stronger. Sore, but stronger."

Vyder's eyes flicked above him, his blue eye exuding a tiny glow. He followed the highlander's gaze and noticed an owl perched on a branch above them.

"Come on, lad, time to eat." Vyder stood and strode away.

When he regained control of his breathing, Henry wiped his brow with the back of his hand and pushed himself to his feet. He returned to the fire, and the trio ate in silence. The meal was scolding, but it tasted divine. The meat falling off the bone, the roots soft and juicy. When he'd eaten the larger chunks of stew, he allowed the water to cool before upending the wood bowl and drinking the remnants of dinner. He gathered the bowls after the others had finished and turned towards the nearby river with a mind to wash them clean.

"You not washing bowls!" Ahitika jumped to her feet. "You chief."

A grin broke Vyder's face. "Prince."

"You prince," the Kalote warrior corrected herself.

Henry stared at Vyder, and then turned his attention to Ahitika. "Are you mocking me?"

"You too important for this," she grabbed the bowls and attempted to pull them from him. "No, no, you too important to wash bowls. You no slave!"

But he kept a firm grip of them, aware of the amused glint in the woman's eyes. "Ahitika, I'll be fine."

She stepped closer so she was inches from him. "I like the way you say my name," she breathed. She flashed him a grin. "I joke, you wash bowls."

He chuckled, turned away, and made for the river.

* * *

Ahitika's heart thundered as she watched the chief walk away from her. She felt light-headed. *Prince!* She corrected herself again.

She turned back to the fire and noticed Vyder watching her. "You like him, don't you?"

She sat by the blaze and poked the burning logs with a stick. *He's a handsome man, strong in his heart, too.* "Maybe."

"Of course you do. He likes you, too, you know?"

Oh, I know that. She nodded, smiling. She'd felt his hardness as she pushed her naked body against him in the river that day. But she wouldn't give herself to any man. A man must prove himself.

"Don't grow too fond, though."

Her smiled faded, and she withdrew the stick from the fire and held Vyder's stare, ignoring the blue eye which seemed to carve the skin from her body. "Why?"

"Tomorrow, we leave the forest behind and enter the plains." Vyder cleared his throat, the distant sound of splashing competing against the campfire's crackle as bowls were rinsed. "And I don't know if we'll be fast enough to make it back to Lisfort before the Huronian Army ensnare and kill us."

III

The incessant drumbeat assaulted the air, ricocheting from the forest around them. The Huronian Army was strewn in a mighty single file stretching for many miles in length, creeping westward towards Wendurlund.

"I don't know why it's so important the ground troops remain in step."

Commander Garx turned in the saddle to appraise the junior officer behind him. "That is what the king has decreed, Lieutenant Sed. Simple as that."

"I know, but it'll give away our position. It just seems such a—"

"Hold your tongue. That is what the king has commanded. End of story."

No need to lose your bloody head over an opinion, whether your spoken thoughts carry good sense or not.

The young man nodded and clamped shut his mouth.

"I've told you before, keep your thoughts to yourself, Sed. Else your neck feel the cold, sharp steel reserved for those judged with insurrection." Sed's eyes widened, and the bump in his throat rose and fell.

"Aye, sir."

Garx faced forward. *King Fillip would have killed you if he'd heard your first sentence, never mind the rest.* Between the monotonous drum beats, a loud peel of laughter echoed from in front, a deep booming rhythm so familiar to Garx. He'd spent enough time in King Fillip's throne room, assisting with the kingdom's petty squabbles, to know the sound of his monarch's laugh. It was followed by a few shouted words, which was greeted with a ruckus of chuckles and claps.

Our mighty liege no doubt regaling his inner most circle of cavalry officers with another of his stories of incredible heroism. Probably only the fifth time they've heard it so far.

He clenched his teeth together, the muscles in his jaws rippling beneath his beard. He'd lost all respect for his king when he'd been instructed to behead the royal diplomat weeks before.

Blake was his name.

He searched the huge boughs, branches, and leaf blotched greenery of the upper reaches of the forest as if it would somehow dampen the memory of cutting Blake's head from his neck. The man had dedicated five years of his life in enemy territory for the love of his Huronian home. When Wendurlund looked to be under threat and weakened, he had reported to his king, whom he'd served with unquestionable loyalty.

And our great king treated him like a fucking criminal and ordered him executed. By mine own hand no less.

The forest disappeared behind his clamped eyelids. Air filled his lungs, his chest pressing against the cold steel of his armour. Garx let it out slow, eyelids parting to reveal the same cavalrymen as before, riding in front of him. *Gods above, Blake, if you can hear me, I'm sorry.*

That same booming noise rose to compete against the drumbeats, accompanied by more shouting and clapping. Anger's searing heat speared through Garx. With great will, he refused to allow the muscles of his face to show the snarl they wanted to form.

At least common sense had prevailed when the small cavalry unit tasked with chasing down the escaping prince had returned. No further groups were sent in chase of the prize.

"I shall capture that bastard runt when I storm into Lisfort!" King Fillip's voice echoed in the halls of Garx's

memory.

The returning group of cavalry had not only failed in their mission, but they'd been cut to pieces. *I could have foreseen the end result, but my mighty liege is all knowing.* The death riders of Wendurlund were designed, amongst other things, to fight guerrilla style. Fast, aggressive, agile, and hard hitting, their skill set was unanswered by almost every unit currently employed by the Huronian Army. The Huronian Cavalry could stand against them, but only on the right terrain and situation. *Sending our cavalry, armed only with curved sabres and spears into thick woodland, to pursue a highly mobile, heavily armed adversary was madness. Like my king, I suppose. Utterly mad.* He spat into the scrub and withheld a curse.

Garx was confident that given an open field of battle, using the cavalry soldiers under his command, he'd be able to destroy any King's Own unit arrayed against him. Provided they were of a similar number, of course. The Huronian Cavalry, particularly King Fillip's household cavalry, were the finest soldiers in the world. But they deserved to be commanded and deployed appropriately. *Something my liege is unable to do.* He cursed under his breath. *Careful, Garx, if Fillip catches you out on your attitude, your head will roll. Just like Blake…and just like the king's loyal cavalrymen.*

The five cavalry soldiers who'd returned from their failed mission, three of them badly wounded, had been dragged away and beheaded for their effort. Their shouts and screams still seemed to echo through the forest around him. At least he'd been spared from carrying out the gruesome duty.

Dusk beckoned and soon night would make its presence felt. It'd be another long, fire-less evening, filled with cold, raw food, and fitful sleep. Ever since

Blake's execution, Garx's slumber was railed with guilt-riddled dreams. *Nightmares more like.*

Shouts ran down the long, snaking file of the Huronian Army, and they came to a halt. It'd be another few hours before the hunting and foraging parties returned to the army and distributed their gatherings. The process was made even more convoluted by the sheer amount of ground upon which the Huronian Army was spread.

Garx dismounted, stretched his legs, and patted his horse. "Lieutenant Sed!"

"Aye, sir?"

"Organise a water party for us."

"Right you are, sir."

The Stream of Taraxon's soft burble issued through the forest now the war drums had ceased their incessant noise. Garx unsaddled his horse, and with a soft cloth, wiped the sweat from the animal's fur. Sed's voice rose above the burble of many voices, caused by thousands of soldiers chatting in hushed tones with one another. The young officer had soon organised a party of forty cavalrymen, each armed with buckets. The group made their way to the nearby stream. They'd be able to gather enough water for Garx's cavalry sub-unit to drink their fill. As was their routine, once this had been completed, their horses would be led to the water to allow the animals to fill their belly with the precious fluid.

His stomach rumbled, but he ignored it, as he did the biting hunger, which had swept his belly for most of the day.

* * *

Before the sun broached the eastern sky, the mighty snake that was the Huronian Army was on the move again. The drums were silent and would remain so now until they neared Lisfort. Garx shifted in the saddle. *Thank the gods.* The dull *thump* of a trotting horse grew louder until the rider in question appeared around a bend in the track, he reined in beside Garx. It was a junior officer with less seniority than even Sed.

"Excuse me, sir."

He glared at the young man. "What is it, sub-lieutenant?"

"Sir, according to my commander, King Fillip would like a word. Please, follow me."

Garx pushed his horse into a trot, following the young cavalry officer. They passed a constant stream of cavalrymen, either talking amongst themselves in hushed tones or lost in their own thoughts. The obnoxious laugh to which he was so familiar boomed out ahead of him louder than ever. Laughter, claps, and praise followed. Garx looked up at the forest's canopy, pleased with himself for hiding what had started as a roll of his eyes. The throng of cavalrymen grew thicker until Garx and the young man behind whom he followed were forced off the track altogether, steering between trees, saplings, and shrubs. Finally, a blob of mounted soldiers, moving at a fast walk, blocked the path, and even pushed out into the surrounding forest, desperate to be near their king and thus be considered part of the monarch's *most trusted.*

Whether through loyal service, backstabbing, or deceit, these were the inner circle of King Fillip's household troop. Their skill in battle was without question, but the morality of their character most certainly was, as far as Garx was concerned, anyway. The sub-lieutenant reined in, and when he was beside the young man, so did Garx.

"Ah, yes here we are, my liege," one of the officers closest the king gestured towards them. "Commander Garx has arrived."

"Garx, you old bastard!" King Fillip called, a menacing grin splitting his lips.

Younger than you, my lord.

"Take one hundred of your cohort and relieve the troop currently scouting our front. They've been out there now for the past five days and deserve a break."

With a clenched fist, he touched the cold metal of his chest armour. "Aye, my lord. As you wish." He turned his horse away and urged it into a canter.

"And Garx!"

He brought the horse to a halt and turned the animal around.

"If you come across an enemy force, destroy them!" The mad king's crazed smile widened further.

Gladly.

"Without question, my lord."

He returned to his soldiers and glared at the closest man. "Lieutenant Sed to me."

The cavalrymen touched his chest and cantered away in search of the lieutenant.

His chest expanded, cool, fresh air rushing into his lungs. He watched a small flock of starlings explode into flight from the safety of a well-hidden branch. They ascended towards the upper most reaches of the forest. It'd be good to be out front of the army, keeping watch. *It'll help alleviate the bloody boredom.* He exhaled through his nose. *Might be a distraction from Blake's haunting.*

The sound of galloping hooves pervaded the cavalry moving in single file at a brisk walk. Garx cast a glance over one shoulder. Sed reined in beside him. "Sir?"

"Gather one hundred soldiers. We're advancing to provide scout cover for the army."

"Right you are, sir."

When the sun had reached its zenith, they were underway. Garx led the small group of cavalrymen at a canter, passing the steady flow of his comrades. Soon, they'd dodged around the blob of cavalrymen encompassing King Fillip.

"Have at it, Commander Garx!" The words were followed by a hollow cheer from the monarch's inner circle.

"Aye, my lord!" he shouted over his shoulder. Then what seemed to be an endless formation of cavalry was behind them, replaced with the general infantry. The walking soldiers were silent, many of them watching the ground with disinterest, probably in their own private hell as they attempted to ignore the pain in their feet and legs.

Occasionally, the gruff voice of a non-commissioned officer boomed through the forest, directed at either a single man, or ordering for the pace to be quickened. Several of the troops glanced at the passing cavalry, but the ground in front of their feet drew their attention again just as fast. When the sun had journeyed a quarter of the way to the western horizon, the last of the general infantry streaked by and were soon lost behind the cantering group of cavalry. They were replaced by a convoy of wagons as far as the eye could see. Some stacked with bales of hay for the horses. They'd been overflowing when the army departed Huron, but at least two were now near empty. There were another forty wagons full with fodder, enough to

see a protracted campaign at an end. When the last of
the hay was fed out of the few near empty wagons,
they'd turn around to revisit the long trip back to
Brencore for resupply.

As the army proceeded on their axis of advance
deeper into enemy territory, supply wagons would
become a constant flow back and forth. The last of the
fodder wagons came to an end and were replaced by
carts full of rations for the soldiers. These were not
usually distributed at the beginning of the march, the
army relying instead upon countless foraging parties to
provide the lion's share of food. One of the dual axle
carts was out of action, pulled off the side of the path, a
broken wheel being replaced by a cursing blacksmith.
Garx and his small group thundered past.

The ration-filled wagons were soon gone, and Garx
stared at horse drawn carriages carrying spare muskets,
swords, armour, boots, cannon balls, massive barrels of
black powder, and first aid supplies. Then they, too, were
consumed by the forest as the group of mounted
soldiers chewed up the ground.

Powerful draught horses towed cannons or
mortars behind them. The convoy of mighty weapons
ran like a giant caterpillar until they disappeared around a
distant bend in the path. Their dark maws were silent for
now, but their roar would echo off the walls of Lisfort
soon enough.

Thick pockets of gunners and mortar-men strode
in between the horse-drawn weapons. Some of the
artillerymen sat upon the colossal barrels in groups,
chatting, laughing, or playing cards. Then the vast power
of Huron's artillery was behind Garx's small force. They
were replaced with the elite formation of The Mortals,
the elite ground troops of the Huronian Army. Five

thousand in number, their red cloaks drew the eye. Even without the aid of the annoying din of drumbeats, they marched three abreast and in perfect step. The columns of red-cloaked warriors stretched far into the forest, forming the spear head of the Huronian Army's advance.

Garx had always thought The Mortals was a senseless name for an elite force. *Why not The Immortals?* That was until he'd overheard an officer explain to a junior soldier that death was part of war, and The Mortals were not afraid of the grave. They'd do their duty knowing their lives were finite. Regardless of their adversary, The Mortals, if required, would fight to the last soldier. Fear of death played no part in the completion of their task.

Imagine if they were trained to fight by horseback? He watched the neat formation of red cloaks slide by. They were worlds apart from the general infantry, who'd been bumbling along, staring at their feet. The elite warriors strode with heads raised, shoulders pulled back, focused eyes staring ahead. *They'd be unstoppable.* Unlike the general infantry, trained in sword and spear, The Mortals, in addition, employed rectangular shields. Garx had seen them training in phalanx formation several times. They were able to change direction fast, providing protection on all sides of their rank and file, including assault from above. Each warrior carried a slung musket, adding to their formidable arsenal. One officer at the front of the formation glanced at the passing cavalry. Garx caught his eye, and the man touched his fist to his chest. He returned the salute. Then The Mortals were behind them. As the sun touched the mountains in the west, the only friendly troops between Garx now were the small group of cavalry scouts somewhere in front of them.

Rounding a bend, Garx slowed his mount to a trot as the Likane Forest came to an end, and he was greeted by the endless, open plains of Wendurlund, painted with the orange of sunset. In the far distance patrolled the small cavalry force he'd been sent to relieve.

* * *

Rone knelt and placed the thick, juicy stem of King's Foil upon a flat stone. To this, he added a Florence Flower and sandwiched the colourful bloom with two leaves he'd plucked from a Targow tree. Using a fist-sized rock, he ground the items together, a pleasing aroma immediately rising to keep the sickly-sweet stench of his comrade's corpse at bay. He continued to grind until there remained only a green mash. To this, he added a touch of water and massaged the liquid in until only a thick paste remained. Scooping this into his palm, he stood, approached his warhorse, and smeared a generous portion of the pleasant-smelling paste around the animal's nose. He then painted a thick line beneath his own nose. Rone mounted, ensuring the dead body draped across the neck of his horse was still tied securely, before urging the destrier into a fast walk. They were well north of the Huronian Army and, come morning, would turn west towards Lisfort. Another few days and they'd be clear of the Likane Forest, travelling instead upon the mighty, open plains. He patted the animal's flank. "We'll be home soon, lad."

* * *

Intermittent, soft breeze kneaded open expanses of knee-high grass with a faint hiss. Occasionally, tiny flocks of birds took to wing, flying clear of the King's Own column as the horses clopped along the path. The sun had long ago fled beneath the distant mountains, allowing stars to blotch their pinpoints of light upon night's black canvas. Baras stared at the moon's bright orb, its dim light casting dull illumination across the open fields unfolding before the force of mounted elite warriors.

Baras touched the bugle clipped to his belt. The instrument was his weapon of choice, more so than the spear sheathed in the leather holster attached to the saddle and positioned forward of his right knee. The curved metal felt cold but gave him comfort. *Thought I'd needed its use a little while ago.* He tore his eyes from the moon and returned his attention to the open fields expanding in every direction as far as the limited light would allow.

Hours before, as the sun had cast hues of pink and orange across the sky, several shouts from the rear of the formation had caught his attention. He'd cantered back, finding six or seven King's Own in extended line, muskets drawn but resting across their laps, facing back the way they'd travelled.

"Huronian cavalry, sir," one of them had called, gesturing at the distant blur of green that was the Likane Forest.

"Are you sure?"

His view had narrowed to a thin line as his eye lids drew closer together. There was a small, brown blob in contrast to the green of the forest, which they'd departed earlier in the morning. But that was as much as he'd been able to see. *Age is a harsh task master.*

"Positive, sir. Maybe one hundred. Probably a scouting party for the main army."

"So then, the Huronian Army is catching us. Time to pick up the pace, I think."

"Aye, sir."

Baras remembered touching the bugle on that occasion as well. "Are they giving chase?"

"I don't think so, sir."

"Good. Keep an eye on them and let me know if they do."

"Yes, sir."

"Let them chase us," another warrior said, chuckling.

Baras flashed a grin. "Aye. We'll get our chance again soon enough." As sunset retreated before the gloaming's onslaught, Baras led the small force onward, where they would normally have stopped for the night. Now that they were upon the open plains, there was nowhere to hide, and while they could destroy a small enemy cavalry force of a similar number, if the mainstay of the Huronian Army reached them, the enemy would overrun them in moments. *We no longer own the element of surprise.*

He stood in the stirrups, stretched his legs, and sat down again, his arse beginning to ache. But he ignored the annoyance. *I hope the prince has enough sense to make a break for Lisfort now the safety of the forest is behind us.* He coughed into a crook of one arm. *And how goes Rone, I wonder?* The man was a fine officer who cared for those under his command. Little wonder the warriors trailing behind Baras would follow Rone through the gates of hell if asked. The moon's shine caught his eyes again. *Myself included.*

* * *

"Here, eat." Ahitika, sitting in the saddle behind him, pushed something into his hand.

The darkness cloaked what it was she'd given him, but judging by the feel, it was the root dug up from beneath a King's Foil tree. Tasty when boiled, but bitter when eaten raw. He held up his hand until the soft glow of moonlight swept his open palm. *As I suspected. King's Foil root.*

"What you wait for?"

He bit off a section of root and chewed the crunchy food into smaller sections. Henry winced against the bitter taste.

"You eat slow!" Ahitika tapped him on the shoulder. "Good for you, you eat more."

He stifled a laugh. "Oh, you want some?" he mumbled through a mouthful, a few small chunks of root exploding from his mouth, glistening with saliva in the dim light.

Her chuckle was almost inaudible. Almost. "No, I not hungry. Kind offer, though."

Henry swallowed and spat out a sliver of tendril. "Are you sure?" He held what was left of the raw foot behind his back to make it easier for the woman to take it from him. "There's bloody plenty."

"No, you eat rest of food. You need more," she squeezed his shoulder. "Good for muscles."

Henry worked his way through the remaining portion of crunchy root with reluctance, wiped his hand clean upon his trousers, and ignored the terrible aftertaste. He took a swig of water, swilled it around his mouth, and spat it out.

"More?"

"Very kind, Ahitika, but I'll be fine until tomorrow." *Is she having a laugh?*

"I have plenty," she patted him on the arm. "You tell me when want more, yes?"

He wasn't oblivious to the tiny chuckle in her voice.

"Oh, don't worry about *that.*" He smiled.

Vyder's powerful horse slowed until the highlander was walking beside them. "Is your horse recovered?"

The man's blue eye burned with a fierce glow, boring into Henry before it shifted to glare at Ahitika behind him. Henry patted the King's Own destrier. The animal had regained its breath, and the fur felt dry.

"Aye, I believe so."

"Then let us increase the pace once again."

Vyder pushed his horse into a canter. Ahitika urged their mount to a similar speed, falling in behind the highlander. Five times throughout the evening, they'd increased the pace of the animals until they began to lose their wind, moonlight glinting from sweat-streaked flanks. Then they'd slow to a walk to allow the mounts time to recover before pushing them on again.

We can only maintain this pace for perhaps another three days at the outside.

"We'll ride throughout the night," Vyder called over one shoulder. "If we can keep up this speed, we'll be at Lisfort by sunset tomorrow."

* * *

For four days they'd maintained a fast walk well in advance of the Huronian Army. The tiny blob of the King's Own unit in the distance remained visible. Garx had hoped the enemy force might have doubled back to offer a fight, but they seemed content to continue their advance for home. He was confident his force could destroy the enemy unit, but he wasn't going to chase them. The horses of his group would be exhausted by the time they caught the King's Own.

Late in the afternoon, a relieving force joined them to allow Garx and his men to return to the main force. They were led by an arrogant, young man by the name of Branf. The lad must have been all of twenty summer's in age. Garx tried to steer clear of the youth at every opportunity.

How in the hell is he in charge of a cavalry force already?

Branf caught his eye and nodded, steering his mount to walk alongside Garx.

"Well met, Garx. What news?"

"Not a lot, lad." He ignored the sharp look with which Branf appraised him. "There's a King's Own force in front of us, but they're keeping to our pace and have remained at a similar distance for the past few days."

"What?" Branf stood in his stirrups and held a hand to shade his eyes from the afternoon glare. "Are you sure they're King's Own?"

"No friendly forces between us and Lisfort. We're leading our army." He fixed his eyes upon Branf. *Remember, dolt?*

"Oh, I see them!" he slumped back into his saddle. "And why have you not chased them down?"

"First, because our horses would be next to useless by the time we reached them." He stared at Branf. "And second, because I don't fucking answer to you, nor do I need to explain myself."

Branf's mouth dropped open. "Well, if you won't do your damn duty, I most certainly will!"

He kicked his horse into a gallop. "My men with me," he roared. The group of cavalrymen followed their officer in his head long charge towards the blob of enemy in the far distance. Garx's force remained in place, following their commander.

"Gormless fool," someone muttered from behind Garx. "The King's Own will tear them apart when they arrive with their horses barely able to walk."

I have to agree. "Now, we have a real problem."

"What's that, sir?"

"We have to backup Lieutenant Branf in his stupid endeavour. If we are found to be sitting back while a friendly force rides to battle, King Fillip will behead us all."

This was met with curses, soft chatter, and grumbling.

"So, let's have at it, men. Stay with me, orders to come once we're closer to our target."

"Aye, sir."

"Curse you, Branf," he muttered and urged his horse into a trot.

While not even close to the speed of a gallop, a trot would eat the ground between Garx's troop and that of the King's Own, while not overworking the mounts.

* * *

The brown plains stretched out before them, ending when they met the line drawn by the sky's blue hue. Baras liked to think the tiny dark blob in the far distance was Lisfort, but they had far to travel before safety of the capital embraced them. *Probably some hillock.* They'd still not caught up with the prince, and the King's Own had been pushing hard. *A good sign.* The pair escorting the young royal seemed to have decided to make a run for Lisfort.

"Enemy charge!" someone roared from the rear.

He blinked, eyes regaining focus. Baras pushed his mount into a trot, turned back, and was at the rear of his force within moments. He re-joined the same small group of soldiers as before, all facing rearward, staring at a dust cloud drifting into the sky. One of the soldiers leaned on the pommel of his saddle, eyes squinted. "Aye, sir," he said without concern. "Perhaps one hundred of them. They're at full gallop."

Baras chuckled. "Senseless. Their mounts will be winded by the time they get close to us."

"Their mounts are probably already winded."

"Re-join the unit. We'll deal with them when they arrive."

The man who'd spoken shrugged. "Right you are, sir."

The tiny group turned away and trotted to catch up with their comrades, Baras on their heels. When they re-joined the force of King's Own, the few soldiers slowed to a walk, Baras continuing on around them at a trot. "We have an enemy force charging towards us," he yelled. "Face front and keep your horses walking at a steady pace. They need to think we are oblivious to their assault. When they are in fighting distance, bugle orders will follow. Clear?"

Baras made three circles of the King's Own unit, shouting the same words until he was confident all men understood what was about to take place. When he was at the front of the column once more, he slowed his horse to a walk. Pulling on the reins, he moved to one side so as to better see around the soldiers immediately behind him. The blotch of dust came into view, a dark smear now visible below the brown mist drifting high into the air. *My eyes grow worse by the year.*

Catching the eye of the soldier immediately behind

him, Baras gestured at him. The man trotted forward a few steps until he was adjacent with him.

"Sir?"

"Muskets at the ready, pass the word."

"Aye, sir."

The warrior slowed his mount to re-join formation and spoke the command to his comrade, who in turn repeated it to the soldier beside him. In short order, the spoken command had drifted across the ranks like wildfire, and the unit of King's Own walked on seemingly without a care in the world, muskets in their hands, the weapons resting upon the manes of their horses.

He guided his horse to the side once more, glaring over one shoulder, the dust cloud, now much closer, came into view behind one of his soldiers. *They're almost here.* He could decipher the tiny shapes of individual horses amongst the dark smear leaving the cloud of dust in its wake.

Baras unclipped the bugle. The cold steel felt good in his hand. It had served him well over the years, not to mention the unit of King's Own behind him. He'd issued hundreds of orders and survived countless clashes with enemy forces. Into the silver metal was pressed a single word. The King's Own war cry. Twisting in the saddle, he could make out individual enemy soldiers, the dull thunder of hoofbeats assaulting his ears. Almost drowned out by the drum roll of hooves slamming against the ground were the shouts, yells, and shrieks of the Huronian soldiers.

He took a deep breath, placed the bugle to his lips, and blew. *About turn, arrowhead formation, full charge.*

The formation of King's Own blurred into movement, pivoting towards the oncoming threat, and within a short space were galloping straight at the Huronian cavalry. Baras positioned himself at the tip of the arrowhead. The destrier settled into the gallop, stretching out, enjoying the speed. Tall grass reaching Baras's stirrups slid by in a blur. His lips touched the bugle. *Fire!*

Muskets crackled to life, sending their shot screeching towards the oncoming cavalry. Within a fleeting moment, the King's Own had galloped through the blanket of gunpowder. *Right and left flanks. Break formation. Re-join at rear.*

The King's Own unit split asunder on the fly, avoiding the enemy charge passing where the King's Own had been moments before. The Huronian cavalrymen found themselves charging at a vacant plain. Baras smiled with grim determination when the confident enemy war cries faded to silence. He led the left flank at a headlong gallop, streaking past their opponents galloping in the opposite direction. The King's Own tactic, from a bird's eye view, displayed the same form as the horns of a buffalo. Baras cast a glance over his shoulder, ensuring the Huronians were clear before guiding his horse to the right, straight towards the oncoming right flank. *Arrowhead!* They met in the middle, turning so they were travelling parallel to one another back towards the adversary. Then they moved into the arrowhead, Baras once more leading the point. The Huronians in front of them appeared in disarray, their commander unsure what to do. They slowed, starting to wheel around.

Baras clenched the bugle in a tight grip, lifted the instrument, and without taking his eyes from his enemy, issued the next order. *Blunderbuss. Fire!* The mighty roar of the blunderbusses spoke in unison, cutting a swathe through the cavalry. Baras estimated more than half of them were dead already. The Huronian horses were lathered in sweat, some of them refusing to comply with the desperate kicks of their riders, unable to accelerate beyond a slow trot. The cavalry formation broke into a messy straggle, a vast contrast to the tight, neat, lethal force approaching their flank. They closed the gap in quick order, and Baras watched the commander cast a terrified glance in his direction. Only then did he realise the youthful age of the officer. He almost felt sorry for what was about to happen. Almost. Baras's lips touched the Bugle. *Battle at will!*

"**Obragarda!**" the war cry echoed across the plain, rising above the noise of thundering hooves and panicked yells.

Baras clipped the bugle to his belt and withdrew his spear. The smooth, cool wood was comforting in his grip. He guided the destrier slight right, towards one man, urging his exhausted horse onward with repeated, powerful kicks. But the spent animal could advance at no more than a fast walk, despite the painful insistence provided by its rider. The enemy cavalryman stopped as he caught in his peripheral vision what was approaching. He stared at Baras, eyes wide as dinner plates, mouth yawning open. Baras leaned forward in the saddle and brought the spear forward in a powerful lunge. The razor-sharp weapon skewered the man's chest, smashing through rib cage, and exiting in an explosion of blood and tiny chunks of bone and flesh.

Baras released his grip of the spear. He'd tried to wrestle the weapon free in a similar situation years before and had nearly dislocated his shoulder. Clashes as steel met steel, *thuds* of weapons plunging into soft flesh, shouts and screams of the wounded, and panicked whinnies surrounded Baras. The King's Own unit barged through their enemy like a sledgehammer, leaving dead and dying soldiers in their wake.

He unclipped the bugle. *At the walk! About turn.* The galloping formation slowed, allowing the warhorses to regain their breath. They swung around, facing their near decimated enemy. *Reload muskets. Advance.* The King's Own unit, remaining in arrowhead formation, allowed their mounts to walk at a sedate pace. The warriors reloaded their muskets with rapid, confident, well-practised movements. Inside fifteen seconds, the last man had completed the task, the weapon placed across the mane of his destrier.

The enemy officer, having so far survived their onslaught, led his men away from Baras at a trot. They were finished, all fight gone from within their ranks. The boisterous war cries replaced by the cries of the fallen and shrieks of frightened cavalrymen.

"Second enemy force!" a man roared from a far flank.

Baras stood in his stirrups and stared at the dark smear advancing towards their rear. He sat back in his saddle, clenched a tighter grip on the bugle and lifted it to his mouth. *Charge!*

The King's Own unit accelerated into a gallop, thundering hooves once more singing their chorus across the open plain. The beleaguered Huronian cavalrymen urged their mounts into a gallop and attempted to swing away from the fast approaching charge, but without success. The horses were exhausted, one of them collapsing to the ground, casting its rider from the saddle.

Fire! The bugle blast cut through the staccato of hooves, musket shots ringing out before the instrument fell silent. The shot ripped through the few remaining Huronian cavalrymen with devastating effect. *Battle at will!*

"Obragarda!"

The King's Own spearhead formation skewered the tiny centre of the enemy force, leaving only death behind them. *At the walk.* Baras leaned forward and patted the warhorse's neck. Although the animal's breathing had increased with the exertion, he was far from winded. He led the unit in a wide circle, until they were facing the way they'd travelled. He clipped the bugle to his belt. Huronian bodies littered the plain, some horses lying beside their riders. The majority of horses, however, had survived the battle. Riderless and without direction, they had fled in several herds in varying directions. The clusters of animals stood together, watching the progress of the King's Own formation, or grazing upon the grass.

Baras focused his attention beyond the scene of death scattered before him at the second enemy force approaching them. The Huronian cavalry were advancing at a steady trot. The enemy commander was more experienced than the first, and the horses of his soldiers would be far more refreshed in comparison to those Baras and his troops recently faced. With the noise of battle finished, there was little need for the bugle.

"Reload your weapons," shouted Baras. "Continue on, I'll catch up."

He pushed his mount into a trot, steering towards the throng of dead bodies lying beside and on top of each other. When he located his spear, he dismounted and levered the weapon free of the dead body. He cleaned the spear tip upon the man's clothes, remounted, and sheathed it. Trotting to re-join his soldiers, he noticed the enemy had split into three small groups. One headed to the left, the other right, and the third maintaining a course straight towards the King's Own formation. When he was once more riding at the head of the spearhead formation, he slowed the warhorse to a walk. *This battle won't be as easy.*

"Finally," a man spoke from Baras's right, "someone who can actually fight."

The trio of enemy groups accelerated into a gallop, a light cloud of dust teasing the air behind each. Ferocious roars of Huronian warriors competed against the thunder of hooves slamming onto the ground.

Baras detached the bugle from his belt. And waited.

IV

At dusk, as the last vestiges of light began to die in the west, Vyder reined in his mount at the insistence of the guards on Lisfort's Eastern Gate.

"Dismount!" one of them commanded.

Vyder obeyed, clutching the reins in his hand, he strode towards the guard, a tall, athletic man. "What business have you here, blue eye?"

"We return with Prince Henry."

The guard grinned. He cast a glance over his shoulder at a small group of his peers standing near the gate, watching proceedings. "Hear that, lads?" he shouted. "It's Prince Henry!" His words were met with laughter and mutterings.

"Listen, highlander, bring your friends back on the morrow when there's more light, we're closing the gates for the night."

Something brushed Vyder's shoulder. He stepped aside. Ahitika had nudged her horse closer, Henry's boot touching Vyder's arm.

"Guard," Henry spoke.

The man looked from Vyder up at Henry. His hooded eyes grew larger, and a sharp inhalation of breath whispered between his lips. The guard dropped to one knee and held a fist to his chest, head bowed.

"My lord," the guard spoke loud enough for his comrades to hear. In a matter of moments, they'd mirrored his movement.

"I have returned and seek an audience with my father. I would prefer to do so this evening."

"Aye,   lord."

"Stand, man, stand."

The guard obliged.

"We have ridden hard, our horses are tired, we are exhausted, and the Huronian Army is on our heels."

"Sir?"

"At least twenty thousand of them, perhaps more. Hence my immediate audience with my father. The king should be the first to know."

"Of course, my liege."

"Wait one hour, and then inform the army of what I have told you this evening. Relay a message to the King's Own and let them know one of their sub-units is fighting a rear guard action against the Huronians. It is the only reason we survived at all. I don't know if the King's Own unit is still alive, however."

"Gods," the guard whispered.

"If you don't mind," Henry gestured at the open gate yawning before them.

"Of course, my lord."

Vyder, stepped back and swung up into the saddle, following Ahitika as she thundered through the gate.

* * *

Henry strode down the palace's long, narrow corridors, navigating through the maze of vacant hallways, and empty courts. He greeted several guards with a cursory nod. A servant with a tight smile. He didn't turn to see if Ahitika or Vyder followed. He didn't need to. The stomps their boots made upon the plush carpet told him they were right behind him.

"Will he be in the throne room?" Vyder asked.

"No, he'll be finished for the day. He's probably eating supper or just finished. So, it is to the main royal kitchen we're heading."

Ascending a short flight of stairs, he turned down another corridor, this one much wider. The guards increased in number. Hands darted to sword hilts as the tiny group strode into view, but the guard commander, eyes growing wide as he watched Henry approaching called his troop to attention, their boots thudding in unison.

Henry held the guard commander's look of surprise. "Is he here?" He pointed at the closed door they protected.

"Aye, sire."

He turned the door handle and pushed, hinges groaned, and he walked through. His father sat at the head of a crowded long table, drinking from a polished, silver goblet. The king's eyes were drawn to the sudden movement as the group entered, and he almost dropped the goblet. He slammed the cup onto the table, wine spilling over the edge to stain the rich, satin tablecloth beneath. The chatter that had been pervading the room stopped, the diners watching their monarch. He wiped his mouth with a cloth and stood. His mouth dropped open, and he made to speak, but his lips clamped shut instead.

Henry stopped in front of the king. "Father, I have returned."

Those sitting at the table turned in their seats, looking at Henry. Recognition glinted in many of their eyes, some smiling, others speaking to those seated close by, gesturing at Henry. A few began clapping and cheering.

King George nodded and cleared his throat. He stepped away from the table strode to Henry and pulled him into a tight embrace. "My son. Gods, I didn't think

I'd see the day."

The king held him at arm's length. His father's eyes narrowed, fury glinting there as he looked Henry up and down. "What have they done to you, son? You look near starving."

He shrugged. "I am alive. That is all that matters. I looked worse before these two arrived." He jerked a thumb over his shoulder at the highlander and Kalote woman.

"You have my thanks, highlander, I'll see you paid after the evening meal," King George said. "Although I am sorry to see you have been blinded in one eye. My thanks to you too, young lady."

"I have bad news, Father."

"Speak."

"The Huronian army marches."

He released Henry's shoulders, his arms dropping by his side. The chatter at the nearby long table increased in volume, some excusing themselves and rushing from the room. "How long do we have?"

"My best guess, perhaps a week."

Henry's father draped an arm around his shoulder. "Best we retire to the throne room, son." He cast a glance over his shoulder at those still seated at the table. "That lot knows too much already," he whispered.

The small group walked out, the king leading the way, a small group of guards falling in behind them. After a short, brisk walk, the door to the throne room *thumped* closed behind them, and they were greeted by deafening silence.

Henry glanced at his companions. "I trust you do not mind their presence?"

The king nodded. "Of course." He held a hand to his face. "What numbers are we talking?"

"Twenty or thirty thousand enemy soldiers, Father. Footmen, cavalry, artillery, mortars, their army in its entirety. But we have that and more." Henry smiled. "We'll see them off within a month."

"Would that it were, Son. While you've been gone..." the king fell silent, took a deep breath and exhaled long and slow, his eyes searching the ceiling. "We've lost between eight and nine thousand soldiers, more than a quarter of the Watch, and at least one hundred King's Own troops."

Dread passed through Henry's body. "How?" he breathed.

He leaned against a chair as his father explained. When the king finished speaking, Henry lowered himself into a chair and rested his head in his hands. "We don't have the numbers to fight them, let alone defeat them."

King George cleared his throat. "I will put a call out to the surrounding towns at sunup, hailing all men of fighting age to attend the capital."

"Farmers with pitchforks?" Henry chuckled, but there was no humour to the noise. "They might bolster our numbers, but they are untrained, nor will many of them be willing to leave their families behind."

"It's better than nothing, my son."

He nodded, staring at the dark, polished hardwood of the table. "They'd probably only hinder our soldiers anyway." He paused, considering his next words with care. "Would it be better to leave the farmers to farm their crops?"

His father sniffed and clamped his hands behind his back. "Very well, you may be right. At the least, I will send supply wagons out to collect what food they can from the farmsteads for storage should this become a siege."

"I may have a solution, sires," the highland accent cut through the musty air.

"Mmm?" The king turned to Vyder. "And what would that be?"

"I could journey into Shadolia and request the help of my people."

Henry turned to the tall assassin, hope sweeping him. "Bring a Highland army south to our aid?"

"Aye, lord. It's worth a try, at least."

"I agree, with a Highland army behind us, we'd see the Huronians off in short order." A smile creased the corners of the king's mouth.

"We have a sordid history with Shadolia, though, father. I can't see a group of Highland clans marching south. But as Vyder said, at the very least, it's worth a try."

"You shall leave in the morning, Vyder," King George said. "I shall triple your pay."

Henry stood, pushed the chair under the table, and turned to his father. "I shall go with him."

"I'll not lose you again, Son."

"If we're asking the Shadolian Highlanders to come to our aid, then it's only pertinent that a member of the royal family from the country they're being asked to support is present."

"I go with them," Ahitika stepped forward.

King George ignored her. "Why not a royal diplomat then?"

"It would make us look weak if a royal diplomat turned up asking for military aid. The Highlanders are a proud, warrior race."

"As I am well aware, my son. It is part of the reason I asked for Vyder to fetch you home."

"Then you can see how it would look, Father, if

anyone other than a member of the Wendurlund royal family arrived in Shadolia, asking for military aid?"

The king sighed, glaring at the thick carpet. "Of course," he whispered.

Henry strode towards the door. "We shall leave at dawn. Vyder, Ahitika, I shall show you to your rooms."

"I'm going to check on Miriam," Vyder said. "I'll stay the night in my home and will return before dawn."

Henry opened the throne room door and stepped through. "Very well then. Ahitika, follow me."

He glanced over his shoulder and hesitated for a heartbeat. She glared at him, a slight smile teasing her lips, her eyes hungry. Henry cleared his throat. "I shall see you on the morrow for breakfast, Father."

"Aye, Son, sleep well."

* * *

Vyder led Storm to the back of his home. The wooden gate creaked open, and he walked the horse through. He placed her in the stable, unsaddled, and brushed her down. Then he ensured she had enough to eat and drink.

He sighed, sadness beating through his veins. He'd hoped to be with Verone, but he knew offering to help fight off the menace on Wendurlund's doorstep was the right thing to do. Wendurlund, afterall, had been his home for the better part of his life. He had to at least try to help them in their hour of need. And if he died in the highlands, then at least he'd be with Verone. He turned away from the content animal and walked towards his house.

"Best to knock on the front door," he muttered.

She still has that hand cannon does she not?

"Blunderbuss, and yes."

He wandered around the front and followed the garden path. Too dark to see, the aroma of flowers and fresh turned earth told the garden had been well-tended. He knocked on the thick hardwood.

"Miriam, it is I!"

Several minutes passed before the handle turned, and the door opened a crack. Miriam, half of her face hidden by the door, stared out at him. "Vyder?"

"Aye, lass, It's me."

She licked her lips, her eyes still wide with worry.

"May I come in?"

"It's good to see you, yes of course." She held the door open wide, revealing the blunderbuss she'd been holding in one hand.

She stared at him, her focus shifting from one eye to the other. "Is that thing still part of you?"

"Aye, Gorgoroth is here. We have an understanding, though. He'll not harm you, Miriam."

She called me a thing! *I must protest, little brother.*

Her face softened, and she stepped into his embrace. "I wasn't sure if I'd see you again," she said.

She pulled away from him. "Have you eaten?"

He smiled. "Always looking after me. I haven't yet, no, but it's no great deal."

"I'll not hear it. Come through to the kitchen, I shall cook you a meal."

Miriam prepared pots, a knife and cutting board, stoked the fire and finally departed to the cold room to select some meat. When she returned, she placed the beef upon the board and sliced it into sections. "So, tell me all about your journey. Did you find the prince? Is Endessa safe?"

As she cooked, Vyder explained what had

happened, from the understanding Gorgoroth and he had reached, meeting the fire spirit, Agoth, the departure of Endessa back to her home in the Waning Wood, to creeping into the enemy camp in search of the prince. He described the actions of Ahitika, Henry, and the King's Own sub-unit, which had ultimately saved their lives.

Miriam was still asking questions when she placed the steaming plate in front of him. He ate with relish, stomach groaning. It'd been so long since he'd eaten a substantial meal. He replied through mouthfuls of hot, tasty potatoes, moistened with thick gravy. When he explained about his mission into Shadolia, her face dropped, and her shoulders slumped.

"You're leaving again, tomorrow morning?"

"I must, Miriam. The Huronians will destroy everything and kill everyone. They'll burn Gorgoroth's home to the ground."

"Can Gorgoroth hear me?" Miriam sat opposite him.

"Aye."

"Gorgoroth, you are a fool! You have brought this down upon us all with your..." she stammered, searching for the words, "your stupid mission to rid the earth of humans. You might have destroyed our empire, including your own home!"

She's a furious little thing. I agree with her, it is my fault. But stay positive, Vyder, we will get to kill more little monkeys.

The highlander refrained from answering the nature spirit, even when Gorgoroth's laughter boomed around his mind.

* * *

Henry lay in the darkness. It had taken the better

part of an hour to wash the dirt and stink from his skin and hair. The soft bedding beneath him was the most comfortable thing upon which he'd rested in gods knew how long. Without any real knowledge of the duration he'd been kept prisoner by the Huronians, it might have been years for all he knew. His eyelids touched, and leaden weights seemed to rest upon every aspect of his body. Exhaustion enshrouded him with a tight embrace, and his breathing deepened.

"Get your arse up, prisoner!" the words were spoken with a thick Huronian accent.

Henry's eyes snapped open and fear bored its way into his stomach, dark, slimy fingers of terror metastasising through his body. He sat up, slumber's weakness long departed. Keys jangled on the other side of the thick, wooden door. Metal scraped on metal, then a click, and the *door was kicked open. Light flooded into the tiny cell, and he threw an arm up to provide shade to his straining eyes, which began to water.*

The guard strode in a step and stopped, feet shoulder width apart. "I said on your feet!" The man took another step forward and paused. Then he laughed. "Look at this!" he pointed at Henry.

A second guard appeared behind the first, he stood on tiptoes in order to better see over the shoulder of his comrade.

"He's fuckin' crying!"

Anger fought a valiant battle in Henry's guts and with its help, he pushed himself to his feet, his arm dropping to his side. He squinted against the light to focus on his captors.

"Oh, there's nothing to worry about, my lord!*" The initial guard advanced, reached up and squeezed Henry's cheek. "There, there, don't be sad."*

Henry snapped his head away from the guard's grip, a frown bringing his eyebrows close together, mouth tightening into a thin line.

"How dare you?" The guard punched him in the midriff and all air burst from Henry's mouth.

He dropped to his knees, holding a hand to his belly.

"I said get your arse up!" The guard's mouth was inches from his ear, the shouted words booming through his brain. "Remember?"

Placing a foot flat on the ground, he pushed himself to his feet, suppressing the grunt of pain that so desperately wanted to claim freedom from his lips.

"We have some questions for you, sir."

He clenched his teeth, looked over the head of the closest guard, and stared at a chipped stone block in the wall opposite.

"That's right, the same questions we asked you yesterday and the day before!" The guard shrugged and giggled with feigned pleasure. "Exciting, isn't it?"

They grabbed him from either side and forced him to walk out of his cell and down the familiar, spartan corridor. When Henry wasn't able to keep their pace, they dragged him, scabs on the bare skin of his toes ripped clear and old wounds reopened, leaving a trail of claret upon the dirty floor.

He inhaled a breath of cool, fresh air, eyelids parting to reveal his bedchamber cast in hues of grey. *Did I hear the door close? Or did I dream it?* Henry rubbed his eyes and sighed. He focused on where the door was positioned, but that corner of the room was pitch black. *Must have been part of the dream.* It'd been some time since he'd dreamt of his capture. At one time, it was a nightly occurrence, but with time, the nightmares faded. However, the memory of his incarceration was still buried deep within his mind. Tonight, the floodgates had opened with fervour.

The whisper of bare feet padded across the room, and the far side of Henry's bed sank, the bed frame creaking under a new weight. A hint of peach perfume washed over him. He sat up, heart thundering. The dark form of someone was sitting on the far side of his bed. A hand curled around the blanket covering him and cast it away. Cold air assaulted his skin. The figure moved towards him. He felt smooth thighs descend either side of his hips and hair brush his face. Hard nipples and soft breasts pushed against his chest.

"You have bad dream," Ahitika's whispered voice filled his ears. "I help."

Their lips met. His arms encircled the naked woman and drew her closer. All memory of his captors and his experience at their hands were gone.

* * *

Rone staved off exhaustion with dogged determination. He lost the battle sometime after sundown and lurched awake in the saddle as dawn's promise painted the eastern sky. The Likane Forest was far behind him. Open plains greeted him in every direction, he was closing upon Lisfort. The officer checked his horse had maintained course while he slept, relief washing over him as he confirmed they were still heading west. He straightened and winced. A dull ache gripped his lower back and neck. He drew the warhorse to a halt.

"Time for you to rest, lad."

He dismounted, untied the corpse and pulled the deceased soldier from the animal. Unsaddling the destrier, he brushed the sweat-sodden fur, offered him a drink, and allowed the horse to graze. He sat, pulled the saddle closer and delved into a pouch, bringing clear the small pot. Opening it, he dipped a finger into the pleasant-smelling mixture and rubbed more on his upper lip. The aroma immediately began to diffuse the growing stink of his decomposing soldier.

The Huronian army was still far to the south of his position but would have covered more ground. He stared at the corpse lying on his back. Apart from his purple-tinged skin and motionless chest, he looked for all the world like he was asleep.

"The Huronians will begin their assault on Lisfort before we arrive home." He tugged clear a blade of grass and chewed it. The King's Own officer was not surprised when his dead soldier did not reply. He spat out a section of grass. "We'll have to negotiate past the capital and enter from either the Northern or Western Gate to avoid the enemy."

He flicked the grass away and chuckled. "Sounds easy doesn't it, brother?"

Only the soft whisper of a gentle breeze massaging the grass around him was his answer.

* * *

Garx pointed at a nearby tree. "Drag him over there. Hurry now!"

They pulled the wounded soldier along the ground and sat him against the trunk. The man's skin was pale, his face screwed up in pain, hand clamped over his shoulder where blood oozed between his fingers.

"Bandage the wound," Garx said, clamping a hand over his comrade's wound and applying pressure. The warrior cried out. "Steady, lad, it'll stem the bleeding. I know it hurts."

"Mind your hand, sir." A pad was placed over Garx's fingers. He lifted his hand clear so the pad nestled against the wound, then put pressure back on the thick fabric covering the terrible hole in the man sitting at his feet. Blood soaked through the bandage, and another pad was pushed onto the first. The bandaging recommenced, this time much tighter. The bleeding persisted.

Garx held out his hand to a cavalryman stooped over a first aid bag. "Another trauma pad. Quickly!"

He felt a tap on his shoulder. "Too late, sir."

The wounded warrior's chin rested on his chest. His skin was ashen grey, and there was no hint of breath.

Garx's dropped his outstretched arm, open palm slapping his leg. "Gods above," he muttered through clenched teeth.

"Tie him to his saddle like the others."

"Aye, sir."

How many of my soldiers have I lost now? He straightened and cast his gaze over the nearby formation of Huronian cavalry under his command. Half of the men were dead, their bodies draped over their horses and tied in place.

They'd dealt an equal level of damage to the King's Own sub-unit, but had it all been worth it? *Had that inept young upstart not charged the King's Own in the first place, we wouldn't be in this position.*

"Sir?"

The voice broke his reverie. He turned back to the cavalryman stood before him. He raised his eyebrows, urging the man to continue.

"Will King Fillip have us beheaded for failing him?"

"I know not, lad," he sighed, "but we must at least return to give a report."

More than likely, though.

"We need a contingency plan. I want the others

sitting before me in a half-circle in five minutes. I have an idea."

The soldier touched a fist to his chest and moved away. "Aye, sir."

* * *

Baras led the men of the King's Own sub-unit at a steady trot, occasionally standing in the stirrups and looking over his shoulder for an enemy force giving chase.

"Any sign?" he shouted over the *thump* of hooves against dry dirt.

"None, sir," a voice roared from the rear of the formation.

Gone were the confident chuckles. Morale was low. He'd underestimated the second force of Huronian cavalry and paid for it. The deceased bodies of half the soldiers under his command lay slung over the saddles of their destriers. The enemy commander, not to mention the fighting skill of the cavalrymen, had been exceptional. Baras's soldiers wanted to face an adversary up to their standard, and it'd happened, the results not as pleasing as they'd assumed.

Rone had temporarily relinquished his command to backtrack for the sake of reaching one of his dead soldiers. *What in the hells will he think when he finds out half his unit were slaughtered in battle?*

Dreas galloped alongside and slowed. "Sir! We must rest soon. The horses are growing weary."

"Soon."

The officer maintained pace beside Baras, forcing the bugler to look at him. The skin of Dreas's face was pale, sunken eyes staring at him from behind a straggly mess of blood-stained hair. One of his arms was bandaged. "Sir, we can't go on at this pace for much longer. We need a break."

"Soon! I want to ensure there is sufficient distance between us and the Huronian cavalry." He gestured over his shoulder. "If they descend upon us while we rest, they'll kill us all."

"Sir, with all due respect, if we don't slow this pace before long, our enemy will play no part in our demise. We'll defeat ourselves."

"Another five minutes and I'll call a halt."

"Aye, sir."

* * *

Garx led his troop towards the advancing Huronian Army. Nervous tension found rest in his gut, ebbing, and then charging in with renewed force that left his legs weak. Fear encompassed his being. He was astute enough to battle the fear from showing on his face, however. *We shall see what King Fillip thinks of our little disagreement with the enemy.* They re-entered the outer edges of the Likane Forest.

He hoped years of dedication to his king and loyalty to Huron would claim the day. But he'd served Fillip long enough to know the monarch would probably order he and what remained of his cavalry put to death for their failure. But he needed to know for sure before he put into action their backup plan.

Failure? We hurt them as much as they hurt us. We sent them running like frightened dogs, tails tucked between their legs. Anger welled up, competing against and defeating the waves of weakening anxiety that had plagued him. He steered his formation to one side of the path, thundering past The Mortals marching in the opposite direction. The commander of The Mortals stared at the depleted cavalry unit, his eyes drawn to the centre, where the dead soldiers lay over the saddles of their horses, arms and legs swinging in time with the movement of the animals carrying them. Garx noticed the commander's eyes widen a little.

They galloped beyond the endless lines of infantry, artillery, and supply wagons. He slowed only when he heard the distant shouts and laughter permeating the forest. *Here we go.*

The first few members of the king's entourage came into view. More of them advanced beyond a bend in the road, their ranks thickening. They laughed and joked amongst themselves. Their horses were well rested, the fur of their mounts glistening in the sun. A far cry from those trotting behind Garx.

He became aware of the frivolity fading away the closer he led his unit. The thick blob of cavalrymen surrounding King Fillip were the next to come into view. They were listening with intent to the loud drone of their king. *Recounting some embellished story, no doubt.*

He looked over his shoulder at the warriors trotting behind him. "Ready yourselves!"

The closest nodded, a tight smile widening his lips. "Aye, sir. We're ready."

Silence now greeted them. The king's dulcet tones faded away, those closest to the monarch watching Garx's encroaching unit with growing interest, which turned to horror.

"What the bloody hell?" King Fillip roared. "What is the meaning of this, Garx?"

Garx reined in, the soldiers behind him halted, a portion of them guiding their warhorses forward into extended line to stand either side of Garx.

"The meaning of what, my liege?"

Fillip's face reddened, his brows furrowing and clenched teeth visible behind parted lips. "*That!*" He pointed at the centre of the formation where half of Garx's force lay dead, slung across their destriers. "And where are the others?"

"That stupid little upstart charged more than three miles at full gallop to close with the King's Own. It was a slaughter. Not a single man from that unit survived." Garx gestured towards his deceased warriors. "We rode in support of our comrades. Yes, we have losses, much to my regret, but we did the same amount of damage to the enemy force as you see here. Send forward another unit and we can destroy them completely."

"I don't want excuses, I want results!" King Fillip roared, veins bulging under the skin of his throat. He took a deep breath and shouted, "I want them executed." He pointed at Garx. "Every damn man of them! Destroy their horses as well."

The entourage surrounding the king kicked their mounts into action, charging towards Garx, drawing swords or brandishing spears.

The time for talk is at an end, it is as I thought. Time now to survive.

"Withdraw!"

The depleted unit turned and galloped away from the Huronian Army. They were now outcasts, hunted, forsaken. Garx urged his mount into a gallop at the rear of the small formation, allowing those at the head, as agreed, to lead the beleaguered force through the forest towards the open plains. The yells and hammering of hooves upon soft earth behind suggested those eager to carry out the bidding of the madman he'd once called king were persisting in their chase.

One wayward horse carrying a dead soldier swerved away from the group. One of his soldiers must have lost his grip on the reins. Garx chased down the horse, leaned over his saddle, and clamped a firm grip of the reins. Guiding the horse back towards his withdrawing force, he re-joined his soldiers. *Who knows what they'd do to the horse.* He cast a glance at the corpse slung across the beast's back. *Or my soldier, for that matter.*

Sadness swept him as trees whipped by. He'd given all his life to the kingdom of Huron, and now it was over. All for nothing. He was a vagabond. He shot a look over his shoulder. Those attempting to follow the commands of their king still chased them. Anger replaced the sadness. *Not for long.*

Garx's unit broke clear of the trees onto the open plains and formed into a tight wedge, their deceased comrades at the centre.

Garx withdrew his spear. "Right wheel!"

His cavalrymen repeated the command, their shouted voices carrying across the plain. The group swung right and continued to turn in a wide arc until they were galloping back towards the Likane Forest.

"Forward!"

The formation stopped turning, heading straight for the centre of the group that had intentions of catching them and carrying out King Fillip's command.

"Charge!"

Spears appeared in the hands of his warriors, and their war cries, shouts, and screams filled the air. The chasing force hesitated, the flanks scattering for the safety of the forest. The centre, too slow to react attempted to swing away from the oncoming threat. Garx's formation slammed into them like a war hammer and split them asunder. Wounding, dying, and dead Huronian cavalrymen were flung from their saddles. Then they were behind Garx's unit.

"Right wheel!"

The tight wedge of cavalry began turning, ceasing the turn only when they were facing the depleted force before them. A few of the hunter force had managed to escape, galloping away into the depths of the forest in ones or twos. The vast majority were still trying to organise themselves, several leaning down and trying to help wounded comrades up.

Garx's eyes narrowed, brows furrowing, his lips peeling apart to reveal clenched teeth. "No prisoners!" he roared.

"NO PRISONERS!" the shout was taken up, spreading across the galloping ranks like wildfire.

They hit them like a battering ram. Garx stabbed his spear through the throat of a man, ripped his blood-stained weapon free, and drove it into another soldier's back. He levered the spear clear before his horse barged past the mortally wounded Huronian soldier. A wide-eyed cavalryman who'd been unhorsed made a grab for Garx, with a mind to pull him from his saddle. Garx withdrew a boot from his stirrup and kicked hard, sending him airborne, clutching his destroyed nose. Garx's unit persisted through the far side of the enemy they had once thought of as comrades and turned again. The few remaining Huronian cavalry lost their will to chase and thundered away into the forest, their appetite to fight long gone.

Garx called a halt. "And what now?" he shouted at the dark forest. "Do you think your king will forgive your failure?" Apart from the faint beat of departing cavalry, only silence greeted him. "You'll be hunted down yourself!"

A hand clenched his shoulder. "Sir! Let us be gone."

"Aye." He stood in the stirrups and cast his gaze over the formation arrayed behind him. "Follow me!"

* * *

Sergeant Graff walked upon the rampart of Lisfort's eastern wall, squinting against the dawn sun. He stopped near a group of soldiers leaning against the wall, talking in hushed tones. He approached them.

"You lads spot anything?"

They turned to him. "No, Sergeant," the closest spoke.

"Don't lie, Dej," another said, a smirk stretching one corner of his mouth. "We've seen five rabbits, a fox, and a flock o' birds."

Dej grinned and rolled his eyes. "No, Sarge, nothing to report."

Graff nodded. "Keep your eyes peeled, lads."

"Aye, Sergeant."

He strode on, leaving the group to talk and laugh amongst themselves.

"Morning, Sergeant!" a soldier called.

Graff didn't stop. He called a greeting over his shoulder, then returned his attention to the eastern horizon. Dawn's golden light shimmered upon the open plains and glinted from dew-covered grass. Somewhere out there, bearing down upon them was the Huronian army. Or so orders suggested. The eastern wall had been bolstered with twice as many soldiers as normal.

"On your feet!" he bellowed at a group sat in a huddle playing dice.

One of them snatched up the dice, shoved them in a pouch, and they jumped to their feet in a blur of motion.

"Sarge! Didn't see you there," one of them said.

"Eyes out!" He pointed beyond the group towards the east.

"Aye, Sergeant." The soldiers turned their backs on him and leaned against the battlements.

Graff strolled on.

He'd lost half his company fighting the giant spiders, which had accosted the western wall. A tingling sensation descended his spine, and he shivered. *Ugly bloody bastards of things.* The army had not fared much better with nearly nine thousand soldiers killed overall. Had it not been for the King's Own that night, the city would have fallen.

Wish we had muskets and blunderbusses. Would have been a different story. He clamped his hands behind his back and sighed. *But they are too expensive to issue to the general infantry, as misfortune would have it.*

"Sergeant! I spotted something." A shout broke his reverie.

He strode towards the voice and shouldered his way through the ranks to stand beside the soldier. "What is it?"

The red-faced man struggled not to laugh. "Sarge, near that small bush over there." He pointed at the smudge of green in question.

Graff squinted, but aside from a dog squatting and excreting, he saw nothing.

"Soldier," Graff said, keeping his focus on the animal. "Do you want to be fucking whipped until the flesh of your back is hanging around your ankles?"

"No, Sergeant," the humour was gone from his voice.

"Then I suggest you take this seriously, lad." He turned to face the young man. "Is that understood?"

The red tinge of the soldier's face had been replaced with a white sheen. "Aye, Sarge. Sorry Sarge."

Graff nodded and turned away. "Out the way!" he roared. Warriors stepped aside to make an immediate corridor, down which Graff strode.

Clamping hands behind his back, he progressed along the wall, nodding at or greeting soldiers. One tiny cluster of men stood to attention when he approached.

"Good morning, Sergeant," one of them said, staring unblinking over Graff's shoulder.

Fresh from basic training. Always so easy to spot.

He smiled. "Mornin', lads, now bloody stand easy." He held out his arms, palms facing them. "Relax. You're not in basic training anymore. This is the real world."

"Aye, sir. Sorry, I meant to say sergeant!" The man's eyes bulged.

Graff chuckled. "It's alright, lad. Now eyes out to the east." He pointed at the horizon behind the soldiers. "Don't worry about me. Get your eyeballs out there."

"Aye, Sergeant."

Graff walked on and sighed. *If the reports are true, and the Huronian army is indeed on our doorstep, those young lads won't survive the first week of fighting.*

His eyebrows rose. *Or the experience may test their mettle, making them even better soldiers, I suppose. Don't be so negative, Graff, me old boy.*

He enjoyed the walk, although his left knee was beginning to ache. *Not as young as I once was.* The throng of soldiers lining the wall thickened and Graff walked on the far-left edge of the rampart, aware of the long drop that awaited him if he misplaced a foot. As the thought broached his mind, a memory flickered from that fateful night facing the spiders. Five of his soldiers charged into the fray, hacking at a massive arachnid. They'd killed it, but even as he ran towards them, the momentum of the spider had carried the group over the rampart and into thin air. Graff watched helpless, the screams of his falling men rent the air, not to mention his soul. They'd been dashed upon the cobbled street far below. Their blood splattered upon the nearest King's Own warriors waiting in extended line ready to fight should the creatures break through the infantry lines.

Graff clenched his teeth together and willed the memory away. The vivid imagery faded and retreated to blackness. Relief washed over him. He stopped walking when he stood above the Eastern Gate. Shouldering his way through the thick throng of soldiers, he reached the wall. The eastern road stretched out into the far distance. Wagons, riders, and pedestrians were dotted along its length, travelling towards or away from the city in an endless stream.

His view reduced to a narrow horizontal band, his eyelids almost touching. Placing a foot on the battlements, he stepped up, keeping a firm grip of the stone to ensure he didn't tumble forward and to certain death. A dark smudge stained the road where the ground met the sky. *My eyes aren't what they once were, but I'd bet money that's a cavalry unit.* Shouting was taken up nearby, spreading across the ranks. Soldiers pointed. *Good, it's not just my addled mind playing tricks on me then.*

"Huronian cavalry!" one soldier shouted.

"Don't look Huronian. Wrong uniform," another said.

"How can you tell? They're too far away," a third chimed in.

Graff held a hand over his eyes to provide shade against the sun's assault. *That young lad is right, they're not Huronian. They look like King's Own.*

"They're ours!" the shout spread across the ranks. "They're ours." Some cheered, others clapped and whooped.

Graff stepped down from the battlements and tapped the closest soldier on the arm. The young man turned to him. "Sergeant?"

"Go down into the centre of the city," he shouted over the noise. "Pass on the message that a King's Own unit is inbound."

"Aye, Sergeant, right away." The soldier forced his way out and ran.

He returned his attention to the closing unit. Individual riders and horses were visible. He leaned forward and squinted, staring at the centre of the formation. *Gods, they are carrying many dead with them.*

The cheering dissipated, the clapping stopped and aside from hushed voices, silence descended upon the wall above the Eastern Gate.

"Bloody hell," a man muttered near him. "They've had a bloody hammering."

"More 'an half of 'em are worm food by the looks," someone said.

A soldier climbed up onto the battlements and turned to face his comrades. He held up a hand, two coins clenched between finger and thumb. "How many dead they got with them? My reckoning is forty-three! Place your bets! Winner takes all."

Within moments, shouting, yelling, laughing, and clapping exploded along the rampart. Bets were taken, and money exchanged hands.

"There are fellow soldiers dead down there!" Graff roared. He felt his skin flush with anger. Those closest to him, stepped away from the sergeant and fell silent. But the noise caused by the others was too much for Graff's voice to quiet.

He pushed his way through the ranks and headed back the way he'd approached. *I need to get back to my soldiers and prepare them. This may start sooner than we all thought. The Huronians may lay siege to us this afternoon.*

* * *

"Ensure you have plenty of food. When the siege starts, lock the doors and don't let anyone in, no matter the reason."

Dawn was breaking, a cool breeze touching his face.

Miriam nodded. "I shall. Hurry back, Vyder."

He hugged her. "I'll be back before you know it." He smiled, shouldered the sack of food, grabbed his weapons, and walked through the door, heading for the stable. Saddling Storm, he distributed the food amongst his saddle bags, handed the empty cotton sack to Miriam. "Take care of yourself, Miriam. Stay safe. This will all be over soon."

"I have a blunderbuss and a kitchen knife, Vyder. Should they breach the city walls, I shall tear them apart." She smiled, but the humour did not reach her eyes. Fear still resided there.

He chuckled, stepped up into the saddle, and stroked Storm. "It won't come to that."

You can't promise that, little brother. It may well come to that. And it is my fault entirely.

"I truly hope not." The smile faded from her lips. "If they breech the walls, we won't last a week."

"The Wendurlund Army are more stoic than you think, Miriam."

No, they are not, and you know it.

Vyder clenched his teeth and bit back a retort. "They shall see the enemy off."

Miriam nodded, her lips stretching in a tight smile. "I shall see you soon."

Laughter echoed in his mind.

I mean I hope you are right, my human brother, I truly do. But I have seen the Wendurlund army fight. Aside from the tiny group of Horse Warriors, they cannot stand against what is marching upon them.

Vyder ignored Gorgoroth. "You shall, Miriam. Stay safe. I will return as soon as I can."

He turned Storm away and urged her into a trot. Casting one last glance over his shoulder, he waved. He pushed Storm into a canter. Miriam lifted her hand, then disappeared behind a building.

* * *

Sitting astride his new horse, Henry relaxed in the saddle, Ahitika mounted upon the King's Own destrier beside him.

"You don't have to do this, my son."

Henry noticed the lines of worry etched around his father's eyes.

"I do, Father, and you know it as well as I. We cannot have an assassin ask a neighbouring kingdom on our behalf for aid in a coming war."

King George stepped forward and held out his hands. "What if I were to send a royal diplomat in your stead?"

"Father, we've been through this. We are talking about the Shadolian Highlanders. You know better than most that they are a warrior race. They value courage and honour above all else."

"Aye, so they do, son." The king's arms dropped by his side.

"Surely then, it will look much better if Vyder, a highlander himself, and myself an immediate member of the royal family travel to the highlands seeking military aid."

"Don't forget you escorted by Kalote warrior," Ahitika said.

He flashed her a smile.

"Very well then." King George shrugged. "I wish you well. Return as soon as you can with reinforcements at your back."

The lines of worry encroaching upon his father's eyes competed with a flush of pride. The king smiled. "You always were a single-minded boy."

"Aye, Father. Mark my words, I shall bring down upon the Huronians a highland army that will send them fleeing for their homeland."

"With any luck, we will have already done that by ourselves."

Henry nodded. "I hope so."

A clatter of hooves grew in volume, distracting Henry from saying any more. Vyder reined in beside him and Ahitika. The assassin's eyes, one a piercing blue, and the other the dark brooding glint attributed to the highland clans bored into him.

"Are we ready, young prince?"

He caught Ahitika's eyes, the woman watching him with a slight smile. He winked at her, then turned his attention to his father. He reached down and clasped his hand. "See you soon, Father." Straightening, he returned his focus to Vyder. "Aye, Vyder, we are ready. Take us into Shadolia."

Part II

Vengeance

V

Vyder led the trio north along the streets of Lisfort. He guided Storm off the cobbled street, casting a glance over his shoulder to ensure the others had followed suit. The massive wagon, taking up almost three quarters of the street rumbled by. On the wagon's tray rested a mighty water barrel, able to contain at least several thousand gallons of fresh water. Three times they'd been forced off the road to allow the behemoths to pass. The water wagons were on their way south to the Therondale River to fill up prior to their slow journey back to Lisfort. If it were to be a protracted siege, then water would be vitally important for everyday life to continue.

He nudged Storm out onto the street and pushed her into a fast walk. Checking, the prince and the Kalote woman were still following, although their horses walked beside one another, the pair talking quietly amongst themselves. Occasionally, they laughed at some jest one or the other made. Vyder turned away from them and smiled.

Oh, they're in love! Gorgoroth's voice echoed in his mind. *How cute.*

"Leave them alone, Gorgoroth," he muttered.

A distant horn echoed across the city, faded to silence, then resounded again. It must have truly been a mighty horn to create such noise. On several occasions in the past had he heard it used. He'd discovered later on each of those occasions it'd been a King's Own training exercise, testing the speed at which the warriors of the unit could assemble at a central point from any area of the city, including their own homes were they on days off. A cold chill swept along the skin of his arms leaving goose bumps in its wake. The clop of a cantering horse approached and Henry reined in beside him.

"I doubt that's a training exercise."

Vyder nodded. "Somehow, I think you're correct, young prince. I only hope it's Baras and his unit approaching, rather than the Huronian army."

We might not be able to leave if the city is laid to siege. Gorgoroth sounded pleased.

The assassin grunted.

Well, I suppose we could sneak out of one of the gates and kill some Huronian soldiers. That'd be fun! We'd have them surrounded in minutes, little brother.

Gorgoroth's chuckle reverberated in his mind.

What say you, my little human brother?

Vyder sniffed and focused on the cobbled road in front of him.

Afraid that little human beside you will hear you talking to yourself?

"Will you shut your trap, Gorgoroth?"

Henry snapped a look at the assassin, cleared his throat, and looked away. "What's he saying?" Henry asked.

Allow me to speak for myself, brother.

Numbness spread across Vyder, his throat tightening and tingling. "I said," Gorgoroth's voice burst from Vyder's lips, "if the city is laid to siege, we may not be able to leave." A grin split Vyder's beard. "And we may be forced to ride straight into the Huronian army and kill them all."

Henry's eyes grew wide, his mouth dropping open. "You're deranged!"

"Why, thank you, human."

"They'd kill us before we even drew close to them."

"You little monkeys are overcautious, sometimes.

You bore me."

Vyder leaned forward in the saddle and coughed. He clamped a hold of his throat and groaned. "Sorry about that, Henry," the highlander said.

The prince offered a tight smile.

"Make way!" a shouted voice boomed from behind them.

The trio barely had time to move to the left of the road. A small formation of King's Own thundered past them, followed the road towards the east, and disappeared behind a group of buildings. Several more King's Own groups ripped past them, following the same route taken by the first unit.

Ahitika reined in on the other side of Vyder. The Kalote warrior stared at the assassin. "Time to leave city. We make highlands? Then we leave now."

"Aye, Ahitika. Agreed, lass."

"Let's make the Northern Gate before it closes!" Vyder pushed Storm into a gallop.

Ahitika let out a loud shriek and kicked her destrier into action, the powerful animal falling in behind the assassin, Henry not far behind.

They progressed across the main intersection, the road spearing to the east thick with King's Own warriors. The trio pushed on to the north. Watchmen galloped past in ragged groups, no doubt on their way to various areas of the city. Vyder cast a glance over a shoulder and noticed another group of watchmen keeping pace behind them, although they were not indicating for the three of them to slow down.

"I think they're on their way to the Northern Gate!" Henry had noticed them, too.

Vyder nodded and returned his attention to the front, steering Storm around a slow merchant cart, and then bringing her to the far-left side of the road to give the huge water wagon room to rumble past in the opposite direction. The crew of the gigantic wagon yelled something at the trio as they thundered by, but Vyder couldn't make out the words.

They followed the gentle curve of the north road, passing slower traffic, dodging oblivious pedestrians and ignoring their shouts of abuse. The Northern Gate came into view. The mighty doors were still open, but the Watch were thronged everywhere inside and outside the city walls. They were allowing people, carts, and wagons to leave in a steady stream, but the thick convoy wanting to enter the city were halted by a veritable army of watchmen and turned away one by one.

"Mind yourselves!" Vyder roared, steering Storm around a group of wagons three abreast.

The trio managed to weave around the outside and closed on the Northern Gate. A panicked merchant barged his way through the line of watchmen and galloped towards the gate and the safety of the city. He was surrounded before he'd travelled fifty paces, a watchman leaping onto his wagon, wrestling the reins from the merchant and turning the wagon around.

A fight broke out when a man tried to usher his family through the lines of the Watch towards the Northern Gate. The city was their only safety from the approaching menace. The man managed to knock one watchman to the ground but was clubbed for his efforts, his wife screaming and lying on top of him to stop the onslaught. He was dragged to his feet and pushed back the way he'd approached, his family, and he denied access to Lisfort.

The massive gates loomed, dwarfing the fast-moving trio. They dodged around slower moving traffic and thundered beneath the Northern Gate.

"Gods, *please* allow us in!" a woman shrieked.

"Step back!" shouted a watchmen.

Vyder glanced at the static line of traffic attempting to gain entry to the city. The woman at the front of the pack, a babe cradled in her arms, was pushed away. She yelled something else, but Vyder was too far away to hear.

Soon Lisfort was a diminishing blob behind them and only then did they allow their horses to slow to a trot and then a walk. They were free of the city, but they'd never be allowed back in, not as long as the Huronian army threatened.

"Only two options now," Ahitika's voice broke the gentle *clop* of horses' hooves.

Vyder swung in the saddle and held the gaze of the Kalote woman.

She grinned. "Victory or death."

* * *

Tork led the King's Own through the open East Gate at a gallop in a column three abreast. Once clear of the city's walls, they broke out into an arrowhead formation.

He caught Roland's eye, who was galloping alongside him. He nodded at Roland. The man brought the bugle to his lips. *Encircle!*

The entirety of the King's Own wheeled around Baras's beleaguered force, providing all round protection for them. One King's Own sub-unit broke clear of the circle and provided a rear guard in case a Huronian advance party had illusions of finishing off Baras and his soldiers.

Tork cantered along Baras's sub unit, taking in the dead soldiers slung across their horses. *Gods! They've had a hard time of it.* He reached the front and reined in alongside Baras. "Well met, Baras."

Baras smiled. "Sir, nice to see you all."

"Where is Lieutenant Rone?" the King's Own commander shot a look over his shoulder at the dead men lying on their saddles. "He in there somewhere?"

Baras explained what had happened.

Tork clenched his jaw and sighed. His eyelids met, and the world descended into darkness. *Rone, you've just given yourself a death sentence. The Huronian army will have killed him by now.* His eyes opened. "I understand why he did it," he finally spoke.

"We would have all gone with him, sir, but he ordered us on."

Pride swelled through him. "I have no doubt. I can only hope he lives and will in time make it back to Lisfort."

"Aye, sir."

"But for now, we should head north to the King's Own cemetery." He jerked his thumb at the dead warriors behind him. "Get these soldiers on their way across the Frost River before the Huronian army put us to siege."

He saw the subtle slump of Baras's shoulders. The dark bags under his eyes, reflected by the members of his sub unit told the silent tale of sheer exhaustion.

Tork nudged Might closer to the bugler's mount. He leaned across and clamped a hold of the bugler's shoulder. "I know how tired you must be, my friend. But this siege may go on for days, weeks, or many months. Our dead brothers need to be buried, or their rotting flesh may cause disease in the city."

Baras nodded. "Given a choice, sir, I think we'd all prefer to bury our men with full honours in the cemetery than burn them like a stack of firewood within the city walls."

"Then let us get it done."

The King's Own headed northwest towards the cemetery that had been dedicated to them for more than a thousand years.

* * *

Rone lay in a hollow in the ground, his dead soldier on one side of him and his horse lying on the other. The King's Own officer crept to the lip of the ditch, musket clutched tight in his hands. He raised his head just high enough so as to see above the grass. The Huronian cavalry force cantered onward, away from him, oblivious to his presence. They carried many dead with them.

What in the bloody hell are Huronian cavalry doing this far north? They were only a small force. *Must be deserters.*

A distant shouted command reached him and the Huronian formation halted, dismounted, and moved out into a circle, their commander standing in the centre. The officer gestured as he addressed them.

His destrier snorted behind him, and Rone flinched. He scuttled back and laid a hand upon the horse. "Quiet, my lad, we aren't in the clear just yet." He patted the powerful neck.

* * *

Garx held out his hands. "We should be safe here for the moment." The dismounted cavalrymen surrounded him in a large circle, listening. Garx stood in the centre of the circle. "I know many of you have families back in Brencore, and I do not blame you for returning to gather them."

Whispers and mutters surrounded him. "But know," he raised his voice to defeat the chatter, "you only have a limited time. When our army returns home, you will be treated as traitors and put to death. That goes for your family as well. Right now, no one back in Brencore knows what has taken place…yet. Once any one of those supply wagons is depleted and makes its way back for resupply, they shall carry word of our," he hesitated and laughed. It was a sound full of sarcasm. "They'll carry word of our sedition." His lips peeled apart to reveal clenched teeth. "Let me be clear that we did nothing but our duty to our empire and our king! We have done nothing wrong."

"What will you do, sir?" a man called from behind him.

Garx pivoted. "I shall stay here. There is nothing left for me back in Brencore. Not anymore."

"And do what?" another asked.

"Fight." He paused. "I don't know against whom yet, but I will fight. And perhaps die."

"I've got nothin' left in Brencore either," said a warrior to his left. "I'll join you, sir. We got nothin' left to lose."

Garx looked at the soldier who'd spoken. "Then there were two."

"I'm sorry, sir. I've a wife and three children. Their safety comes first. I must return and get them away from the city."

He turned to the speaker and nodded. "I completely understand and hold nothing against you." He raised his voice. "Nor would I hold anything against any of you who choose to return for the sake of your families."

"I'm with ya, sir!"

"Me too."

"Good luck to you, sir. I must return to my family."

Eventually, twenty cavalrymen decided to remain with Garx, while thirty-one chose to return to Brencore to secure their families and spirit them away before harm could visit them.

"Then we are decided!" Garx called to the cavalrymen encircling him. "But before we part ways, let us at least bury our brothers and send them on their way."

After many hours, the job was done and the soldiers sat together, talking in quiet voices about the dead, laughing at some of the memories, speaking in sombre tones about others. Then they mounted up, muttered their farewells to the makeshift graves where the bodies of their brothers would rest for eternity. The last remnant of sunlight speared the sky purple, and the two groups of Huronian cavalrymen parted. One heading deeper into Wendurlund territory, the other steering back to their homeland.

* * *

Fishermen teamed at the water's edge of the Wendurlund Port, carrying wooden crates or baskets full of fresh fish from their boats towards the fishmongers. The smell of fish pervaded the area. Gulls wheeled, dived, and bickered with one another for scraps. Vyder smiled. The aroma brought back memories of days gone by. In the water, tied to the wharf, were all manner of boats, ships, and barges bobbing with a gentle rhythm as the ocean moved beneath them.

Merchants wandered along the stalls of the fishmongers arrayed in neat rows, selecting fish, crabs, squid, and even selections of shark. Once they'd purchased their produce, their journey to Lisfort or outlying towns would be a mad dash before the seafood turned bad. Vyder didn't understand why merchants entered the seafood game, it was such high risk, not to mention expensive. If an inn, fellow merchant, or kitchen chef did not purchase their product, they were out of pocket. If one wagon-load failed to sell, or the produce went off, it'd see the merchant at an end.

Vyder turned to the pair walking behind him, leading their horses. "I missed that smell. I often worked at Shadolia's Port as a lad for one copper a week."

Henry glanced at the highlander, his mouth down-turned, nose crinkled. "Trust you to miss a smell like that. I suppose you highlanders are a sea faring nation, so it makes sense."

Ahitika laughed and slapped Henry's arm. "You too soft, too pampered."

The prince's eyebrows shot up, and he chuckled. "Perhaps I am."

A highland longship was moored further down the wharf, several Shadolian highlanders standing on the jetty in front of the ship and talking amongst themselves. On the bow of the ship, large highland runes were carved into the wood. "Sea Serpent," Vyder muttered.

The highlanders wore a thick tartan cloth diagonally across their chests, the square colours of black with red centres denoting the crew belonged to clan Steelforge. At their hips were holstered muzzle loading pistols, and on their backs, point facing towards the ground, were sheathed swords. Vyder changed direction towards the group.

"Ho there, highlanders!" he called to them.

They ceased talking and turned to Vyder. One of them, a tall man with flame hair and beard, stepped forward. Like all highlanders, the iris and pupils of his eyes were dark. He looked Vyder up and down and sneered.

"What do ya want?"

Vyder swept an arm behind him to encompass the two behind him. "We seek passage to Shadolia."

Flame Beard tucked his thumbs into his belt. "Do ya?"

"Aye."

Flame Beard stepped past Vyder and addressed Ahitika. "This true, Kalote?"

The Shadolian and Kalote empires shared a close bond, each sharing a history of hardship and oppression at the hands of Wendurlund and Huron respectively. Vyder did not blame the flame-haired highlander for immediately distrusting him.

"It true," Ahitika replied. "He good man." She pointed at Vyder. "Crazy as wounded dog," she tapped her chest, "but good."

Flame Beard stepped back and held Vyder's stare. "Crazy, are ya?" his lips parted to reveal yellowing teeth. "That makes eight of us, then."

The highlanders behind Flame Beard burst into laughter.

He became stern again and pointed at Vyder's one dark eye. "I see you have highlander blood too, crazy one."

"Aye, I do."

"Which clan?"

"Ironstone."

"Strong clan that one." He grinned again. "Almost as strong as Steelforge. But where is your tartan?"

"I left it behind as a young man when I travelled south over the sea to Wendurlund. We are despised there. Wearing my clan colours would have done me no favours."

Flame Beard sneered. "No." He gestured at the highlanders standing behind him. "*We* are despised in Wendurlund. You are as good as someone of Wendurlund stock now." He stepped closer to Vyder. "Besides," he motioned towards Vyder's darker eye, "tartan or no, it is easy to see you have highland blood. So why not wear your clan colours? Ashamed of them, are ya?"

Vyder's jaw bulged. "Of course not."

"Could have fooled me," one of the highlanders behind the flame haired warrior muttered.

"This is goin' 'round in circles, Snarri," another spoke. "The wares are here. Best we be off."

Vyder touched the charcoal disk beneath his shirt and remained silent.

A wagon-load of fine rugs, blankets, and clothes rumbled to a halt behind Vyder. Another highlander jumped down from the driver's seat, a wide grin adorning his face. "A good bargain this time, Snarri," he addressed Flame Beard.

"Snarri," Vyder said. "We can pay."

Snarri's eyes left the wagon and returned to Vyder. "Oh, you'll pay, Wendurlund. One gold coin per person."

The chuckles and snorts of the highlanders standing behind Snarri faded to silence when Vyder produced the payment. Even Snarri's eyes bulged a little.

"That pays for the travel of both us and our horses."

Snarri nodded. "Fair enough, Wendurlund."

"My name's Vyder."

Snarri shrugged and spat upon the thick wooden planks upon which he stood.

"This is Ahitika and Henry," Vyder motioned at the pair behind him.

Snarri appraised Henry with a sneer. Turning his attention to Ahitika, he smiled and nodded. "A pleasure, Ahitika." He shot the highlanders standing idle behind him with a glare. "Let's get this wagon unloaded!" he roared.

When the wagon had been unloaded, the trio were motioned onboard. First, they were made to lead their horses up a wide gangplank onto the aft of the longship and into a large, dark enclosed area. The enclosure was awash with the stink of animal urine and shit. It was too dark for his eyes to focus at first, but he was not oblivious to the cries and bleats of cows, sheep, and goats all around him. Blinking, the blackness receded into shades of grey and gloom. Vyder noticed various species of stock were stabled. Vyder led Storm to an empty stable and locked the horse away. The area his horse was enclosed was wide and long enough for the animal to turn around and even lie down if necessary. He checked the water pail hooked on the rails was full.

"You have any fodder?"

A highlander approached him and shoved a bale of hay at him. "Here."

He cast the hay over the enclosure railings, and then reached through and cut free the bindings holding the bale tight. Checking Henry and Ahitika had done the same for their mounts.

"Through this way!" shouted a highlander standing near a door leading towards the bow.

He'd travelled upon a similar longship when he'd departed Shadolia as a young man. Large as it was, the ship was long and narrow, allowing it to cut through the water much faster than most other sea craft.

They ducked through the doorway and down a narrow walkway, oarsmen sat on either side, preparing themselves to begin rowing out of the harbour. Some of them bound strips of leather around their hands to ward off blisters. Others stared at the newcomers, particularly Vyder and their eyes were far from welcoming.

"Mixed blood," one muttered as he strode by.

"There's the half-blood," another whispered.

A third growled something Vyder missed, but the oarsmen nearby erupted in laughter.

"What's a Wendurlund dog doing onboard?" one of them shouted from behind.

Vyder turned. The highlander cast down his oar and burst to his feet, his face red, teeth clenched, and brow furrowed. But he wasn't looking at Vyder, he was glaring at Henry.

"Brings nothin' but bad luck." He pointed at the prince. "He'll send us to the bottom before we see Shadolia!"

"Aye!" another joined in.

The highlander leading the trio brushed past Vyder and faced the furious oarsman. "Stow it, Bowold. They have paid for their passage."

"Aye, and we likely to see any of that coin?"

The highlander nodded. "Snarri's good for it, you know that."

That seemed to appease Bowold, although his dark eyes glinting with controlled violence returned to Henry.

Bowold sat upon his rowing bench with lack of speed, his stare never leaving the prince's face.

The highlander turned back to the three newcomers and took the lead once more. "Come," he said over one shoulder. "I shall walk you to the top deck."

* * *

Remaining prone, Rone waited for long hours as the nearby enemy cavalry unit buried their dead. He often withdrew with slow, deliberate movements to check on his horse. The warhorse remained lying and seemed to be calm. *Can't be comfortable though.*

The Huronians finished the task, and then split into two groups. One continuing on towards Lisfort, the other departing in the opposite direction. When they were gone, and he could no longer hear the plod of their horses' hooves, he dragged his dead comrade onto the horse and tied the corpse in place. "Gods you stink, brother."

He coaxed the horse to its feet, stepped into the saddle, and as darkness descended upon the land, urged his mount onward towards Lisfort and the safety of the city's walls.

* * *

The bright glow thrown by Finkam the Hunter glittered upon the surface of the ocean. Ahitika leaned upon the rail of the top deck and stared out at the harbour. She steadied herself as the ship accelerated and decelerated beneath her. A tell-tale sign they were travelling under the power of oars.

126

"Nice night," Henry spoke, moving alongside her.

"It is."

The ship was negotiating out of the harbour. The surface of the ocean was still and flat, the longship cutting through the water at speed.

Henry's arm encircled her shoulders. "Where's Vyder?"

She jerked a thumb behind her. "He sleeping."

A raven landed on the handrail nearby and cackled. Ahitika noticed one of the animal's eyes shimmered a gentle blue. "Maybe he not sleeping." She nodded at the bird. "He also witch doctor."

Henry laughed. "You think Vyder is controlling the raven?"

She shrugged out of his embrace and fixed him with a baleful glare. "These things no laughing matter. I saw Vyder speak with fire god. Long before your rescue. He not just man. He something else as well. Something," she paused, "not man."

"His mind is just injured, Ahitika. I've seen it before. We call it a split personality."

"You wrong, Henry." She leaned on the rail again, staring at the raven. "I right."

The bird glared at her with its odd eyes, stretched its wings, cackled, and flew away.

Henry clutched a hold of the ship to steady himself as the deck rolled and pitched beneath his feet. A shouted command in the highland tongue and a team of sailors untied a thick rope, allowing the sail to descend to its a full length with a powerful *snap*. Wind billowed the sail, powerful lines holding it in place creaking against the strain. The longship accelerated. Muffled shouting below decks suggested the oarsmen had been commanded to cease their work.

A small group of highlanders moved to the bow and stern, fixing a dragon's head and tail respectively. Ahitika had seen many longships adorned in such a way.

She noticed Henry watching the groups as they hammered the carvings in place. "To ward off evil spirits."

He nodded, his brow relaxing.

"Best get some rest," Ahitika said.

"How long does the journey across the Shadolian Sea take?"

"We arrive tomorrow evening." She clutched a hold of his hand. "Come, we rest until Yanahee's Fire splits the sky."

Henry grinned. "We're going to rest, are we?"

She smirked at him and winked. "Maybe. Maybe not."

* * *

Vyder jerked awake and sat up. He'd been allowed to sleep on the centre of the longship's top deck. *Something's wrong, brother.*

For the first time, Gorgoroth sounded concerned. Perhaps even frightened.

"What is it?" he whispered.

We are not alone.

Vyder snorted. "We're on a longship full of highland warriors, Gorgoroth. Of course we're not alone."

Well, well, what have we here? A new voice, higher pitched than that of Gorgoroth blasted through Vyder's mind.

A crushing pressure pushed down upon his chest, and despite his attempts to resist the weight, Vyder was forced back into a supine position. A flicker of lightning lit the deck up for a fraction of a moment, followed by a blast of thunder.

A nature spirit out here upon *my* ocean?

Vyder attempted to sit, but despite the burning of the muscles in his stomach, he remained flat upon the wood of the longship's deck. "What is happening, Gorgoroth?"

Like I said, little brother, we are not alone.

Gorgoroth is it? I've heard of you. You're the shepherd of the Waning Wood.

I haven't heard that title in a long time.

Thick clouds blotted out the moon's glimmer and a second flash of lighting descended towards the ocean nearby, the deafening *crack* of thunder shuddering through the longship.

Have you heard of me, Gorgoroth?

It's a little difficult when I know not your name.

Thoron.

Vyder attempted to squirm sideways, but he was held firm against the longship's deck. Torrential rain slammed down upon the longship, turning dry wood slick within a matter of moments. The sail, sodden, hung limp. The storm descended upon them, but no wind filled the sail.

You are a rarity indeed. Vyder. We are in the presence of royalty. Thoron is both a water and air spirit.

"Pleasure to make your acquaintance," Vyder spoke through gritted teeth. He wiped a hand across his brow, eyes clenched against the torrential rain. "Tell me, are you known by we highlanders as Thros, the storm goddess?"

The very same.

Fear speared Vyder, numbness spreading through

his extremities. "So, now I'm talking to a highland deity," he muttered to himself.

You might have asked my permission before you embarked upon your journey, Gorgoroth.

I did not know you guarded this area, Thoron. Had I known, I would have.

Well now you do know. So, what say you now?

May we pass?

Perhaps.

The weight faded from Vyder's chest, allowing him to scramble to his feet.

Perhaps not.

Lightning seared the dark sky, a clap of thunder shattering the air around the longship.

Something smacked into Vyder's chest with a dull thud. He blinked through the heavy rain and looked down to see a hand holding a wooden pail against his chest. Following the hand, and the arm to which it was attached, he looked into Snarri's face. The longship's captain squinted through the blinding weather, water streaming from his thick beard. "Make yourself useful! Start bailing," he roared, pointing below decks. He stepped closer to Vyder, a wide grin splitting his beard. "Thros is giving us a show, is she not?"

"Aye," he leaned toward the captain's ear and cupped a hand against his mouth. "Although I think it's more than a show! She means to kill us!"

Snarri threw his head back, droplets of water flying from his hair. He laughed and held out his hands, then returned his attention to Vyder. "We must all die." He looked at the dark, grey sky around them, "and today is as good a day as any. Yes?"

Vyder thought of his wife, Verone, waiting for him on the far side of the Frost River. He smiled. "Death holds no fear for me, Snarri." He clasped the pail and pulled it free of the captain's grip. "If today is the day we are sent to the bottom of the ocean, then so be it."

Snarri slapped him on the shoulder and strode past, shouting orders.

Vyder climbed down the ladder. He jumped onto the deck and stepped clear of the ladder. The cold rain faded to be replaced with heat, the stink of body odour and shouting. Oars were stacked in neat piles in the centre of the floor. Highland sailors ran towards another ladder, descending into the bowels of the ship. They carried pails, similar to that clutched by Vyder.

Rain water streamed between the planks of the top deck, splashing to the floor at Vyder's feet, where it seeped between the boards.

"The bottom deck is flooding," shouted one sailor, brushing past Vyder. "We must bail the water clear, or the ocean will claim us."

And will you claim us, Thoron?

We shall see.

VI

Shouting awoke Ahitika. She rolled out of the hammock, her feet slammed onto the deck, and she steadied herself, her hand clenched upon the hilt of her knife. The other touching her bone breastplate. The longship pitched and rolled beneath her. Thunder reverberated through the ship, rain water streamed through the gaps in the ceiling, cold against her skin. Henry landed with a *thud* beside her, his face calm, but his eyes belied the fear she knew he experienced.

Highlanders ran towards a ladder, climbing down deeper into the longship, wooden buckets in their hands. She spotted Vyder amongst them and called to him, but the assassin disappeared into the depths of the longship. She turned to Henry.

"Safer up top." She pointed towards the sky. "If ship sinks, we jump off." She pointed at her feet. "If we down there and ship sinks, no good." She passed an extended index finger across her throat. "We good as dead."

"Right you are," Henry said. "Upwards it is."

They walked to the ladder leading towards the top deck and stepped aside as several highlanders came sliding down, landing one after another, running for the lower decks, wooden pails in their hands. Ahitika took the ladder in her hands, glared up and for the first time caught a glimpse of the ferocious storm high above them. She squinted against the incessant rain and climbed. Her soft moccasins were slippery on the ladder's rungs, but she persisted, pulling herself clear when she reached the upper deck. A sudden flash competed with the strength of Finkam the Hunter, and then faded to gloom, followed by a deafening blast of thunder. She ducked to her haunches, her soaking hair plastered to the skin of her cheeks. Henry cleared the ladder and stood beside her, pulling her to her feet.

"Are you okay?" he shouted.

She grinned. "I good. Not dead yet."

Waves half again the height of the longship rolled towards them. The captain had been skilled enough to turn the ship to face the oncoming threat. The deck ascended beneath them as the longship broached the wave, forcing the pair to squat in order to maintain their balance. Henry vomited upon the deck, the skin of his face whiter than normal.

Ahitika laughed. "You no sea dog!"

The longship crested the mighty wave, and then the bow descended. Ahitika reached behind her with both hands and threaded her fingers between a gap in the planks of the deck, holding firm. Henry copied her but vomited again.

"When ship level, we run for mast!"

Henry nodded his understanding, wiping vomit and tendrils of saliva from his mouth.

The ship became level as it reached the trough between the waves and the pair dashed for the mast pole. They raced the next huge wave sweeping towards them. As the deck ascended, they clenched a firm grip of the mast. Sea water swept across the deck, threatening to wash her feet from beneath her. Seaweed snared against her leg. She plucked it free and threw it clear.

The frothy water swept clear of the deck leaving several fish floundering upon the wood. Lightning made the ocean daylight for a fleeting moment and thunder tore the sky asunder, her ears ringing. The longship rode the peak of the giant wave and pitched downward. Henry slipped, one of his hands coming free of the mast.

Ahitika crouched and grasped his wrist, water streaming down her face and soaking her to the bones. She pulled him towards her until he managed to snatch a hold of a rope tied around the mast. He shouted something, but she could not hear him over the hiss of rain, intermittent thunder claps, not to mention the incessant rumble of the powerful ocean around them.

A group of highlanders approached them in a tight group. *They're probably going to seek shelter with us, or aid us to a safer location.* The ship tilted as it ascended the next great wave and the highlanders crouched, their balance impressive. When the longship reached the apex, they sprinted for the mast and surrounded Henry. The men grabbed him from all sides and hauled him towards the gunwale, shouting, although she knew not the words.

Lightning flashed, and it was only then she saw the anger creasing their faces. *They must believe Henry has brought the storm upon us.* She snarled and shrieked a war cry, unsheathing her hunting knife. They began their steep descent towards the bottom of the wave, and Ahitika released her grip of the mast. Her feet left the ground, and she dropped towards the group beneath her, smashing into them, sending several highlanders to the deck. One of them slid away across the slick wood, scrambling for a hold to arrest his movement. He failed and disappeared over the edge of the ship to be claimed by the furious ocean.

Henry fought his way clear and punched one man in the face. Ahitika jumped at another highlander who'd snaked a forearm around Henry's throat. She clenched a fistful of hair, pulled back his head and drew the razor-sharp knife across his throat, splitting the skin. Blood gushed from the wound, spilling to the deck. The liquid was pleasantly warm as it rushed down her arms, across her neck, and soaked into her clothes. The highlander released Henry and dropped to the deck where he died.

Pain exploded in her cheek and the longship rose to meet her face. An assailant squatted over her, a blade of his own in his hand, the tip pointing at her throat. A wicked grin adorned his face. She kicked him in the groin. He fell backward. Ahitika rolled away and managed to wedge her fingers between a gap in the deck planks. They climbed the next wave, and Henry tumbled towards the edge of the ship, embroiled in a wrestle with the last highlander. When they reached the wave's peak, she released her grip, ran to the man who'd so recently squatted over her, drew back his head and cut free his scalp. His scream was a drawn out, high-pitched wail. She stood and held the bloody section of hair and skin high, shrieking, fury consuming her. Blood ran down her arm. She threaded the hair through her belt. They rushed towards the trough, waiting for them between the wave they'd conquered and the next rolling towards them. She knelt to regain her balance.

Henry broke clear of his assailant's grip and kicked him, his boot slamming into the man's midriff and spinning him from his feet. A wave crashed across the deck, sweeping the highlander away. Thigh deep water threatened to pull the Wendurlund prince into the eternal embrace of the ocean, but he clamped upon the gunwale and held firm. The longship reached the trough, the deck evening beneath her. She ran for Henry, clasped a fistful of his shirt, and pulled him away from the ship's edge.

"Back to mast!" she shouted. "Come!"

***

Freezing ocean water sloshed around Vyder's hips. Fresh rain water streamed down through the cracks in the planks of the deck above, soaking him, his hair plastered against his face. He stood in an extended line, passing pails filled with water to the man next to him. The wooden containers, one after another, flowed down the line until they reached the last man, who emptied the water out an oar port and held the empty bucket out to a man standing opposite. The empty pails then made their way up another line in preparation to be refilled. Adept as they were, the highlander sailors were only able to maintain the water at the same level. If they slowed their effort, the longship would sink within minutes.

"Faster!" someone further down the line shouted.

"We're going as fast as we can!" another roared in reply.

Muffled thunder shuddered through the ship.

You've made your point, Thoron. I apologise for not asking your permission to seek passage through your area of the world.

I wonder, what brings the guardian of the Waning Wood this far north?

It's a long story sister, but my forest is under threat. The Huronians have invaded and will burn my land to the ground. They'll kill my children. I can't allow this to happen, so it is to Shadolia we travel in search of reinforcements.

I could not bear to lose my land, much less see the creatures under my protection forced into extinction.

Gorgoroth did not reply, but Vyder, his muscles aching, sensed the sadness sweep his being.

I give you safe passage. May the creatures under your custodianship live.

The incessant rumbling of the storm outside, muffled by the ship's framework, faded to silence. The water, streaming between the planks above their heads like a river, ebbed to slow drips.

"The storm is at an end!" a highlander roared. "Thank Thros!"

"THROS!" the others shouted. They laughed, cheered, and joked, but at no point did they slow their bailing.

A hand slapped Vyder's back. "You might be a half blood, but you work like a highlander."

The water level gradually dropped. The buckets full of water were passed up the line and once emptied, streamed back down the men standing opposite just as fast. Soon, the water that had once threatened to consume the longship, lapped at Vyder's feet.

A halt was called and the sailors, relief palpable throughout the enclosed space, moved towards the ladder and climbed upward, out of the ship's bowels towards the dim light above.

* * *

During the storm, the majority of the highland crew had darted below decks to help bail water. Snarri knew his crew would work like draught horses to assuage the ocean from sending them beneath the waves and into the silence-enshrouded pitch depths where only death waited. On top deck, there'd been a skeleton crew who'd hauled the sail up to avoid the power of the wind snapping the mast in half. Snarri had been steadfast, both hands upon the handle of the steer-board. The wooden handle of the steer-board had, on several occasions, almost been ripped clear of his grasp by the ocean's power swelling beneath the hull. He'd struggled to keep the longship pointing towards the oncoming waves, but deft skill and decades of experience had won the day.

Snarri had not been oblivious to proceedings between his skeleton crew and the pair of newcomers who'd positioned themselves at the mast, clutching the thick wood for dear life. He'd yelled at his highlanders to stand down. Much as he disliked the thought of a full-blood Wendurlund man onboard, especially one of royal blood, they'd paid for their journey.

One corner of Snarri's mouth stretched upward. *And paid well.*

But his crew hadn't obeyed him, or didn't hear his command over the storm's noise. When the fight broke out, he thought the newcomers wouldn't stand a chance. But the Wendurlund man had fought well given the situation. But the Kalote woman? She was something else.

"She must have highland blood," he muttered, watching the pair sitting together near the mast.

She'd taken a highland scalp, and then finished the others off, kicking the dead bodies overboard. Or that's how it'd looked through the darkness, not to mention the heavy rain and blustering wind.

Movement caught his attention, and highlanders appeared one after another from below. They laughed, bellowed at one another, or simply strode in silence across the deck, ringing water from their soaking clothes.

"Ho!" one yelled at Snarri. "Boss, where are the others?" He spoke of the skeleton crew who'd been left on the top deck.

"Claimed by the ocean."

Some nodded and passed a hand across their chest. A silent acknowledgement of their comrades' memories.

Snarri stumbled a step forward, strong wind

pushing at his back in line with their direction of travel. Rarely did the wind in the Shadolian Sea blow in exactly the desired direction of a sailing longship. Often the sail needed to be trimmed to catch the breeze.

He cupped his mouth. "Drop the sail!"

Highlanders reacted immediately, running to the mast. The Wendurlund prince and Kalote warrior scrambled clear. The huge woven wool sail, painted with vertical black and red stripes descended under the power of teams of sailors hauling on ropes. Within minutes, the sail filled with a loud *snap*, and the longship lurched forward, gliding across the ocean towards Shadolia. The ship cut a wide arrowhead wake through the sea.

Snarri tightened his grip on the steer-board and chuckled. "At this rate, Thros will have us in Shadolia before dawn!" he shouted.

* * *

Vyder, saddle slung over his shoulder, led Storm up the wide plank from the longship to the Shadolian wharf. The dawn sun painted the world orange. Henry and Ahitika followed him, their mounts in tow. They negotiated the gangplank and exhaustion overwhelmed the trio when they stood upon the flat, stationary planks of the wide wharf. Half the crew of the longship were nearby in a group, talking and laughing. Some of them smoked pipes, others greeted family members who'd awoken early and walked to the coast to wait. No doubt the rest of the crew's family would travel to the wharf later in the day when the longship was scheduled to arrive.

Brushing encrusted salt free of Storm's fur, Vyder cast the saddle upon the horse, buckled it tight and

139

stepped into the stirrup. The pair behind him followed suit, and they moved away down the wharf, past the empty stalls of the fish mongers, the faint smell of seafood still permeating the air, despite the absence of the traders and their produce.

"Thank you for the hospitality!" Vyder shouted over his shoulder at the group of highlanders. "We'll be back sooner than you think."

Some of them waved, a couple turned their backs to the departing trio. Snarri, halfway up the gangplank to the wharf waved at them. "Wind at your back!" he roared in the highland tongue.

Henry fixed his gaze upon Vyder. "What did he say?"

"Just slang for a formal Highland farewell." Vyder explained what Snarri had said. "Rather than say 'Goodbye friend and may the wind always blow at your back,' it's faster to say what Snarri did."

Henry nodded. "Fair enough. So where are we off to now?"

The highlander urged Storm into a canter. "The highlands."

Henry came alongside him, a look of mock disbelief lining his brow. "Really? I had no idea, Vyder!" The muscles of his face relaxed. "Where are we going?"

Demanding little human, isn't he, brother?

Vyder returned the prince's stare. "He is."

The bump in Henry's throat rose and fell, but he maintained his focus upon the highlander.

"We're heading north west towards the village of Yorv. Ironstone land. It was where I was born."

"You still have relatives there?"

The highlander nodded. "Aye, my brother lives there with his family. My parents died a few summers before I left for Wendurlund."

"How long the journey?" Ahitika asked from behind.

"If we push throughout the day, I hope to arrive come evening."

Henry shot him a glance. "*This* evening?"

"Aye, young prince."

"Shadolia is smaller than I thought. How many swords do you hope to raise?"

"Our land might be small, Henry, but we are warriors. In Lisfort, you have bakers, farmers, blacksmiths, clothes makers, road sweeps, merchants, wagon drivers, cooks, the aristocracy and, of course, the army. We have those trades, too. But the difference here in Shadolia is any one of those skills are secondary to the sword, spear, musket, and blunderbuss. Our primary profession is one of soldiering. We are, and always will be, a warrior race, so don't worry yourself with the size of a village."

They rode in silence, the sun rising, casting warmth upon the land and drying sea-drenched clothes. Vyder scratched his arm. Dry salt settled upon his skin where ocean water had once soaked him. He brushed the white, powdery substance clear. The first tiny village came into view. Three longhouses built in a square horseshoe, the clear land in the centre was ploughed, a thigh length crop glistening green against the sun's power. In the centre of the crop stood several highlanders holding watering pails. They wandered down the lengths of the plough lines, watering each plant. All but one was bare chested, and brown trousers and black boots covered their legs and feet. The colours marked upon the tartan sash draped diagonally across their upper bodies suggested they belonged to clan Steelforge. The same as the sailors who'd brought them across the Shadolian Sea.

The highlanders stopped their work as the trio passed. Vyder waved at them, but his gesture was not reciprocated. One of the highlanders straightened, stretched his back, and rested a palm upon the butt of the pistol sheathed at his hip.

Henry cantered alongside Vyder. "They're a friendly bunch, aren't they?"

The assassin grunted.

"Vyder." Henry paused and stared up at the single, small cloud drifting with lazy speed across the sky. He licked his lips. "I need you to be honest with me."

Vyder appraised the young man, one eyebrow arching.

The prince tore his gaze from the cloud and returned the highlander's piercing glare. "Are we going to die?"

He shrugged. "Who knows, young prince? Maybe. Maybe not."

"Well!" Henry took a deep breath and let it out with a mocking sound of refreshment. "I feel *so* much better!"

"We highlanders believe that Othin, the father of the gods, weaved our lives before we are even born. We call it our skane. The time and day of our death is marked out for us."

Unless there happens to be a Wiccan nearby. Isn't that right, little brother?

Gorgoroth's laughter boomed in the vaults of his mind.

Vyder shifted in the saddle. "We cannot control the time of our deaths, or the way in which it occurs. So, there's no need to worry about it. If we die," Vyder held out his hands, "then we die."

Henry sighed and refocused upon the cloud, hands clenched so tight upon the reins his knuckles turned white.

"You worry too much," Ahitika broke the silence. "Live more in now." She came alongside Henry, reached across and held a hand upon his chest. "Live here." She pointed at the cloud. "Not out there."

Henry took Ahitika's hand in his and kissed it. He smiled at her, then looked at the assassin. "My skane, you say?"

Vyder nodded. "Your skane."

***

By mid-morning, Henry's clothes were dry, although remnants of salt imbued into the cloth of his shirt drifted to the skin of his back. He scratched at the grit beneath his shirt.

"Need wash."

He grinned at Ahitika. "I stink that bad, do I?"

She pinched her nose between index finger and thumb and winked. "Worse than dog turd."

He chuckled.

They rode on through midday, eating in the saddle. The trio travelled near and sometimes through small villages. The colours and shapes of the tartans worn by the highlanders were the same for several villages, but as they advanced deeper into the highlands, changed to represent a new clan. One thing always remained the same, however. The highlanders watched them with distrustful glares, although Henry was aware most of the distaste with which they were welcomed was aimed at him. One man who Vyder later explained was the chieftain sneered at Henry, shouted a string of Shadolian words. Henry smiled at him and waved, but the chieftain's response was to drag an index finger across his throat. Despite the language barrier, the gesture was clear enough.

They really don't like we Wendurlund people.

Ahitika reined in beside Henry. "When we arrive at Yorv, I watch your back. But highlanders hate your people as much as my nation hate Huron."

"I understand." He smiled at the Kalote woman. "If I need to fight, I will."

"No if, my love," she reached across and squeezed his hand. "You…" She paused, searching the sky for the words she chased. "You need prove yourself. You *will* fight. No need to stand tall, but you must stand up." She tapped her hunting knife. "I fight alongside, but strike fast when threatened. You understand?"

He nodded. *You're the one who wanted to be a warrior king. You can't be a warrior without being willing to fight to protect yourself and those you love.* Images of Steef, and the other guards who'd made his life a living hell inside the Huronian dungeon, drifted across his mind. *I've been in worse situations.* Anger, fury, and hatred soaked through his body. He gritted his teeth and snarled. "I understand." Henry offered a tight smile.

When the sun touched the treetops carpeting the forest in the west, Vyder called a halt.

* * *

Vyder turned Storm to face the pair riding behind him.

"Soon, we will arrive in Yorv." The highlander stared at Henry. "I fear my people are like no other you have come across."

"I'm sure I'll manage, Vyder."

The assassin paused. There was a flicker of something in the prince's eyes he hadn't seen in the young man since the day the King's Own, outnumbered and surrounded, hammered through the Huronian army, carrying their prince to safety.

Just more little monkeys, brother. Gorgoroth's voice pervaded his mind. *They might dress a little different or speak another language. The kin of your blood may live in a lifestyle foreign to Henry, but to me? You are all the same. I will uphold my promise, however. Only those deserving of death's touch will I send to the Frost River.*

"Pleasing to know," Vyder answered both Henry and Gorgoroth. He swung Storm away and urged her into a canter. When the sun disappeared beneath the western horizon and daylight started to die, Yorv came into view.

The southern entrance was as he remembered, save that the thick posts, once rising more than three times the height of a tall man standing either side of the road, were nothing more than blackened stumps. They passed through the entrance, and Vyder hesitated. The first home, belonging to a young couple close friends with his brother was an abject ruin. It'd been burned, one wall completely destroyed. Looking in through the absent wall, it was clear the dwelling was abandoned.

"This doesn't look good," Henry whispered.

A small family Vyder didn't recognise stood outside another home. The walls and roof were partially blackened where flames had once long ago attempted to consume the building. The man held a musket in his hands, and the woman clutched a spear. Behind her skirts peeked a little girl, her eyes wide.

"We are friends," Vyder said.

The man took a step forward, his index finger touching the weapon's trigger. "I won't take your word for it. Ride on through, stranger."

Vyder reined in. "I am Ironstone, although I have been away a long time. What has happened here?"

"Clan Firestorm swept south across the Highlands year before last. They hit us, Windeagle, Waterborne, Earthforge, Coppersmith, Wintercreek and," he paused and searched the ground, "Forestlake," he said, tapping the Forestlake tartan slung diagonally across his chest. He gestured at his wife. "We were the only survivors of our clan."

"Gods." Vyder's heart quickened.

"How did the rest of Ironstone fair?"

The man shrugged. "Ironstone is a powerful clan, but Firestorm is bigger. Ironstone lost a quarter of its number I guess."

"A quarter?" whispered Vyder. He scowled, clenched his jaw and nodded at the family. "My thanks."

He nudged Storm into a canter. They passed crops, the smell of freshly tilled earth drifting to his nostrils. The trio swept past a cluster of homes, some people glancing out of doorways at the small group. Vyder thought he recognised some faces, but with the advance of age that touched their skin, he couldn't be sure. One thing remained in common. All of the homes were either destroyed by fire, or at least bore the scar of flame.

Vyder guided Storm down a side road, galloped between buildings, ignored curses or shouts of people stepping aside, turned down another road, dread and fear swilling in his gut. The further they travelled, the greater the damage to each dwelling. Like the first house he saw at the southern edge, each house was a blackened ruin. He skidded to a halt outside one particular home. Like the others, it was a sight of destruction. Fire had consumed the wood, leaving nothing standing.

A few clicks resounded from behind, and Ahitika reined in beside him. "This mean something to you?" she gestured towards what remained of the wooden structure.

He nodded, jaw bulging. "My parent's home," he managed. "They died before I travelled south, but my brother and his wife moved in."

Vyder swung a leg over Storm and stepped out of the saddle, his booted feet hitting the ground with a *thud*. He offered the reins to the Kalote woman. "Can you hold Storm?"

She smiled and took the lengths of leather from him.

He walked through the opening that had once been the front door. The destroyed structure came up to his chest at its highest point. The roof, which once towered high above him, was long burned away. It was difficult to make out the layout. He'd been away so long it was hard to remember where his childhood room would have been. Brushing a hand against what was once a wall, chunks of charred timber came away in his fingers.

Moving to the rear of the dwelling, he noticed the tops of what looked to be two headstones planted in the overgrown back garden. Lips curled down, he sniffed and wiped his eyes. Stooping, he tore out clumps of weeds and grass, casting them away until the first headstone came into view fully.

Magdolin Ironstone
Aged 32 years
Killed during Clan Firestorm raid
IV

Is it who you expected, little brother?

"My sister-in-law."

What does the four mean?

"The number of raiders she killed before succumbing to her wounds."

Tough woman.

Vyder moved on, more clumps of grass sent skyward, roots and all, to land nearby.

Raif Ironstone
Aged 39 years
Killed during Clan Firestorm raid
IX

He didn't die very easily.

"No," Vyder chuckled, although tears slid down his cheeks. "We're Ironstone."

He knelt before his brother's grave and lifted the Ironstone tartan from the headstone. Passing the narrow, long band of material over his head, he tightened it diagonally across his chest. He stood, turned away, and almost tripped over on a large stone. Reaching down, he touched a third headstone, much smaller than the others. He closed his eyes. Clearing the long grass away, he passed a hand over the letters etched into the stone.

Abigail Ironstone
Aged 6 years
Killed during Clan Firestorm raid
I

"A niece I didn't know existed." He wiped his nose with the back of a hand. Gorgoroth was silent, but Vyder was aware of the sadness pervading the nature spirit.

He sniffed, stood, and walked back through the house. Nodding his thanks to Ahitika, he took back the reins, stepped into the saddle, and led the trio towards the centre of Yorv and the town's long-hall. In less than five minutes, they stood before the beautifully constructed long-hall.

"Who lives here?" asked Henry, admiring the structure.

The building was at least twenty-five metres long and six metres high. It was built in such a way so as to resemble an upturned longship.

"The Ironstone chieftain, Olsen." He pointed at a tie up rail near the closed, mighty doors of the entrance.

Henry shrugged. "I can stay out here and watch the horses if you want?"

Vyder dismounted. "Not by yourself, you won't, Henry. Plus, I may need your aid inside." He tapped the knife at his belt. "If you know what I mean?"

Henry's eyebrows disappeared beneath his fringe. "Ah, I see. Not a friendly visit then." The Wendurlund prince groaned as he swung out of the saddle.

Vyder finished tying Storm's reins to the rail and strode to the doors. He pushed them open, the heavy wood groaning upon the powerful hinges. The longhouse languished in gloom, aside from a heap of glowing coals in the centre of the building, a hint of smoke drifting up and disappearing through the circle cut out of the roof above the fire pit. On the far side of the coals, his face illuminated a dull orange, sat the chieftain. But it wasn't Olsen. The young, overweight man glanced up at the newcomers, a flicker of annoyance passing across his face.

"Who are you?" he snapped, his double chin

wobbling.

"I might ask you the same thing, laddie," Vyder spoke through clenched teeth. "Where is Olsen?"

"Uncle?" the young man flicked his hand at the fire in a dismissive gesture. "He's dead. He died in the raid, as did his son and wife." The fat man sat straighter. "I am the only one of the blood line to survive, so the role of chieftain fell to me."

Vyder stopped in front of the seated man. "Did it?"

He's a rather rotund little monkey, isn't he, brother?

Vyder grunted in response to Gorgoroth.

"And what was your course of action after Clan Firestorm finished murdering half of our people?" Vyder sat in front of the chieftain, glaring into his soft eyes. "Including my own brother and his family, I might add."

"I struck a deal with them, of course. We give them a portion of our harvest each year, and they refrain from striking us again."

"I'm not sure you're aware of the clansmen and women out there," Vyder jerked a thumb over his shoulder at the open door through, which he'd recently walked, "Chieftain," he added, looking the young man up and down. "But they're half-starved."

The young chieftain spread his hands. "Needs must, I'm afraid. Clan Ironstone must survive, and in order for that to happen, we must pay tithe. Times are tough."

Vyder's jaws bulged, and he pointed at the chieftain's midriff. "Not that hard for you though…Chieftain. You seem to be doing well for yourself."

Ahitika chortled behind him.

"How dare you?" the man lurched to his feet with

an effort, lost his balance, and almost fell to the ground. Eventually, he stood looking down his nose at Vyder. "Get out of my longhouse!"

Vyder pushed himself to his feet, towering over the flabby chieftain. "I'm a highlander of Clan Ironstone," he tapped the tartan cloth stretched diagonally across his chest. "And we bow to no man and no clan. Or did you forget?"

"Of course not!"

Vyder took a pace forward. "And what is your name, Chieftain?"

The overweight young man thrust back his shoulders. "I am Neyarl."

"Well, Neyarl, my name is Vyder of the clan Ironstone, and I challenge you to combat for the role of chieftain."

Neyarl shrugged and nodded. "Fine." He withdrew a long skinning knife sheathed at his hip and lunged with lightning speed.

Vyder felt numb as Gorgoroth took control, sending him tumbling away from the razor-sharp blade. He somersaulted backwards, came to his feet, and leapt over the fire, his knife appearing in his hand.

I fear we may have misjudged this fat monkey, brother.

Vyder grunted again.

"I've been challenged seven times for the role of chieftain following the raid." Neyarl's mouth widened in a death's head grin. "I killed them all." He patted his substantial gut. "I wasn't always this shape. Do you remember the orphan boy adopted by Chieftain Olsen's brother?"

"I remember. A violent little boy prone to anger. Pretty handy with a weapon, though, as I recall. Why?"

Neyarl stood rooted to the spot, held his hands out

either side of him, his eyebrows arching.

"I don't recall you ever being called Neyarl, though."

The chubby highlander shrugged. "It's just a name. Easy enough to change."

"You want me to kill him?" Ahitika strode toward the chieftain, smiling.

"No. This is between us, to the death. If he kills me, scalp him for me."

The Kalote woman grinned. "Pleasure."

Neyarl paused, his eyes widening. "I don't understand what you two are saying, but I know it is the language of Wendurlund you speak." He pointed his knife in Vyder's direction. "It seems you are a traitor."

"Amusing coming from you."

Vyder continued taking paces to his rear, he shot a glance over his shoulder to ensure he was aiming for the mighty doors through which they'd walked.

"Scared are you, Vyder?"

The highland assassin ignored the well-fed chieftain. His intention was to bring the fight outside the longhouse and into public view of the villagers. They'd then see with their own eyes it'd been a fair fight and Vyder hadn't murdered Neyarl in cold blood. If they suspected the latter, they'd never follow him as chieftain. Much as the rotund man may be disliked, if the challenge hadn't been carried out according to Highland Law, Vyder's claim to the leadership would be forfeit.

He glanced over his shoulder again, and Neyarl took the opportunity to run at Vyder. The assassin sidestepped the charge, blocked a knife thrust with his forearm, and hissed as the blade cut his skin, blood dribbling down his arm and dripping from his fingertips. He held firm pressure upon the wound.

"Lucky block. That was intended for your guts. You ever seen a man die from a gut wound?"

Vyder burst out laughing. "I have indeed, laddie."

"Then you'll know it's no laughing matter." Neyarl attempted to flank the assassin, to cut off his exit.

The chieftain wasn't fast enough, and Vyder stepped outside, walking backwards past the tethered horses, keeping his eyes fixed upon his adversary. Neyarl followed at a sedate pace, relaxed. The chieftain held his knife upright and always seemed to squeeze shut his eyes for a brief moment before he attacked.

Vyder switched to the Wendurlund language. "Henry, Ahitika," Vyder called to the pair following behind Neyarl. "There is a highland word, it is pronounced *aforthafik*, it means someone has challenged the chieftainship. *Aforthafik*. Can you remember that word?"

Both said the word, stumbling over it several times before it started coming easier to their tongues.

"Good. Start shouting that word. Loud as you can!"

Ahitika brushed past Neyarl, offering him a look of hatred, striding towards the homes in the near distance. "Aforthafik!" she yelled, veins bulging at her throat. She roared the word again. Henry bellowed the word, adding to the chorus.

One corner of Vyder's mouthed tugged upward. "We have to follow traditions, don't we, Chieftain?"

"This constant walking is boring me. Let us get this over and done with."

Vyder glanced down at the belt stretched taught across Neyarl's belly. "Need a break, do you? This is probably the furthest you've walked this month."

Neyarl's eyes snapped shut, and Vyder darted to

one side, avoiding the knife thrust. Carrying his blade with a reverse grip, he held his other hand out before him, open palm facing the chieftain. Vyder slowed his rearward progress, the hoarse voices of Henry and Ahitika fading into background noise.

The plump man stepped backward, but Vyder remained in place. He'd fight the chieftain on his own terms. Following his adversary would take the initiative from Vyder. The assassin began retreating again, aware that the calling of Henry and Ahitika were being taken up from all around the village. In his peripheral vision, he saw movement. People came out of their homes and walked towards the fight in small groups.

Neyarl tutted and walked after Vyder again. "You're a damn coward, aren't you?"

"Aye, whatever you say, laddie."

Vyder halted, bunched his legs beneath him and sprinted straight at Neyarl. He jumped and kicked out with both legs. His boots slammed into the chieftain's chest, sending the fat man to the ground, his breath exploding from his mouth. The assassin landed in a crouch and slashed down at his opponent, the blade opening a cut on Neyarl's arm. He'd intended for the wound to be fatal, but the chieftain, flabby as he was, moved fast. He'd rolled away from Vyder and already regained his feet, albeit with a groan.

Red-faced, jaws clenched and eyes narrowed, Neyarl came for him at a head long charge. At the last moment, he twisted away, side-stepped and then lunged at Vyder's flank. The assassin leapt back, the razor-sharp metal barely missing the skin of his throat.

"Only a matter of time, Vyder."

"Bit short of breath there, Chieftain? Need a rest?"

Neyarl's eyes snapped shut, but this time Vyder

stepped in, grabbed his opponent's wrist, twisted it away, and slammed his knife into the chieftain's chest. The blade ground against a rib, and Neyarl's shirt around the embedded knife turned claret. He kept a tight grip of Neyarl's wrist, acutely aware that even a dying man could still strike a fatal blow. The chieftain dropped to his knees, then collapsed onto his side, Vyder released his wrist, the arm flopping to the ground. Neyarl's last breath passed his lips with a soft whisper.

Cheering exploded around Vyder, and the assassin jumped. He'd not been aware of the circle the clansmen and women had formed around the pair, so focused had he been on the fight.

"A new chieftain!" roared an older highlander, stepping into the circle, and stopped beside Vyder. The older man turned to Vyder, and his face softened, eyes widening. "I know you! You're Ulf and Frayona's lad, the boy went south in search of riches. Is it Vyder?"

The assassin smiled and nodded. "Thrane? You were a fine friend to my parents."

Thrane grinned. "The very same!" He slapped Vyder on the back, took a deep breath, and yelled, "Vyder, chieftain of Clan Ironstone!"

Shouting, cheering, and clapping pervaded the area. Thrane grasped Vyder by the arm with a firm grip. He leaned towards the assassin to be heard over the noise. "Tell me, lad, did you find riches?"

He thought of the mansion he owned, the bags of gold stored in the bank, and the coins he carried in the small purse attached to a string around his neck. But then Verone's face drifted to him and the city he now called home under siege by an enemy determined to eradicate the kingdom of Wendurlund forever.

"In a manner of speaking, yes…but also no."

Thrane released his grip and nodded. "It sounds to have made you wiser. Although I'm sorry to see infection has ailed your eye." He pointed at the stark, blue eye.

"Aye."

That's a little harsh to call me an infection, little brother.

Vyder held up his hands for silence. "When was the last time there was a feast held in the longhouse?" He gestured behind him at the building behind him, once inhabited by Neyarl.

"Before the raid," a highlander said.

"And do we have the food to provide a feast?"

"Aye, chieftain," another called.

"Then tonight, we drink and we feast!"

Cheering, laughter, and clapping boomed around the clearing. Clan Ironstone had a new chieftain. It was time to be strong again. It was time to stand back up.

VII

Flames licked at thick pieces of wood sitting upon the fire pit in a pile tall as a man. The flickering, bright orange glow lit the longhouse in a way the people of Clan Ironstone hadn't seen in years. Vyder stood in one dark corner, nursing his deer horn cup of mead. He'd positioned himself in such a way so as to watch the clan mingling with one another. No one had yet spotted him, aside from Ahitika, her eyes keen as a hawk. She sat upon the floor beside him, back leaned against the wall, sipping her mead, Henry alongside her. The couple spoke together in hushed whispers, their words lost amongst the laughter and merriment.

On several occasions highlanders walked past Henry, barging into him and offering a string of curses at him. One man, a black-haired rogue with scars adorning his face, leaned over Henry and knocked his cup over. Ahitika stood and muttered something to the man, her eyes murderous. Henry caught her hand and pulled her back to her seat. The highlander laughed and strode away.

That will only get worse, will it not, Vyder?

"Aye," he said. "Eventually Henry will probably have to fight one of them if he is to get any respect. Especially as he is allegedly a prince of Wendurlund.

Allegedly? But he is a prince is he not?

"We're in the highlands now, Gorgoroth. Prince is just a word, it means nothing to these men and women. A title is earned here, not simply inherited."

Some people brought in step ladders, placing them beneath shields, blunderbusses and, of course, the clan colours, which was attached neatly beneath a set of crossed swords. The items adorned the wall high above

the head of the long table. The decorations were dull,
their sharp glint long faded to the persistence of dust and
cobwebs. One man placed his foot on the bottom rung
of the stepladder.

"Ho, Olaf!" he shouted at another standing nearby,
thrusting his deer horn cup at him. "Hold my drink." He
turned to a clanswoman nearby. "Wish me luck,
dearest!"

She shrugged. "We all must die someday husband.
Today is as good as any."

"Wisht, Helga!" He bellowed through a chuckle,
ascending the stepladder and almost losing his balance.
"Today isn't my skane, lass."

The weapons were lifted down with care and
passed to various members of the clan standing in a
group at the base of the ladder. Each adornment was
carried to the long table where clusters of clansfolk sat
together talking, laughing and cleaning away the dust,
cobwebs and restoring the sharp sheen the weapons had
once enjoyed.

Vyder pushed himself away from the corner,
stepped into the light and finished his mead with several
swallows. He strode to the long table, stepped over the
bench and lowered himself amongst a group of
clansfolk.

An older woman smiled at him. "Chieftain!
Wondered where you'd got to."

Her face was familiar, but he couldn't place her
name.

"It is Gwinifred," she said. "I remember when you
were just a wee lad, Vyder."

"Of course! Now I remember."

His empty deer horn cup was whisked away and a
full one placed in front of him accompanied by a slap on

the back. "Good to see you chieftain," the clansman said, striding away to help another group cooking the food.

A young man sitting opposite, polishing a blunderbuss glanced over the butt stock at him. "So, Vyder, our tithe to Clan Firestorm is due in a few months."

Vyder gritted his teeth. "Is it?"

"Aye, I think we have just enough grain to meet their requirement for the year."

"We have enough grain to feed our clan, lad." Vyder took a gulp of his mead and placed the cup upon the table, holding the young man's stare. "No more and no less."

"But what about the tithe?"

Anger warmed him. He shrugged. "What of it?"

"If we don't pay our tithe, they will crush us. They've threatened as much!"

"I care nothing for their threats." Vyder rose to his feet. "Ho!" he roared. The chatter died to silence and the eyes of those in the longhouse rested upon their chieftain.

Vyder drew a breath. "It has come to my attention that our tithe to Clan Firestorm is due in the near future."

A couple of mutters met his statement.

The assassin placed his hands upon the table. "That grain is for our clan and our clan alone. The tithe is at an end." Vyder snarled. Heat touched the skin of his face, anger all but consuming him. "We are Clan Ironstone!" he shouted. "Always!" He looked from face to face. Fear touched the eyes of some, anger shone from others and pride from the rest. "It's about time we remember who we are and for that which we stand. We are highlanders! We are Ironstone!" He slammed a fist upon the table. "We are warriors!"

"And if Firestorm attack us? What then chieftain?"

"Then we fight them."

The clansman shrugged, his eyes shone with fear. "And if we lose?"

"Then we die. But at least we'll have met our skane upon our feet, instead of existing on our knees."

A group at the rear cheered. Others shouted, "Ironstone!"

"Tomorrow," Vyder shouted over the noise. "I'll ride for Clan Windeagle. The day after for Clan Waterborne." He leaned forward. "Then I'll head for Clan Earthforge, and the next day? Clan Coppersmith will welcome me to their hearth. Clan Wintercreek will be my final stop. And when I can convince enough warriors to ride with me, there will be one last clan I will visit. Firestorm!"

Shouting, cheering and arguing erupted around the longhouse.

Vyder's chest expanded as a large breath filled his lungs. "Who will ride with me?" His voice rose above the crescendo.

Men and women stepped forward, some adding their voices to the noise, veins pushing against the skin of their throats, their eyes bright with fervour. A few remained at the back or stepped away, fear evident in their demeanour.

He appraised the large group who surrounded him still adding their voices to the boom of dissonance bouncing around the longhouse.

"Good!" he roared. "Then let us eat!"

* * *

Storm nuzzled his chest. He stroked her nose and ran his hand along the sleek, powerful neck. The rising sun painted the horse's flank in hues of soft orange and pink. Vyder stepped into the saddle.

"Back on the road again, lassie," he whispered to the horse. Storm's ears flicked back at the sound of his voice.

Behind him a long column of Ironstone warriors mounted in a similar fashion. If he was forced to guess, Vyder estimated four hundred clansmen and women would ride with him. Another three hundred of fighting age remained at home, although if Vyder was successful in his bid, he hoped they would decide to join him.

Ahitika reined in beside him. "How far to next village?"

He patted Storm. "We'll be there by nightfall."

She nodded. "Highlands much smaller than Wendurlund."

Henry brought his horse to a halt near Ahitika.

"And how do you fair, young prince? At least you look healthier now."

There was flesh upon his bones, the muscles of his arms becoming more defined, thanks to the daily exercises Vyder had given him. His appetite had returned, Vyder noticed.

The young man shrugged and smiled. "I feel good, better than I did a month ago." He shifted in his saddle. "Although I seem to have made an enemy. An ugly man with hair the colour of a raven's feathers."

"Aye, I noticed that."

"I've tried ignoring him, but it does nothing. I intend to gain his trust eventually," Henry said.

Vyder sighed. "You won't ever gain his trust, Henry. And as long as he taunts you, your image as a warrior prince amongst the highlanders will diminish, until they too begin to hate you."

"What then is the answer?"

"You will have to face him sooner or later. At best a fist fight, at worst a fight to the death."

The young Wendurlund man nodded, broke Vyder's stare and focused ahead of them.

"I'm sorry it has to be this way, Henry. It is the way of things here in Shadolia. Do not mistake me, this rogue is a man of little honour, and even less integrity, but his treatment of you is doing damage to what reputation you might have had." Vyder lowered his voice. "And if we want highlanders to march south in aid of your country, you will need to be viewed as a strong leader in your own right. Not a meek man cowed by a bully."

Henry snapped his attention back to Vyder. "I am not cowed!"

"*I* know you're not." He jerked a thumb behind him. "But *they* don't."

Henry fell silent.

Ahitika leaned across and slapped Henry on the leg. "You too soft," she chuckled and gestured at herself, and then Vyder. "We make you strong."

The woman is good for him, little brother.

Vyder nodded. He swivelled and looked down the column of mounted clansfolk behind him. Many of them were chatting amongst themselves, some groups chuckling as a man, gesturing wildly, was probably regaling some story. One man was sitting on his horse in silence, the skin of his face pale. He was staring at the ground in front of him. His name was Torgun from memory.

Vyder turned Storm around and trotted to him. "You alright, lad?"

The clansman lurched in his saddle, startled by Vyder's voice. "I'm fine, chieftain," he smiled. "Just seven or eight too many meads last night. My gut churns and my head hammers."

"Sip some water."

"I fear my breakfast will be all over the horse if I drink any water."

"Trust me, just sip some, Torgun."

The highlander pulled free a water bladder and sipped some of the cool liquid.

Vyder grinned. "Better?"

Torgun laughed. "No, but I'll be better by noon."

Vyder turned Storm away and cantered back to the head of the column, stood in his stirrups and signalled they were on the move. They travelled at a slow trot, fast enough to chew through the distance, but slow enough not to exhaust the horses. During the journey, Vyder rode up and down the column, often stopping to talk. Some of the people he remembered from childhood, others younger than he, he'd never seen before. Many of them introduced themselves to him and try as he may he was unable to remember all their names.

The group of Ironstone highlanders stopped at noon for a brief meal, to rest, feed and water the horses, and then they were underway again. Vyder slowed beside Torgun. Colour had returned to his cheeks, and he looked more comfortable.

"You look a bit better, Torgun."

"Turns out you were right, Vyder." Torgun patted the near empty water bladder tied to his belt. "The water works."

"Good to hear." He pushed Storm on and advanced along the column towards the front again. "You looking forward to a mead tonight?" he shouted over his shoulder at Torgun.

The booming laughter of the young highlander echoed out.

They entered the township of Windeagle as the sun touched the western horizon. The houses looked much the same as the village of Ironstone. Those on the outer edges were utterly destroyed or blackened by the assault of flame. Clans folk stood in doorways watching the procession ride through their village towards the centre, where lay the chieftain's longhouse. Fear filled many eyes. But glinting in those of a precious few was the power of anger, fury, and an obvious lack of fear. One Windeagle highlander with shoulder length flame red hair and beard strode out into the middle of the dirt road and held up a hand. The column stopped. The powerfully-built man held Vyder's stare, then noticed the tartan sash, although his index finger did not leave the trigger of the musket he held across his body.

"Ironstone, eh?"

Four men and two women crouched in doorways or knelt, taking cover behind a corner of a building, watching the newcomers. Each of them held muskets or blunderbusses at the ready. Although they did not point the weapons directly at Vyder, they'd be able to bring the muzzles to bear in the blink of an eye.

Vyder held up his hands, palms facing the man. "We travel in peace." He looked over his shoulder. None of his clansfolk had drawn a weapon. They simply watched. The last thing Vyder needed was one of his clan pointing a musket at the warrior barring their way.

"Aye? And what is it you seek?"

"Retribution."

The man's lips parted, revealing clenched teeth. "And what have we ever done to Clan Ironstone?"

"Nothing. It is not against you we seek retribution." Vyder swung in his saddle and pointed behind him at the blackened houses. "Is that the work of Clan Firestorm?"

The highlander hawked and spat. "Aye," he growled.

"That is the clan upon whom we are taking our vengeance. We are simply here to ask if you'd consider joining us."

The man slung his weapon and walked off the road to make way for the column to pass through. He pointed towards the centre of the village where the distant longhouse awaited them. "It isn't my decision, Ironstone. Speak to the chieftain, but I'll wager you'll have an addition to your number one way or another." He winked and grinned.

Vyder nodded his thanks and pushed Storm onward. The horse stopped before the longhouse, and Vyder stepped out of the saddle. He tied her loosely to the tie-up rail near the mighty front doors. The majority of Ironstone warriors remained atop their horses, although some dismounted and stood in groups talking. Henry, Ahitika, Torgun, and a few others who could not be dissuaded otherwise accompanied Vyder into the longhouse.

The chieftain, a short, stick-thin man sat at the head of the table, elbows upon the wooden surface, the fingers of his open hands making a pyramid upon which he rested his chin.

That is not the chieftain.

Vyder grunted his agreement with Gorgoroth.

"That is chieftain?" Ahitika whispered, although Vyder was not oblivious to the slight chuckle which accompanied her question.

"It can't be."

I'm telling you, little brother, that is not the chieftain.

"Let's find out, shall we?"

Stubborn little monkey.

Vyder stopped, withdrew his dagger and handed it to Henry. "Hold that, lad." He gestured at the small group. "You lot stay here, as some of you well know, it is an offence for a foreign clansman to carry arms when in the presence of any chieftain."

The assassin strode on, holding the thin man's watery, weak eyes. "Greetings, Chieftain, I am Vyder Ironstone, chieftain of Clan Ironstone and wish to seek your council."

The spidery man shifted in his seat and shot a glance towards the doors Vyder had recently walked through. His attention returned to Vyder.

"My name is Arn, you are welcome at my table." He pulled out a chair nearby.

Vyder sat. "I see Firestorm hit your clan, as well."

Arn's eyes narrowed and suddenly he did not look so weak. His brows creased. "Aye, some time ago. We hit them in reprisal but lost nearly half our number in the battle." He drew a breath, his eyelids closing. "We've been living on our knees ever since."

Vyder leaned forward and placed his forearms upon the table. "I'm sorry to hear that, Arn."

The assassin allowed the silence to grow, interested to see how or if Arn would fill it.

"I'm not sure what kind of council you seek, Vyder, but I fear I may not be able to help."

Vyder stared at the chieftain, sitting slumped, looking downtrodden. "I was once told that the highlands are a tough place, filled with some of the fiercest warriors ever to have walked. I was advised that I didn't have to stand tall. But…" he stopped and waited until Arn turned to hold his stare, before continuing, "if I wanted to succeed, that I must stand up."

Arn nodded. "I haven't heard that in a long time." A weak smile broke his lips, and his back straightened a little.

A blur of movement caught Vyder off guard, and the flame-haired warrior sat beside him. "You already have your answer chieftain. Name's Bordrog."

"Vyder." He clenched the proffered hand. "So, I take it you are the true chieftain of Windeagle?"

"You're an observant lad, aren't ya?"

Arn stood. "If I'm no longer needed?"

"Aye, Arn, thanks."

The fake chieftain excused himself and walked away. Vyder noticed his back was ramrod straight.

"An interesting tactic you have there, Bordrog."

He shrugged. "You can never be too careful, especially in such a weakened state as we are. Deception is the only way when outnumbered."

"Good point."

"How many swords do you need?"

"As many as you can spare."

"I shall speak with the clan tonight and have an answer come the dawn. Will that suffice?"

"Aye," Vyder stood and shook hands with Bordrog once again. "It will."

"While the clan is meeting, there is a town square half a mile east of here. You are welcome to feed and water your horses there. I'll see that fodder for the animals and meals for your clan are brought."

The assassin smiled. "You have my thanks."

Clan Ironstone weaved along the narrow streets, watched all the while by curious groups. Some of the

Windeagle clansfolk carried weapons and looked more than ready to use them. Others shrunk into the shadows, their wide eyes belying the fear assaulting them.

Torgun walked his horse beside Storm. He glared at one such terror-filled family. "They have forgotten what it is to be highlanders."

"Perhaps." Vyder shifted in the saddle. "Time heals many wounds. In the following weeks, they may defeat their fear."

"Doubt it."

"Never be so sure, lad. A hero can only be such by defeating bone-numbing fear. Some of the bravest warriors I've ever seen were riddled by fear until circumstances demanded their action."

Torgun grunted.

As the gloaming settled upon the village, Vyder and his clan spread out into a large square upon the flat, open ground of the village green.

As promised, over the following few hours, food was delivered to both horse and rider. Vyder ensured Storm had eaten before settling down to eat the hot stew from a deep, wooden bowl. When he'd finished, he sunk to the ground beside storm and lay on his back, hands behind his head. Ahitika and Henry lay together on the far side of their horses. They whispered to each other. Vyder concentrated, although he had no interest in what the lovers spoke to one another. He was more drawn by the dull noise of the clan meeting in the distance. Cheers, clapping, shouts, both of glee and anger, rolled across the village in a muffled bur. Silence followed for a moment, then jeering and booing broke free. Storm stopped chewing on her meal and swung her powerful neck towards the sound, her ears flicked forward.

"It's alright, lass." Vyder reached across and

stroked one of her forelegs. "Nothing to worry about."

Vyder closed his eyes and allowed exhaustion to sweep over him. A rapid thudding filled his ears. It was the beat of a tiny heart. He searched through the darkness and was drawn to the branch of a tree high above him. The beating was coming from a bird.

It is a sparrow, little brother. Shall we?

"Aye," he whispered.

His stomach lurched, and he flew upward, speeding through the cool night air faster than a bolt of lightning. Coming to a sudden halt, his eyelids parted to reveal the open expanse of the village green far below. Directly beneath him lay his sleeping body, hands resting behind his head.

Are you up to flying?

Vyder tried to answer, but only a series of chirps echoed from his beak.

Good, you have control, little brother. I only have one request. Be careful and don't hurt the bird.

Vyder chirped, stretched his wings and leapt free of the branch. They soared across the night, banking to avoid trees, flapping to gain altitude. They flew over the village, aiming towards the chieftain's longhouse. They closed the distance, and with the sparrow's sharp night vision, Vyder saw clansfolk unable to fit into the crowded longhouse, standing on tiptoes at each of the longhouse's doors, struggling to listen to the meeting.

They swept above the heads of the highlanders and flew into the longhouse, ascending to the upper beams high above the long table. The room was packed with the people of Clan Windeagle. Bordrog sat at the head of the table, elbow on the surface, head in hand, listening to a nearby man.

"I mean, can we trust them?"

The red-headed chieftain leaned back in his chair, his chest expanding and contracting fast. "Horkon, I told you I've spoken to Vyder chieftain to chieftain, and it is my belief he and his clan can be trusted. Is my word not good enough?"

Horkon held out his hands. "Oh no, it's not that, it's—"

"Shut up, Horkon!" a massive highlander roared from further down the table.

Horkon lurched to his feet. "How dare you interrupt me during a clan meeting?"

The man mountain jumped to his feet and waded through the clansfolk until he was staring down his nose at Horkon. "I told you to shut the fuck up, Horkon," he spoke through clenched teeth. "I want to know what my chieftain has to say, not listen to the drivel of a weasel."

Horkon's eyes were wide, his face losing colour by the moment. He licked his lips and chuckled, although the sound was a high-pitched staccato. "A weasel, is it?"

"You heard me, Horkon."

Bordrog cleared his throat and stood. "Lads, that's enough. Horkon, Harald, take your seats. There is no reason to be bickering."

"I lost my family during that raid," Harald shouted. "My wife raped and cut open like a fish while I lay unconscious, bleeding to death. Although she killed three of the bastards." He lifted his shirt to reveal a large scar across his midriff. "Sometimes, I wish the healers hadn't done such a good job reviving me." His huge chest expanded. "And I wasn't the only one who lost loved ones." He swung around to face the crowd of highlanders crammed into the longhouse. "We all did!" he bellowed. He turned to stare at Horkon. "Well, *most* of us," he muttered. "So, if another clan comes in peace, seeking revenge upon the people who slaughtered my family, I'll bloody well listen!"

This was met by roars of agreement, cheers, and clapping.

Bordrog held out his hands. "I agree, Harald," he shouted over the noise. "But sit down, so we may continue." The chieftain's eyes flicked to Horkon and bored into the smaller man. "And you. Keep your trap shut this time."

Horkon's jaw bulged, the fingers of one hand curling into a fist. Finally, he nodded and sat. Harald grumbled under his breath and strode away to retake his place.

"As I was saying, I trust Vyder and his clan. My mother and father were burned on funeral pyres because of the Firestorm raid. As Harald said, we all lost something in that raid. Later, we learned we could not defeat Firestorm by ourselves."

"If we had an army of clans, we'd wipe the floor with them!" a woman shouted from one of the doorways. Her words were met with tumultuous agreement.

"One thing at a time," roared Bordrog. "For now, let's take a vote. Who's for joining Clan Ironstone?"

The noise that followed reverberated around the room, vibrated through the floor and rattled windows.

I take it that is a yes, little brother.

Vyder replied with a *chirp.*

Vyder leapt off the beam, plummeted towards the long table far below and flapped his wings, sailing around the room before shooting over the heads of the clansfolk wedged against the open door at one end of the building. Darkness and cool fresh air were a welcome relief. When he'd regained his night vision and bearings, he banked towards the village green and perched in the same tree he'd left from. He peered down at his sleeping form.

The little one does not appear to be hungry or thirsty, so we shall leave it and return to our body.

Vyder chirped, and his stomach lurched once more. He descended with rapid speed towards the ground, fear enshrouding his body, the grass ascending to meet him. He braced for impact, waiting for the pain to explode through his body, but his eyes snapped open instead, and he inhaled a deep breath. Vyder sat up. He stared at the closest tree towering over them. The sparrow sat statue still for several long moments. Then it shook its head, stretched its wings, and called into the darkness. A similar call answered it from a nearby tree. The bird took to wing and disappeared into the night.

* * *

After dawn broke, soaking the land in a mash of pink and orange, Vyder encourage Storm to drink what remained in the water bucket nearby. She stood in front of the pail looking at him, then nudged his shoulder.

"You can lead a horse to water," he muttered, stroking her face.

Quiet movement came from all around as people awoke. A yawn, cough or groan accompanying a stretch spoke the end of slumber. A loud fart echoed around the village square.

A woman tutted. "You're such a pig of a man!" she hissed.

"Sorry, dearest," the clansman boomed and farted again. He held out his hands, mouth open, eyebrows arching. "I couldn't help that one."

She glowered at him, but amusement twinkled in her eyes. She turned away to roll up her bedding.

Vyder watched the exchange, chuckling to himself. A flap of wings caught his attention. Two sparrows sat beside one another on a branch, looking down at him, twittering to each other.

That is an old tree that one, little brother. At least seventy years in time as you know it.

A blur of motion across the sky, and a hawk slowed, performing a perfect landing on a branch in the tree's upper canopy. It appraised Vyder with glowering eyes.

"It seems the animals are aware of your presence, Gorgoroth."

Storm finally drank her fill and raised her head from the empty pail, pushing a wet nose against Vyder's cheek.

"In a minute, lass," he laughed, patting her neck.

He saddled Storm, and when the rest of the clan was ready to move, he stepped into the stirrups and swung up onto the horse's back. He walked Storm to the head of the column and led them away from the village green towards the northern entrance.

Torgun cantered up beside him and slowed. "I take it Windeagle decided not to join us, Chieftain?"

"Aye, lad, it'd appear that way. It was worth a try."

The heavy weight of disappointment pulled at Vyder's guts. The meeting of Clan Windeagle had appeared to be successful. Perhaps more bickering had occurred after he and Gorgoroth had flown clear of the longhouse?

Who knows, little brother? We'll smite these Firestorm monkeys by ourselves if need be.

Vyder smiled.

"It was worth a try." Vyder looked at Torgun. "We'll take Firestorm down by ourselves if we have to."

"I'm glad you think so," muttered the younger man.

"We are Ironstone, lad. Don't forget that, Torgun. Some of our people have forgotten what it is to be highlanders, let alone Ironstone." He held Torgun's stare. "Don't be like them, lad. We are Ironstone, now and forever."

Torgun's jaw bulged, his brow furrowed and a fierce glint entered his eyes. The younger man nodded.

Shouting erupted from the rear of the column, the shrieks and bellows drowned out by a thunder of hooves. Vyder stood in the stirrups and stared over his shoulder. A column of riders galloped towards them, a cloud of dust drifting into the sky behind them. Cloaks billowed from shoulders, but the piece of tartan fixed diagonally across each chest told the assassin all he needed to know.

He smiled. "Clan Windeagle."

Bordrog reined in beside him, the man mountain, Harald, slowing on the far side. The flame-haired chieftain grinned. "Trying to steal away in the wee hours without us, Vyder?"

"The wee hours?" Vyder laughed. "We slept in!"

Bordrog chuckled. "Aye, we of Windeagle do enjoy our sleep, I'll not lie!"

"I'm glad you joined us, my friend."

The smile departed the redhead's face. "If it means taking those bastard Firestorm devils down, I would have come alone if the clan opposed the suggestion."

"No, you wouldn't, Chieftain," rumbled Harald. "There would have been two of us."

Bordrog jerked a thumb in the giant's direction.

"That's Harald." He pointed at the assassin. "Harald, that's Vyder." The highlanders nodded once at one another in greeting.

Vyder swept his eyes along the column of mounted Windeagle highlanders walking in file behind their chieftain. "A concern you need not entertain by the looks."

"Aye, we bring two hundred swords to the fight."

"We now have five hundred highlanders."

Bordrog patted his horse's neck. "Where to next?"

"By nightfall, I hope to make the village of Clan Waterborne."

"Easy done," said Bordrog.

The two clans melded into one large column. Several sets of bagpipes were retrieved from saddlebags and soon highland songs were peeling out over the landscape surrounding the riders. Some sang to the haunting tunes, others sat in their saddles, staring into the distance, no doubt thinking of happier times before Firestorm's raid had swept Shadolia.

By late afternoon, Vyder and Bordrog sat weaponless before Rafe, the chieftain of Clan Waterborne. Rafe was a well-built highlander of medium height, jet black hair reaching beyond his shoulders. His dark, brooding eyes were hard to read. The warriors standing behind Rafe, hands on sword hilts looked ready to kill to protect their leader.

When Vyder finished speaking, Rafe leaned back and snarled, fury washing over his face. Vyder clenched his fists, braced and prepared to fight a battle he knew neither he, nor Bordrog could win. They were outnumbered and unarmed.

Rafe turned his bright red face to the rafters, veins bulging from his neck. "Those bastards killed my daughter," he roared. He slammed a fist onto the table and returned his attention to Vyder, a murderous glint in his eyes. "I want to kill every last one of Clan Firestorm. I will come with you, and I'll bring two hundred and fifty swords."

"There's more than five hundred warriors in the clan, Chieftain," one of the highlanders standing guard behind Rafe spoke.

Rafe turned in his chair. "What of it? We need fighting men and women to stay at home to protect our village."

"Aye, I know, but I want to be one of the two hundred and fifty."

"Me too," the second muttered.

"Aye," the third said.

Rafe swung back to Vyder, a grin breaking through the snarl. "You'll not want for swords, Vyder."

* * *

On the evening of the third night, Vyder sat unarmed before Bulvye, the chieftain of Clan Earthforge. On Vyder's right sat Bordrog and on his left, Rafe.

When the assassin finished talking, Bulvye remained silent, his hands splayed upon the table. The chieftain was balding, but his dark green eyes were piercing, missing nothing. Tiny scars littering the skin of his forearms belied the rumour Vyder had heard that Bulvye was no warrior. Rumours were mostly always false he'd found from experience.

The balding, heavily bearded-man sat forward and held Vyder's eyes. "You wish to destroy Firestorm?"

"That's probably a little harsh." Vyder paused, gathering his thoughts. "What we wish," he gestured at

176

the chieftains either side of him, "is a chance for retribution and to place Clan Firestorm in such a position that they can never again sweep the highlands as they have done in the recent past."

Bulvye's eyes twinkled with humour. "And how is that different to destroying them?"

"I mean to spare the life of any innocent person and all children. I don't know about Clan Earthforge, but that was something that was never afforded to our clans when we were attacked." He indicated the chieftains seated either side of him.

"I shall bring two hundred and fifty swords to the fight. We shall join you come dawn."

* * *

Sundown on the fourth day saw Vyder and the three chieftains who'd agreed to join him sitting beside one another opposite Holrik, chieftain of Clan Coppersmith. Vyder was still part way through the explanation when the short, stocky Holrik held up a hand. "I've heard enough. We'll join you. We can add two hundred and fifty highlanders to your number."

By mid-afternoon the following day the column of one thousand highlanders, snaking its way along the northern road, reached the village of Clan Wintercreek. While the five chieftains rode into the village, the highlanders made an encampment on the outskirts and prepared for the evening. Horses were taken in groups down to a nearby river to drink their fill. People washed themselves, clothes and refilled water bladders.

Vyder led the way, walking Storm along the main street, which was nothing more than a wide dirt road. Worried eyes peered at them from doorways. One man

177

clutching a musket stood out the front of his house, his wife beside him, a sword gripped in her hand, the blade resting on her shoulder. They glared at the newcomers.

"They're still ready to fight," Rafe's booming voice echoed from the nearby buildings.

"Aye, a good sign," said Bulvye.

Within the hour, unarmed as always, the men sat before Hyglak, a tall rake thin man and chieftain of Clan Wintercreek.

After Vyder finished speaking, Hyglak frowned. "And if you lose? What then?"

"I hadn't entertained the thought, if I'm being honest."

Hyglak pointed at the assassin. "I'll tell you what happens. Firestorm will launch a counter offensive except, this time, they'll leave no one alive. They won't just want a small tithe and portion of our food, they'll take it all." He swept his arms around at the room surrounding him. "Everything. And they'll burn us to the ground."

"And do you think if we fail and Firestorm sweep the highlands once more, that your clan will simply be left untouched because you didn't take part?"

Hyglak leaned back in his chair, his heavily bearded jaw bulging.

"Because from what I saw on the ride in, you were hit pretty hard by those bastards."

"Aye, we were. Probably lost half of our clan. We weren't strong enough to fight them then and we're certainly not powerful enough to resist them again if they attack a second time."

Vyder gestured at the chieftains seated either side of him. "Neither are our individual clans. But together? We can make a mighty force to ensure Firestorm's actions can never be repeated."

Hyglak nodded. "I understand what you say. You have convinced me, but I can only offer one hundred highlanders to your cause."

Vyder spread his hands. "It is a hundred more than we had a few moments ago. You have my thanks. And Hyglak? It is not my cause, it is the cause of all of us seated here at this table, not to mention the people of our respective clans."

Hyglak offered a tight smile. "We do not have enough food or supplies to cater for all the clansfolk encamped outside our village, but you chieftains are welcome to join us this evening for a small feast."

Vyder's stomach grumbled. "Aye, it'd be our pleasure."

* * *

What is this drink, brother? It makes my head spin like that honey drink you highlanders like so much.

"This wine is good!" Vyder slurred, placing the wooden cup upon the table top.

Ah, wine. Yes, I've heard of it. Made from crushed berries.

"It's made by fermenting crushed grapes," Vyder blurted by way of explanation to Gorgoroth, forgetting no one else around him was able to hear the nature spirit.

Rafe paused, a chicken leg half way to his mouth. "Gods, I had no idea!" he roared with laughter. "Thank you." He giggled and almost dropped the food onto the floor.

"So, Vyder, tell us of that blue eye," Bordrog spoke. The red head leaned forward so as better to see down the long table.

179

"It belongs to Gorgoroth." The assassin upended the goblet, and as soon as he put it down, it was refilled by a clansman standing behind him.

"And pray tell, who in the fuck is Gorgoroth?" Rafe asked, swaying in his seat.

Numbness swept Vyder's body. His throat felt as if it was constricting, and his limbs became heavy. "Well," Gorgoroth's voice erupted from his lips, "that would be me, little human!"

Rafe's eyes narrowed, anger glinting there. His mouth retracted into a tight line, a hue of red tinging the skin of his face, veins in his neck bulging. The black-haired chieftain paused, leaned back in his chair and burst out laughing. "So, you, too, are a berserker?"

"I don't know what a berserker is, human."

The other chieftains were frozen in place, watching Vyder with wide eyes.

"Er, it is one who is not of…" Holrik shifted in his seat, "sound mind. Good to have on the field of battle, though."

"Well then, yes, Black Hair, in that case, I am a berserker."

Rafe raised his cup at Gorgoroth. "To the berserker chieftains," he roared, downed the drink, and slammed the wooden goblet upon the table.

Vyder leaned forward, coughing. Feeling returned to his arms and legs. He cleared his throat. "Sorry about that," he muttered. "At least you know now who Gorgoroth is."

The chieftains seated at the long table seemed more relaxed, having come to terms with Vyder's affliction, or that would be how they viewed it. One thing he'd missed about the Shadolian Highlands and its people, was that they were so accepting of what other cultures would deem inappropriate or worthy of banishment.

Hyglak pushed his empty plate away. "One thing you are not…is a chieftain."

"Am I not?" Vyder was unarmed and knew if a fight broke out, he and the others would be surrounded and killed within moments. He touched the blackened piece of round charcoal resting against the skin of his chest. He could take one man out of the fight immediately, but if he could bring the hidden token to a source of flame, he'd be able to summon Agoth within moments.

"No."

"Are we to fight an aforthafik over this feast?"

Hyglak chuckled. "No, you mistake my meaning. Clan Ironstone is without a chieftain. They will need to decide on a new leader. Because you are no longer a chieftain, certainly not of a single clan. You are now a highland warlord, Vyder."

"He's right," Bulvye spoke through a mouthful of food. "You have united some of the most powerful clans of Shadolia."

"There hasn't been a highland warlord in more than a thousand years," muttered Holrik.

Gorgoroth's laughter boomed in his mind. *You're welcome, little brother.*

<h1 align="center">VIII</h1>

The highland army was camped in the forests to the east of the large Firestorm village.

"So, what thoughts on bringing Clan Firestorm to heel?" Vyder sat cross-legged upon the ground. He spoke in the tongue of Wendurlund so that Ahitika and Henry could also understand what was being said.

The other chieftains along with trusted warriors and advisers sat with him in a tight circle, away from the army, where they could plan and discuss in peace.

Rafe cleared his throat. "I say we surround the village and kill them all!"

Vyder picked up a twig and broke it in half. "We need our force together in one place, not stretched thin encircling the village of Firestorm."

"So, we need to draw them out of their village," Bulvye said.

"Aye, and then smash them in an area of our choosing," added Holrik.

Vyder dropped the broken twig upon the ground. "I agree. But how?"

It is quite simple, little brother.

He ignored the nature spirit.

Hyglak shrugged "Send in a messenger and invite them to battle. Perhaps appeal to their sense of highland honour?"

Rafe spat and wiped his mouth with the back of his hand. "Those bastards don't have any bloody honour!"

Vyder felt his throat constrict, and his limbs become heavy and numb. He attempted to resist Gorgoroth, but the nature spirit had other ideas.

"Forgive me," Gorgoroth's voice boomed from his lips. "I have been trying to explain how to do this, but

Vyder keeps ignoring me."

Rafe chuckled. "Bastard's gone berserk again. I like it. What's your plan?"

"A group of us steal Firestorm's version of this," he pulled at the tartan cloth depicting Clan Ironstone's colours adorned diagonally across Vyder's chest, "and then walk into their longhouse."

"Just stroll on in?" asked Holrik.

Gorgoroth leaned forward, glaring at the chieftain. "It's easier than you think, little human."

"It may well work," said Bordrog. "It's certainly worth a try."

"And if we die?" Hyglak asked.

Rafe shrugged and grinned like a death's head. "Then we die. If today is to be my skane, then I am ready."

"There will be dying to be done, of that there is little doubt," Gorgoroth's voice boomed. "But it won't be any of us."

Vyder's arms and legs became less heavy and his throat tingled. He coughed. Clenching and unclenching his hands, he waited for the pins and needles to subside.

"Now we just have to work out how to engage them once we've drawn them out of their village," Vyder muttered. He coughed again and cleared his throat. He looked around at the circle of highlanders. "The King's Own, or the Horse Lords as you know them, use an instrument to control their formations during the noise of battle. It's called a bugle. Highlanders don't use bugles, but we have from time to time been known to use war horns."

"Aye, you mean like this?" Hyglak unclipped a war horn carved from deer antler from his belt and held it up.

"Exactly like that. I have an idea."

* * *

Henry finished his exercises and stretched out the muscles of his arms and shoulders. Although he was still slight, he'd put on weight. Under the skin of his upper body was a layer of thin muscle, which seemed to be more defined with each passing week. His strength increased with each day.

Regaining his breath, he rolled his shoulders to help relax the tight muscles. A highlander, the raven-haired ugly one, spoke a long sentence in his native tongue and barged past Henry. He'd been subject to verbal aggression. He'd been unable to understand the words, but the body language had been enough to explain the intended message. He'd walk past groups of highlanders and hear a shouted sentence followed by laughter. The first few times, he'd cast a glance over his shoulder. The highlanders would be chuckling, watching him with hatred in their eyes.

But this had been the first time he'd faced physical aggression from the highlanders. Probably because Vyder and Ahitika were no longer present. He clenched his teeth together, his jaw bulging.

It was only a matter of time.

If he'd learned anything from his short time with the King's Own, not to mention the hell of the Huronian dungeon, it was to stand up and account for yourself. To submit was to lose. Vyder himself had said as much. Even if defeated, it was better than submission. A rustling from nearby drew his attention. Raven Hair was knelt by his saddle, rummaging through his saddlebags.

He allowed the anger to flow through him,

184

although stopped it from overwhelming him. Anger was important, but dangerous. It could motivate action or be as oppressive and ensnaring as fear itself. Another lesson he'd been forced to learn whilst riding with the Unit. Harnessing both anger and fear were techniques parallel with one another.

He turned towards the highlander and walked towards him. "Stop!" he shouted, the skin above his nose creasing, drawing his eyebrows together. His mouth widened and lips peeled apart to reveal clenched teeth. The highlander paused, looked up at him and laughed before dragging free a bladder of water. He pulled free the stopper and took a long swig, then threw the bladder to one side, where precious, fresh water flowed out of the container. He delved a hand back into the saddlebag.

The benefits of diplomacy is sometimes exhausted. Ironically, then, for peace to reign, only the fight remains. He recalled the words in silence, although he'd forgotten where he'd heard them.

* * *

Vyder strode through the forest, the dry leaves crunching beneath his boots. Ahitika walked on one side of him and Torgun on the other. Henry had been intent on joining them. He'd argued, but eventually rescinded his eagerness when Vyder continued to refuse.

"The Firestorm people will see you are of Wendurlund stock and distrust us on sight, or try to kill us."

Hyglak and Rafe also accompanied them, Hyglak because he could use the war horn to signal the highland army when they were still some distance away. Rafe because the berserker would be handy to have nearby

185

when things turned to shit.

And things will turn to dung, little brother.

"I know," he muttered.

Rafe looked at him with a quizzical glance, then stared beyond him to catch Hyglak's eye. "I think he's going berserk again," he whispered, grinning.

They reached the main road leading into the Firestorm village in less than half an hour. Vyder removed the tartan cloth adorning his chest and folded it away.

"Waterborne now and forever," Rafe muttered under his breath, removing his tartan and putting it away.

Ahitika touched her chest plate, then brushed her hands across the dried scalps tied to her belt. They were left to their thoughts, but Vyder was confident each knew battle was not far away.

The village of Firestorm was huge, spanning more than two hundred acres, by Vyder's estimate. The perimeter was guarded by a ten-foot wooden wall, made from straight tree trunks, each thicker than a man's leg and the apexes carved into a sharp point. The road down which the small group strode led to an open gate.

"This is the Eastern Gate," Hyglak offered. "The north, west, and south entrances possess such a gate as well."

They walked through the open gate and blended amongst the villagers, few people having spotted their lack of tartans. The ones who seemed to notice weren't bothered. Vyder stepped aside to allow a merchant wagon to rumble past. A group of young, drunk Firestorm highlanders formed a circle on the far side of a merchant square yelling and cheering. Two of their number conducted a fist fight in the centre of the circle.

The group carried on down the dirt road, turning

off and heading into a residential area. Homes stood huddled together, a small garden adorning the front of most. It appeared the occupants of some dwellings grew vegetables, others sported well-tended beds of flowers and several had been allowed to go to ruin. Weeds having long taken over. Vyder opened a rickety old gate, strode through the thigh high weeds and rapped his knuckles against the hardwood of the front door.

Ahitika stopped beside him. "What you doing?"

"We need Firestorm tartans. These people are going to give us theirs."

The door opened to reveal a poorly-dressed man who stank of stale sweat. Dried puss crusted one eye half-closed. He held a knife in one hand, although the blade appeared to be blunt and half rusted.

"What do you want?" He snarled.

Vyder appraised the man from foot to head. "Obviously, the chieftain isn't distributing the tithe very well, is he?"

"I asked—"

"Were you involved in the raids your clan was responsible for that swept Shadolia a few years ago?"

"Damn right I was! It's about time the rest of the clans learned their places."

Vyder stepped forward and slammed an open palm into his throat, sending the highlander stumbling backwards. The assassin strode through the door and pushed the wounded man further into the house, allowing the others to enter behind him. The Firestorm highlander only stopped when he slammed against a wall and slid to the ground.

Vyder kept his eyes on the man who was on his knees, holding both hands to his throat making choking noises. "Close the door."

"Gladly," Rafe growled.

Straining hinges groaned under the weight, ceasing their noise only when the door closed with a loud *thud*.

"Capell! What is wrong with you?" shrieked a woman.

She ran into view, knelt beside the man, a hand on his shoulder. Noticing movement, she looked at the advancing group. Her eyes bulged, but Vyder was not oblivious to the fury that replaced her surprise. She fled the room.

He bent down, grabbed a fistful of the wounded man's shirt and dragged him to his feet. The choking highlander, his face turning a tinge of blue, reached down, his hand coming up with a knife. He lunged, arm reaching out with a clumsy attempt to wound him. Vyder slapped the hand away, disarmed him, and stabbed the knife into his throat. Kicking his legs out from under him, Vyder allowed the critically wounded man to gurgle and writhe at his feet. He reached down and pulled the Firestorm tartan free of the dying man, passing it over his head and one arm to settle diagonally across his chest.

"Bastards!" the woman screamed, running back into view holding a musket and preparing to fire from the hip.

Before Vyder could react, Rafe brushed past him, grabbed a hold of the weapon's barrel, turned it towards the ceiling, and wrestled the musket free of her grasp. Reversing the weapon, he clubbed her in the head with the butt stock. Standing over her, the berserker continued battering her until the floor around her head was slick with fresh blood, small chunks of flesh, and splinters of skull.

Rafe stooped and pulled the tartan clear. "Right!"

he turned back to them, his face and beard painted with flecks of blood. "That's two tartans. We just need a few more."

Vyder headed back to the entrance. "Let's call in on the neighbours."

* * *

"Get your stinking hands out of my belongings!" Henry said.

The highlander chuckled and continued to ignore him. He cursed, aware there was an audience. Highlanders from all directions were advancing upon the altercation. They formed a wide circle around the pair, some talking, others laughing. They watched Henry, curious to see what the Wendurlund man would do.

Only the fight remains.

The last time he'd been so openly ridiculed and disrespected was at the hands of Steef, one of the Huronian soldiers tasked with guarding him during his time as a prisoner. Steef's ugly face hovered in his mind and a wave of fury swept over Henry. He clenched his fists.

"Piece of shit!" Henry said, although unbeknown to those standing nearby observing, he'd been addressing Steef's memory, not the highlander hunched over his belongings.

He jogged the last few strides and launched a kick straight into the highlander's face. The man rolled away with a grunt and came up holding his face. He spat out a glob of bloody phlegm, grinned and unsheathed a knife. Henry reached behind him and withdrew his own blade, sheathed at the small of his back.

The dark haired warrior spluttered a sentence in his

native tongue and feigned an attack, his grin widening when he saw Henry flinch.

"Come then coward."

The sadistic grin vanished, anger flashing in his eyes.

He knows that word at least.

"Have at it, *coward.*"

Raven Hair spat a few words in the Shadolian language and Henry guessed at the meaning.

"Oh yes you're a coward, alright. Are we doing this or not, *coward?*"

The highlander roared, veins bulging against the skin of his throat. He came at Henry in a sprint, dark eyes glinting with fury and violence. He stepped aside and kicked him in the stomach. Doubling over, the highlander held his midriff. Henry hissed at the pain lancing his calf. He checked his leg. His adversary's blade had sliced the skin, although it was only superficial.

"That all you have, coward?"

The Shadolian straightened and lunged at him. Henry leapt back, the knife only inches from plunging into his guts. Again he attacked and Henry lost his footing, tumbling to the ground. He regained his footing in time to dodge another stab that would have skewered his chest. The highlander was grinning again, his teeth painted claret and a strand of bloody saliva hanging from his beard. This was a fight to the death. The Shadolians were a proud, warrior race and few challenges would end with a handshake and shared beer. With that thought in his mind and with his muscles already tiring, he had to end it fast, or he'd be crossing the Frost River sooner than he'd like.

Henry met his next attack on the front foot, jabbing a fist straight into the nose of his opponent. The highlander backed away, blood streaming from his nostrils. He attacked again shouting what sounded like a war cry. The man's eyes, filled with tears from the blow to his nose, slashed his blade wide, missing Henry by a hair's breadth. The Wendurlund prince strode in and slammed the knife into the throat of his enemy. He stepped back and kicked the man away, although he remained on his feet. Even as life blood gushed from the wound in rhythmic spurts, Raven Hair stared at Henry, hatred never leaving his dark eyes. He dropped to his knees, the glint of life fading. Then he fell forward.

Henry cleaned his blade on the dead man's shirt and sheathed it. He wiped sweat from his brow and regained his breath with slow deep inhalations. Looking around at the crowd of highlanders surrounding him, he expected to see hostility, renewed hatred, he even expected to die under an army of swords and knives. But he found nothing of the sort. Something else found residence in the stares of the men and women. Respect.

* * *

When all but Ahitika owned a Firestorm tartan, they headed for the longhouse at the centre of the village.

"I no highlander," Ahitika said when Vyder offered to provide her with one. "Kalote no wear tartans."

The group walked together in a loose formation, all but Rafe relaxed. The berserker, who'd since wiped his face clean of blood, was constantly reminded to relax, his face often shifting from a neutral look to one of blood curdling fury as he watched Firestorm highlanders stride past.

Vyder negotiated amongst a throng of people. Clan

Firestorm was so large, he had no concern he or anyone in the group would be questioned as to their identity. Kalote people were often travelling to and from Kalote into the Shadolian highlands and vice versa, so Ahitika, too, was safe. The further they travelled, it was more obvious they were entering the richer area of the clan.

Beautiful homes clustered together, painted in soft hues of cream or white, a thin, dark streak lining the perimeters of windows. The dirt road ended, and a cobbled street began.

Vyder's boots thumped upon the firm surface. "Fancy. They're living the high life."

"Not for long," Rafe said, his voice cheery.

People looked well fed, strong, and content. Unlike the vast majority of clans spread across Shadolia, working tirelessly to eek a living from the land, only to have half of their crop taken in a tithe to be given to Clan Firestorm.

This group of little monkeys need to be purged. Cleansed with fire and sharp steel.

Gorgoroth sounded angry.

"I agree."

Hyglak looked sidelong at him. "With what?"

He smiled. "Nothing, just talking to myself."

Ahitika tapped him on the arm. "What crazy one saying?"

"He wants to kill them all."

Rafe grunted, his eyes glazed with fury. "Tell him I agree."

A group of merchant wagons were parked close beside one another. The horses used to haul the vehicles were detached from their harnesses and stood in a large temporary fenced area nearby, munching upon a few bales of fresh feed. The wagons had been unpacked and wares of all shapes and types placed on tables. People browsed the wares, haggled, or as in Vyder's case, walked past, ignoring the calls of merchants, attempting to draw more people in to purchase their goods.

The longhouse came into view at the end of the main road. Two guards holding spears stood at the entrance. Few people approached the area, and the several who did were turned away.

Torgun cursed. "Just stepped in horseshit."

The young man scraped his boot against the cobbled road.

Hyglak chuckled. "Isn't that meant to be good luck?"

Torgun stamped his boot upon the ground. "Doesn't bloody smell like it."

Vyder watched the young man. "I'm sure you've smelled worse than horse dung, surely?"

He jogged a few steps to catch up with the group. "True," Torgun said.

Vyder swung around and walked backwards, looking from one person to the next. "We stick to the plan."

They all nodded. Vyder stared at Rafe. Although handy to have in a fight, a berserker would also be an unpredictable asset. "Agreed?"

Rafe smirked. "Aye, of course. I'll stick to the plan, and then I'll stick every bastard in that longhouse."

The assassin turned around and continued striding towards the building. The pair of guards outside were watching the approaching group. One of them leaned towards the other and muttered something.

Vyder forced a smile. "Good morning!"

A guard stepped forward and held up a hand. "Stop there, laddie, Herdrike is not accepting visitors today. Come back tomorrow."

"Strange." Vyder frowned, stopping before the guard. "We were summoned here by him."

"Still, laddie—"

"Vyder."

The guard held out one hand, open palm facing the group. "Vyder, we've been instructed not to allow anyone to pass."

"I don't care what you've been told." He pointed at the closed door behind the pair. "We've been summoned here. I'm one of Herdrike's senior advisers, I know you're just doing your duty, but is it worth losing your head?"

The bump in the soldier's throat rose and fell.

"Because, that's what's going to happen if you don't allow us to pass."

The guard stepped aside and gestured for his comrade to do the same, then waved a hand towards the closed door.

"A wise choice," said Vyder, striding past.

"I didn't know they had senior advisers," whispered Rafe.

"Neither did I," muttered Vyder, clutching the steel handle, turning it, and pushing open the door.

Herdrike sat on a large wooden chair at the far end of the longhouse, hands clamped upon the fur lined armrests. Head lolled against the backrest, his eyes were closed. Four guards stood nearby, two on either side, spears clutched in their hands.

Sitting cross-legged beside the fire in the centre of the huge room were two Kalote warriors. One man, the other a woman. They wore shabby clothes, eyes downcast, metal collars upon their necks, chains attaching the collars to the ground. One of them reached across and added a fresh log to the blaze, then returned to staring at the rich carpet upon which they sat. Fresh sparks drifted from the blaze, disappearing through the hole in the roof high above. He'd never seen Kalote slaves before. The only people from their neighbouring country he'd ever known had been much like Ahitika. Free, proud, and fierce. Not to mention the fact the countries of Kalote and Shadolia enjoyed an alliance. In his peripheral vision he saw Ahitika stiffen and did not need to look to know her face would be creased with fury.

A massive, black war hound lay on the floor at Herdrike's feet, jowls resting upon its paws. One baleful eye opened, then the other, and the hound raised its head, brow creasing with interest, alert eyes watching the approaching group. It snarled and barked, the powerful sound echoing around the longhouse. Herdrike lurched in his chair, bleary eyes opening.

"Wait until we are closer, do not attack until I give the signal, understood?"

A strange, intermittent, low-pitched noise moved with the group advancing upon the sleeping Firestorm chieftain. Vyder swept his gaze across the group, his attention coming to rest upon Rafe. The man was growling with each exhalation, his lips pulled apart in a snarl, eyes wide with fury and madness, a tendril of saliva hanging from his beard.

"Rafe!" he hissed. "Rafe, get a bloody hold of yourself."

"What is the meaning of this?" Herdrike shouted.

The war hound barked again, the animal's deep growl promising a bone crushing bite should the newcomers move any closer. Vyder looked into the dog's face, staring into those dark eyes.

Hello, my daughter. Aren't you a lovely one?

The hound's face relaxed, and her tail thumped against the floor. She licked her lips and whined. Climbing to her feet, she padded forward a few steps, her tail wagging from side to side so fast it was nothing more than a dark blur behind her.

"We are here as you requested, my chieftain," Vyder called.

The guards on either side of their leader relaxed.

The hound darted forward at Vyder's voice.

"I didn't request your presence. You'd best leave or she'll tear you all limb from limb."

The black hound, her head reaching Vyder's waist, skidded to a halt in front of him, stood on her hind legs and placed a paw on either shoulder, licking his cheek.

Vyder squinted against the onslaught of affection, stroking her, but attempting to push her away. The animal was having none of it. She licked his face, Vyder eventually having to resort to covering his mouth with a hand. When she'd finished, she dropped back onto all fours and stared up at him, her tail slapping against the thigh of Torgun standing nearby.

He knelt beside the animal and scratched her head. "It's been a while, girl!" he said loud enough for the chieftain and his guards to hear. "My apologies, my lord, there must have been some mistake. We were told to come to the longhouse as soon as possible for a meeting with you."

"What's that Kalote slut doing here?" Herdrike roared.

It was lucky for the chieftain Ahitika could not speak or understand the Shadolian language, else Herdrike would be without a scalp.

Vyder shrugged. "She cooks." He smiled. "Attends

our needs." He'd be less his scalp if Ahitika knew the words *he* spoke. Maintaining the smile, guilt stabbed him. Verone's face drifted into his mind's eye.

Herdrike laughed. It was a harsh staccato of sound. "I do not recall summoning you, especially that drooling dimwit amongst your number, but you may stay briefly."

He looked at Rafe and noticed the berserker's eyes rolled back in his head, several tendrils of saliva hanging in various lengths, vying to be the first to drip to the floor.

Vyder's arms and legs became numb. He allowed Gorgoroth to take control without complaint. He stroked the dog, and she nuzzled his cheek.

"You see that little bastard sitting in the chair over there?" he looked at Herdrike.

The hound followed his gaze and whined.

"Soon, I'm going to kill him and the men standing guard over him."

The whine changed to a deep, aggressive rumble.

Gorgoroth stood. He appraised the group around him with a lethargic sweep. "Is everyone ready?"

Ahitika snarled, Torgun nodded, Hyglak muttered something under his breath, and Rafe growled, one tendril of saliva finally touching the ground.

Hand still upon the hound's head, he strode forward. "Then let us get it done."

Gorgoroth pulled the hunting knife free of its sheath held firm by the belt beneath his shirt. He broke into a run, darted around the seated Kalote slaves, and charged at the chieftain. Herdrike was on his feet, struggling to draw his sword in desperation. "Kill them!" he screamed at his guards.

Gorgoroth plunged the knife into the man's throat. The sharp blade sliced through soft flesh, and Vyder kicked the dying man to the ground. The hound leapt upon the closest guard, her jaws fracturing his arm with a sickening crack. The man, off balance, fell to the floor under the dog's weight, screaming in agony. The animal released his arm and bit down upon his throat. The screaming ended.

Vyder coughed and rubbed at the tingling ache in his throat. Feeling returned to his limbs. He knelt beside the dying chieftain, grabbed a fistful of shirt and hauled him into a semi-recumbent position. He stared into his eyes. "That's for my family and my clan, you stinking pile of shit. I am Clan Ironstone." Herdrike's eyes, fast losing the light of life, bulged. He released him to fall to the ground. "Now and always."

When he stood, Rafe had killed one clansman and had the other in a headlock. Ahitika had dispatched the final man and the group stood watching Rafe. The berserker screamed like a wounded animal, spittle flying from his mouth. The guard struggled in Rafe's grip and finally landed a powerful blow on the berserker's back. The force of the punch would have given most men pause, but Rafe screamed at the roof of the longhouse, veins bulging in his throat and forehead. The glint of madness lit his eyes.

"Crazy as wounded dog," Ahitika muttered. She cleaned her blade upon the shirt of one and sheathed the weapon. Vyder half-expected her to scalp the guard, but she refrained. Instead she turned away and walked to the seated Kalote slaves watching proceedings, hope flickering in their dark eyes.

Torgun stopped beside Vyder and gestured at the struggling pair. "He going to kill him? or keep playing at wrestling?"

He shook his head and shrugged, lost for words.

"What in the name of the gods are you doing, Rafe?"

Tightening the grip on his throat, the guard buckled at the knees. Only then did the berserker release the hold. The purple-faced guard clutched his neck, gasping in a deep breath.

"Thros!" screamed Rafe, looking to the rafters. "Thros, bring us luck!" He drew a knife from his belt. "For you!" he yelled, pointing the weapon at the ceiling and the sky beyond, then dropped his arm and slashed open the guard's throat.

"Ah, a sacrifice," muttered Torgun.

Something wet touched Vyder's fingers, and he glanced down. The hound nuzzled his hand, her tail wagging. He squatted beside the animal.

Vyder stroked her head. "Good work, lass. I need to think of a name for you, don't I?"

Prying a spear free from a guard's dead hand, Vyder rose and approached the slaves. Ahitika sat near them talking in their native tongue with soft tones.

"Can you tell them we're going to free them?"

Ahitika swung around. "Done already."

"I'm going to use the spear to pry lose their collars."

She turned to the pair and switched back to her native tongue.

"I'm not going to hurt them."

Ahitika translated.

They appeared unsure, yet hopeful. The closest felt her collar and found the locking mechanism fastening the device around her neck. She slid around to present it towards the assassin, then arched her head to give Vyder space. In doing so, she exposed her throat, entrusting a man she'd never before met with her freedom and her life.

He placed the spear head into the lock and pried the rusted metal apart. She winced at the pressure. The metal held, the lock bending completely out of shape. Then it snapped. Ahitika pushed the spear away and opened the collar. The woman, once a slave rubbed her neck, wide, disbelieving eyes staring at the man sat opposite. She looked at Vyder and waved her hand at her comrade.

Vyder nodded. "Yes, he's next."

He walked around to the far side and performed the same rudimentary operation. The pair jumped to their feet and embraced each other, laughing.

Rafe, who looked more human following the brief fight, and having obviously wiped his beard, held out two spears. "You'll need these."

The Kalote couple nodded their thanks, then snatched one each. The male brushed past Vyder, approached the corpses littering the ground at the far end of the longhouse, and with a high-pitched whoop, slammed his newly acquired spear into Herdrike's chest. He ripped it clear and stood over each dead body, doing the same.

The woman stood before Vyder and spoke a few sentences in her native tongue, then reached out and tapped his chest.

"She say, 'You good man and strong warrior. She also see you touched by a god.'"

Ahitika turned away from Vyder and replied to the woman, who burst into laughter. "I tell her, no god, you just crazy. Crazier maybe than him." She pointed at Rafe.

The door through which Vyder and his small party had recently walked was thrown open. The guards he'd convinced to allow them access stood there, their figures silhouetted by the fresh light flooding in behind them.

"What is the meaning of all this screeching?" They advanced into the room together. "Chieftain? Chieftain! By the gods. By the bloody gods." The man who must have been the senior guard glanced over his shoulder at his comrade. "Send for help. Go!"

"But, sire…"

"Go now! Quickly."

The dog leaning against Vyder's leg stiffened, her muscles bunching. She growled. He dropped a hand to brush her head. "Nothing to worry about my lass." And then in a louder voice. "And what do you think you're going to do against us? You're outnumbered."

"Not for long, traitor. You and yours will be hanging in the village square within the hour."

"Will we?" Vyder asked in a quiet voice.

A high-pitched shriek exploded around the longhouse, and the Kalote woman who'd recently been a slave, sprinted past Vyder and threw her spear. The weapon streaked through the air and plunged into the guard's chest before he could take evasive action. He crumpled to the floor in a growing pool of blood. She stood over the corpse and spoke in her native tongue, her face creased in a snarl. Ahitika offered the woman her knife, but the once-slave shook her head and spat a word.

Vyder ran across the floor and out the longhouse. He jumped clear of the stairs and sprinted away. "Let's go, follow me!" he bellowed.

The group streamed out after him, Ahitika ushering the Kalote pair onward. When he reached the closest building, he stopped and gestured them past him.

"Hyglak, lead them to the merchants' wagons. Take their horses. I'll be along soon."

Ahitika halted beside him. "I stay with you."

"No, you go with them, lass."

She looked to be considering arguing. "I'll be fine, Ahitika. I'll be right behind you."

The Kalote warrior snarled, brushed past him, and sprinted to catch up with the others.

Vyder crouched and patted the hound. She licked his face and sniffed his hair. "By what name should you be known?"

She tilted her head, ears cocked, staring at him. Shouting erupted in the distance, growing louder by the moment. The drum of many boots mingled with the voices. An enemy horde approached.

The war hound looked beyond Vyder, her lips parting to reveal razor sharp fangs. A growl rumbled deep in her chest. He rose to his feet and turned towards the approaching din.

He patted the hound's back. "Another time perhaps."

The group of guards surged into view, scattering people out of their way. The only remaining survivor of Vyder's assault led the way. He was red-faced, eyes bulging with either anger or fear, his spear clutched in a tight grip. So focused upon the longhouse were they that not a single guard noticed Vyder and the hound standing beside the closest building. They hammered up the stairs and entered the building, shouting and shrieking. The narrow entrance provided a choke point for those at the back, eager to advance into the longhouse and close with the enemy who had claimed the life of their chieftain.

Vyder tossed the spear into the air, caught it mid-haft, broke into a run and threw it. The weapon sailed through the air towards the throng.

"Your enemy is behind you," he roared.

The hound barked, flecks of saliva bursting from

her great maw. Those at the back of the group turned to face him. A brief moment passed as they registered what it was Vyder had said. Then their war cries filled the air, and they charged. Vyder's spear skewered one through the chest, the highlander's legs collapsing beneath him. His fury-filled face morphed into one of pain, and he grasped the embedded weapon as if that would somehow save his fleeing life. He disappeared beneath the boots of those behind him, jostling with one another to be the first to reach Vyder and claim his life.

"Bring your clan!" He walked backward, whistling for the hound to join him. "I have a Highland army with me. We shall meet you in battle near the eastern forest."

Some laughed, a few jeered but most ignored him. A couple threw their spears at Vyder, but they were aimed with lack of skill, slamming into the ground a few paces in front of him. One man slowed, peeled off, and sprinted away.

"Good lad," muttered Vyder. "Gather your army that we might smash you from existence."

He gestured at the spears embedded in the ground nearby. "Is that all you have?" he shouted. "Pathetic!"

He turned from them and sprinted in the direction of the merchant wagons. "Come, lass!" he yelled at the hound. She offered the advancing group one last powerful bark, then followed her new master.

Vyder ducked down an alley. A spear clattered against a brick wall behind him. He stopped, sprinted back and picked the weapon up. He managed a quick glance at the chasing group. They were much closer than he'd anticipated.

We should fight them, little brother.

"They'd kill us, Gorgoroth."

You underestimate me.

"No, I don't, they outnumber us."

Only by a little.

"I was never good with numbers, but if you call thirty to one good odds, then I'd say you're not of the betting persuasion."

Vyder's legs ached, and his lungs burned. He turned down another side street, the hound keeping pace with effortless grace.

"Watch out!" He barged through a small group of people walking on the narrow road.

They cursed, one woman screamed.

He cast a glance over his shoulder. The group through which he'd charged were pressed against the walls of the buildings either side of the road to allow the group of guards to pass. One of the guards threw his spear. Vyder sidestepped, the weapon hissing past his face and sliding along the cobbles.

Vyder turned a corner, increased his pace, and ignored his body's protests. He went around another corner, and the merchant wagons came into view. The merchants were standing in a group, shouting, yelling, and threatening the highlanders who sat upon the horses the merchants used to pull their wagons.

"Hurry up, Vyder!" called Hyglak.

"You don't say?" he managed between breaths.

He reached the closest animal and clambered up behind Ahitika. "Let's go!"

The group galloped away, leaving the merchants calling insults.

Rafe turned in his saddle. "Tell the guards of the theft!" He laughed, eyes wide.

"You see if we don't," one merchant threatened, holding up a fist.

"Now's your chance. They're right behind you!"

Vyder shot a glance over his shoulder. The guards scattered the merchants, one rather rotund man falling to his buttocks. He grinned and faced front.

"You alright, lass?" he called down at the hound running beside him. She glanced up at him, tongue lolling from one side of her mouth. She wasn't even struggling to keep pace.

She's enjoying herself.

The fond tone in Gorgoroth's voice was difficult to miss.

Hyglak, leading them, often waved his arms and hollered to make way, lest people be run down by horses. Most people complied, but others, whether hard of hearing or simply stubborn, leapt clear at the last moment. One man shrieked like a child. They swept through the eastern gate and made for the forest in the distance.

Vyder cupped a hand around his mouth. "Hyglak!"

The highland looked back at him.

"Call make ready!"

The warrior turned away, pulled clear his war horn, brought it to his lips and blew two long blasts.

The horses were breathing hard, sweat turning their fur slick. It'd been a long time since they were asked to work so hard. Highland warriors streamed out of the forest and formed up in a square, round shields in one hand, swords in the other. Ahitika brought the horse close to the army and dismounted smoothly, closely followed by Vyder.

Ahitika tapped him on the arm. "I get my horse, I also lead your horse and his horse." She gestured at Hyglak dismounting nearby. She appraised the two former Kalote slaves. "I bring horses for them, too."

Henry came alongside her. "I'll come with you."

There was blood on his cheek noted Vyder.

Ahitika smiled and nodded.

"Aye. Thanks, lass."

She and Henry jogged towards the forest.

He patted the animal's powerful neck. "Thank you, great one." He placed a hand on the shoulder and pushed. "Now away with you. This is no place for you." The horse nuzzled him. Vyder clapped his hands. "Go!" he yelled.

Startled, the horse galloped away, tail raised in the air, the other animals following suit. They fled together in a tight herd. He strode to the front of the army, Hyglak beside him. The war hound was racing up and down the length of the formation, barking and yipping in excitement. The highlanders laughed, cheered and called to the animal. But it was one word that was repeated from all quarters that drew Vyder's attention. Saigh. The Shadolian word for arrow.

Spotting Vyder, she bolted toward him, circled he and Hyglak, and finally stopped beside him looking up at him panting. He knelt and took her wide head in his hands. "I think we have your name, lass. We shall call you Saigh. What say you?"

She barked, placed a paw on his shoulder, and then licked his face. He ruffled her ears, stood, and turned to face the highland army.

"Soon, battle will find us. Muskets and blunderbusses in the second rank." He spotted one man in the front rank, clutching a musket. "You!" he pointed at the highlander. "Step back."

The warrior, red-faced, jostled backward, and was replaced by a short, powerfully-built man hailing from Clan Coppersmith.

"Everyone remember the horn blast for shield

wall?"

Silence answered him.

He leaned into Hyglak. "Call black powder," he whispered.

Hyglak brought the war horn to his lips and blew four short blasts.

Some warriors in the front rank turned side-on as they'd been trained, while those in the second rank brought muskets or blunderbuss to bear. Most of the warriors in the front seemed bewildered, looking around, realisation only dawning on their faces when they saw their comrades standing side on.

"Hold your fire!"

Vyder punched the air. "Pathetic! Remember, four short horn blasts are for black powder!" he tapped his temple. "Burn the command in up here, because if you don't," he turned to look at the distant city, "then we're done for."

The Firestorm army was yet to appear, but if Vyder's message was delivered, it would not be long before they marched out the gates and onto the plain towards them.

"Be patient, Vyder," Hyglak muttered. "These clans have never fought together before like this, and this tactic," he lifted the horn in his hand, "is all new. Give them time."

"There *is* no time, my friend. Call shield wall."

The war horn spoke again.

Round shields clattered together followed by the rolling voices of highlanders. "*Skyaldborg!*" the Shadolian word for shield wall peeled across the plain and echoed through the forest in the near distance behind them. The warriors in the front rank interlocked their shields in front of them, while those in the third rank stretched forward and interlocked their shields above the heads of those carrying muskets and blunderbusses in the second rank. Those ranks behind did the same until the only rank whose heads were unprotected was those standing at the rear.

"Now, black powder."

Hyglak blew the war horn, and this time, the front rank reacted as one. They stood side on, their shields still in position. Then the shields dropped and the second rank appeared, already aiming down the metal sights of their flintlock weapons.

"Hold your fire! Better! Okay, everyone, relax for the moment. Now we wait. Where are the horses?"

"We brought them forward. They are all tied up just shy of the forest edge, lord," Bulvye called from the front rank.

If Firestorm decided to fight from horseback, it would be pointless to try and counter them with infantry tactics.

Vyder stepped towards the chieftain of Clan Earthforge and held out his hands.

"Do not correct him on your title," warned Hyglak. "If that's what you were about to do, of course. You are a warlord now, Vyder. You earned it, you melded our tribes together, so own your title. Do not apologise for it."

"Thank you, Chief Bulvye." He faced Hyglak. "Thanks for the reminder, my friend," he whispered.

"You're welcome, my lord," he said, a smirk twisting his lips.

Shouting erupted from the highlanders. Some were pointing towards the Firestorm city. Vyder swung to face the distant eastern gates. A column of Firestorm highlanders appeared, marching on foot. Row after row appeared from behind the colossal gates. It was a seemingly endless stream. When the last row appeared, Vyder hazarded a guess at twelve hundred warriors.

He strode to his army and walked along the length of the front rank. He allowed the clansmen to shout, jeer, and roar at their adversary for a while. When he reached the end of the rank, he turned around and walked back, stopping at the centre.

He held his hands high above his head. "Silence!" he yelled. "Quiet!"

Silence never approached, but the din lessened enough for him to be heard.

"Remember those bastards?" he thrust an arm out behind him at the Firestorm highlanders, negotiating the plain in their direction. "Remember what they did to your families? Your homes? Your *clan*? Never forget it! Not ever."

Hooves thumped against the ground. Ahitika and Henry rode towards him, leading Storm and a few other mounts. He nodded his thanks, took the reins from her, patted Storm's neck, and mounted. Hyglak did the same. The two Kalote warriors leapt into their saddles, shrieking and whooping, each clutching a spear, their fierce eyes never leaving the approaching enemy.

Pushing the mare towards the formation, Vyder held out his hands. "They were expecting to face a clan. But instead, they're facing a highland army! We have Waterborne." He pointed at the cluster of men and women hailing from Clan Waterborne. They roared and began chanting their clan's war cry over and again.

He gestured at another section of the formation. "Windeagle!"

The voices of Clan Windeagle joined in with their own clan's war cry.

"Earthforge!"

A new section of the formation broke into a powerful chant, the war cries rolling across the plain.

"Coppersmith!"

New voices joined the cacophony.

"Wintercreek!" although Vyder could barely hear his own voice, his finger was enough indication for the clansmen and women of Clan Wintercreek to shriek their clan's war cry.

"Ironstone!" he roared.

He could not hear Ironstone's war cry of 'victory or death!' but he spotted members screaming the words, their faces creased with savagery and fury.

He caught Hyglak's eye. He cantered to him and cupped a hand to his mouth so as to be heard over the booming mash of noise behind him. "When the fighting starts, we stay mobile around our army. It's the benefit of having a horn to signal commands."

Hyglak wiped a hand upon his trousers and unclipped the war horn from his belt.

"Where do you want us?" Henry called.

Henry, Ahitika, and the pair of Kalote warriors stood in a loose group.

"You stay mobile, don't get too close to the Firestorm formation, but harass them when you get the chance."

Henry nodded but he seemed hesitant.

"Stick with Ahitika, fast moving guerilla tactics is a Kalote speciality. She'll show you the way."

The Kalote woman whispered something to Henry and chuckled. The skin of his face flushed , and he smiled. She turned her horse away, and the trio followed.

"And don't get killed!" Vyder yelled.

The cries of the Highland army intensified,

individuals shaking swords, muskets, or shields above their heads, screaming and shouting. He twisted away from the departing group and focused upon Clan Firestorm. They were charging in an arrowhead formation.

"Call shield wall!"

He pushed Storm into a trot, Hyglak not far behind. The horn's call pierced through the storm of furious voices, and some complied. Many of them ignored the call, their blood up and their focus entirely on the enemy.

Vyder pushed her into a gallop. "Again!" he shouted over his shoulder.

The war horn spoke again. Saigh barked and streaked after Storm, her ears tucked against her skull.

"Shield wall, damn you!" Vyder bellow, sweeping along the front rank, Storm's hooves ripping up chunks of earth and flinging them into the air behind her. "Shield wall. Bloody listen!"

Hyglak called the command again. Shields clattered together, overlapping one another. The Highland army disappeared behind a fortress of round shields, although they continued to shriek their war cries.

He slowed Storm to a trot and turned her so they were traversing the rear rank. Thanks to the horse's height, he looked over the shields. Firestorm were closing the distance fast, their own voices creasing the sky and echoing from the forest in the distance.

"Hold!"

Hyglak lifted the horn to his lips and blew.

Draw in those little monkeys, brother. Then unleash hell.

"Great minds think alike, Gorgoroth," muttered Vyder. "Come on, just a little closer."

"Signal it again, Hyglak."

The horn cut through the noise, and the shield wall remained steadfast, like some monstrous, frozen beetle. Vyder's brow creased. Clan Firestorm slowed and stopped, forming their own shield wall.

"Bastards want us to come to them." Hyglak laughed and spat on the ground.

"Then we shall oblige them."

"Advance!"

Hyglak took a deep breath and pursed his lips around the horn's mouthpiece.

The Highland army took two paces forward and halted. A guttural grunt accompanied each footstep, then the war cries started again.

"Advance!"

The shouting stopped, another two paces forward, a powerful rumble booming out as each boot struck the ground. Then the shouting recommenced.

"Again!"

The highlanders were used to fighting in shield wall formations and had done so for centuries. But introducing the black powder element in such a focused, organised way was something entirely new.

"I just hope it works," he whispered.

The two formations were within a stone's throw.

"Forward!"

The horn blasted, and two more paces brought the formation within spitting distance of their enemy.

"Hold!"

Vyder remained trotting along the rear rank, Hyglak beside him. "Ready?"

Hyglak clutched the war horn in his right hand, his fingertips white. He nodded once.

Vyder took a deep breath. "Call black powder!"

He trotted up the flanks so as to better view the

front rank.

The instrument's voice pierced the roar of voices. The front rank turned side on as they'd been trained, maintaining the position of their shields. Then their shields dropped, and the front two ranks disappeared in a cloud of burnt gunpowder. The *crack* of muskets and *boom* of blunderbusses dominated the ferocious words issuing from thousands of throats. The front rank brought their shields back into position and the second rank dropped to their knees to commence reloads.

Vyder advanced a few more paces, the acrid smell of burnt black powder bringing a cough. The shouts that had been so aggressive from Clan Firestorm persisted, but screams, pain-filled yells and groans of the wounded mingled with the noise. The cloud dissipated, and he saw the front rank of the enemy shield wall had been decimated, many of their number either dead or dying.

"Advance and engage!"

Hyglak blew the command and the Highland army jogged the last few steps of open ground separating the two forces. Their shields slammed against those of the enemy, and they pushed them back. Swords appeared beneath shields to slice, cut or stab at feet, ankles or calves. Working in tiny teams, those in the front rank called for those holding shields above them to provide a gap, whereupon they stabbed their swords above their shields and down upon the enemy. Once the sword arm was retracted, the gap slid closed.

"They're fighting well, lord!"

Vyder grinned. "By the gods, they are!"

He trotted almost to the fray, and stared down at the first couple of ranks of his fellow clansmen. "Second rank!" he shouted. "How goes it?"

"We're reloaded, lord!" the muffled voice shouted

back from beneath the ceiling of shields protecting them.

"Right then." Vyder flinched as a spear sailed past his nose. Saigh barked and sprinted for the man who'd thrown the weapon at her master. "Saigh!" he bellowed. "To me, girl! To me!" He turned Storm away, the hound at the horse's heels, and they trotted to the rear of the shield wall formation. "Call withdraw."

Vyder's force disengaged from the enemy and withdrew two paces. "Black powder!"

The muskets and blunderbusses spoke again, spewing another cloud of burnt powder to drift over the field of battle and blotting out those in the first few ranks of each opposing force.

"Advance and engage!"

The roars of the Highland army reignited anew, and the shield wall slammed home against those of their enemy, pushing them back further than they had before. When the cloud had dissipated, the efficient, lethal power of the black powder weapons was obvious. The projectiles had cut the second and some of the third row down, splitting the enemy shield wall open like a rotten log.

Sensing their opportunity, the Highland army pressed forward, cutting down their foe in scores. Vyder pushed Storm back to the front.

"Hold the wall!" he shouted. "Hold your formation!"

Some highlanders may have been tempted to break free and storm in amongst their enemies, inadvertently weakening their own shield wall. But they remained true, advancing against Clan Firestorm together, keeping the shields interlinked.

"Second rank?" he roared.

"Reloaded, lord!" the same muffled voice yelled.

Firing the weapons while engaged with an enemy force was a risk.

"Lord, if the front drop their shields while fighting, it'll leave them vulnerable to counter attack."

He twisted in his saddle and appraised Hyglak. "I know, but if we disengage, it will give the bastards precious time to reorganise. Call black powder!"

Hyglak blasted the order and mere moments passed before the deafening explosion of flintlock weapons sang their lethal song. The screams of the wounded and moans of the dying drowned out the shouts of the Firestorm highlanders. When the smoke dissipated, the opposing shield wall back to the fifth rank was decimated.

Vyder's army didn't need the order, they pressed forward, shattering the enemy's wall and dispatching them in short order. Clan Firestorm broke and ran towards the protection of their city.

"Hold!"

The horn's blast echoed over the field of battle, and although the Highland army continued to yell, jeer, and roar obscenities at their retreating foe, they held firm the shield wall. High-pitched screams pierced the sky, and Ahitika led the loose formation of galloping horses. They tore across the ground towards what remained of Clan Firestorm. Henry was at the rear, spear in hand. The former female slave lifted a leg over her horse's neck, leapt clear of the saddle, and hit the ground at full sprint, slamming into a highlander and bearing him to the ground.

Her hand, clenching a knife, rose and fell and continued until the struggling man lay still. She changed the grip on the weapon, leaned over her adversary, and sliced. Vyder only realised what she'd cut when she stood over the downed warrior and held the scalp above her head, her face creased in a snarl and eyes glinting with fury.

Holding his spear double-handed, Henry stabbed a highlander through the back, but the haft was ripped clear of his grip when the wounded man fell to the ground. He tried to rise, but his legs collapsed beneath him. One fleeing warrior swung his sword at Henry, but the horse was past him before the blade could connect. The Wendurlund prince turned his mount around and charged the highlander, the horse's powerful chest battering the man to the ground. Henry dismounted, retrieved the weapon, and killed the man with his own sword, then climbed back into the saddle.

Ahitika loosed arrow after arrow. Her mount moved at such speed, some of the projectiles missed their intended targets. But many did not. The former male slave jumped from his horse and landed on the back of one unfortunate Firestorm highlander running from the battle. His death was quick. As fast as they'd ridden in, Ahitika led the group out of the fray, leaving even more enemy dead or dying behind them.

A hand slapped him on the back, and Vyder looked away from the tiny force galloping clear.

"I think we won, lord," Hyglak bellowed, a wide grin splitting his beard.

When the last of the Firestorm highlanders disappeared into their city, the gate was closed and probably barred.

"Back to the forest!" Vyder encircled the army shouting the words over and over until they broke their shield wall and streamed back to where they'd started.

"Gather your horses and prepare to move!"

Hyglak helped spread the word amongst the army.

Their blood was still running hot, and many of them were shouting, laughing, recounting stories from the recent battle, making good natured jests, or helping tend to the wounded. A small group carried the fallen. Vyder counted eight dead, and perhaps three times as many wounded, of which most were minor lacerations.

Hyglak reined in beside him. "We got off lightly, lord. Your tactic worked well."

"It was a risk, but it worked. I'm not sure it'd work again now Firestorm know what to expect. They may even try to replicate it."

"Doubt it. They won't be replicating much for many a year." Hyglak turned in his saddle and looked out at the open ground between them and the enemy city. "See for yourself."

Vyder turned Storm around. Saigh sat nearby, her tongue lolling from her mouth. He swept his eyes over the enemy fallen in the distance. They littered the ground in a heap of cluttered and broken shields, weapons and bodies.

You and your little army have done well today, brother.

A broken Clan Firestorm flag lay amongst the dead, wind teased one corner of the fabric causing it to flutter. Vyder had never been good at estimating numbers, but he assumed there were several hundred bodies lying upon the field of battle.

Hyglak leaned a forearm on the pommel of his saddle. "Five hundred is my estimate. We cut their clan in half. It'll be some time before they consider sweeping the highlands again."

Vyder grunted. "Good."

Within the hour, the Highland army was mounted and on the move, winding through the forest towards their respective clan homes. Vyder, riding at the front of the army seized the opportunity.

"Chieftains to me!"

Hyglak and Bordrog were already nearby, but the others took some time before they cantered up the flanks of the army and joined him. Holrik was humming a tune when he slowed to walk his mount beside Vyder.

"You're in merry spirits, my friend."

"My family and clan have been avenged," the chieftain of Clan Coppersmith smiled.

Bulvye arrived next, dark circles beneath his eyes. He yawned.

Rafe galloped into view, his horse skidding to a walk. He cheered. "A victory, Warlord!" The whites of his eyes were bloodshot, probably remnants of his berserk rage during the battle.

"Aye, Rafe, our clans fought well today."

Vyder took a deep breath and clenched the reins in a tight grip. "Now that Firestorm have been dealt with and rendered incapable of storming the highlands for many years to come, I have news from further afield."

Rafe laughed. "Another clan whose arse needs handing back to them?"

"Not quite. Have any of you been south into the lands of Wendurlund?"

Rafe spat and looked away.

"As a child, briefly," Bulvye said.

Bordrog shrugged. "Not me. I'd like to see the lands that once belonged to our ancestors, though."

Holrik nodded. "Lisfort is a nice city. Although the people were hostile."

Hyglak remained silent.

Rafe leaned forward in his saddle, eyes boring into Vyder. "Why, lord?"

"They are under siege by a much larger Huronian

army. Who knows, they may have already fallen."

Rafe shrugged. "Not my fight. Not any highlander's fight."

"I know what you're saying, Rafe, but it will be your fight when Huron subjugate all of Wendurlund and sweep north to plunder our beloved highlands."

"And why would they do that? It makes little sense," said Bordrog.

"Do you know of King Fillip?"

Silence answered the question.

"He's a madman, an utterly deranged madman devoid of logic, and at his hands is one of the largest armies ever known to our history. If Lisfort falls, they will take over Wendurlund, enslave or kill the people. And then, have no doubt, King Fillip's eyes will turn north."

"And if we refuse?" asked Bulvye.

Vyder shrugged. "Then you refuse. But regardless, Ahitika, Henry and I will travel into Wendurlund to help. No, they are not our allies, but things can change with the advance of centuries. If we do not face this great threat now while the army of Wendurlund still has some strength, then we will be left to fend for ourselves and believe me, the Huronians will destroy us."

"Will you return here once it is done?" Hyglak's voice broke the quietness.

Vyder shifted in his saddle. "I will die there, my friend."

"You can't know that," Bordrog said.

"I know that I will. When it is done, I will die." Verone's face appeared in his mind. She was smiling.

"I will come with you then, lord," said Rafe. "If I am with you, death will be too afraid to approach!"

Vyder chuckled.

"But it is the choice of my clan whether they join me," said Rafe.

"I understand."

Holrik cleared his throat. "You have done us a great service by bringing our clans together so that we might avenge our loved ones, Vyder."

"Lord," corrected Hyglak.

Holrik ignored him. "So, I will join you. Tonight, I will put it to my clan, but like Rafe, I can't guarantee they will join me."

Hyglak unclipped his war horn and held it up. "You'll need someone to signal your commands upon the battlefield, I suppose?"

"Aye, I will."

"A temporary chieftain will be appointed while I'm away," said Bordrog. "But like the others, it may just be me if my clan chooses not to join me. Fighting the war of another country is a choice they have to make on their own merits."

Bulvye sniffed. "I, too, will join you, my lord."

"Thank you all. As you say, when we rest this evening, put it to your respective clans, and if you choose to change your decision, then I will lose no respect for you. For any of you."

"When do we leave?" asked Rafe.

"Right now, my friend. We're on our way right now."

Rafe grinned. "Let's show those southern bastards how a Highland army fights."

Part III

Hold the Wall

IX

The sweeping, grassy planes of Wendurlund offered no place to hide. Only the veil of darkness gave refuge from prying eyes. So, Rone moved at night, always heading west towards his home city of Lisfort. Sometimes he dismounted and walked, allowing the powerful horse to rest. There was enough of the paste left to stave off the stench of rotting flesh, until he was able to bury his soldier at least.

Dawn announced its arrival, bringing a halt to their advance. Rone stepped from the saddle untied his dead soldier from the mount's back and pulled the corpse clear, lying him on the ground. Then he unsaddled the animal, brushing the slick fur down. Strengthening light invaded the sky, sending stars into full retreat. Ignoring the horse grazing in the near distance, the King's Own officer crouched, his eyes just above the top of the thigh length grass.

"What the hell are they doing?" he whispered.

The blob of Huronian cavalry moved west in a tight formation. Rone couldn't see them individually, but dogged experience told him there were perhaps twenty or thirty of the enemy soldiers.

If they're deserters, why are they still heading into the fray? Why are they not running from the war?

Every morning they were there. Sometimes south of Rone, other times north, but they were always heading in a westerly direction. It seemed they chose to move during daylight, whereas Rone rested while the sun shone and travelled when the moon rose. So, each night, he closed the distance between them. He watched them, noting they were heading in a slight south westerly direction. When evening came, he would move in a west or even north westerly direction to ensure he would not stumble upon their camp during the night.

He slumped to the ground beside the deceased soldier. Even the thick, pleasant smelling paste was on the verge of not being enough to stave off the stink. But it would do for now.

"Only two days before we can lay you to rest," he muttered.

The dead man remained silent and still while the horse, oblivious to Rone's thoughts, continued to take its fill from the plentiful grass. If he had his bearings, there was a small lake a little way to their north. When it was time to move, he'd deviate in that direction so the animal could quench its thirst, and he could refill his water bladders.

Rone lay on his back, rested hands behind his head and closed his eyes. The gentle heat of the sun on his skin was soothing. Combined with the occasional snort and chewing of the destrier nearby, it was enough to bring sleep to him. He awoke once at midday, rolled onto his side, and noticed the warhorse standing over him, legs locked straight, dozing. Closing his eyes, exhaustion swamped him, whisking him away into the ether of slumber.

He jerked away when something soft touched his face. Rone's eyes snapped open to find a horse nose inches from his face. The nose descended towards him and nuzzled his cheek again.

"Alright, alright." He stroked the soft skin and sat up. "I'm up."

He saddled the warhorse, asked the animal to kneel, and lifted the body into place, securing his soldier with rope. Rone straddled the saddle, then coaxed the destrier to stand, and they were underway. The lake was closer than he remembered. It did not take long for the animal to take its fill of the precious resource. After he refilled his water bladders, they departed westward.

The night passed in a slow, tiring grind. When the dawn announced its imminent arrival, they stopped, and he repeated the process he'd carried out the morning before. The horse, now clean skin, grazed nearby. Rone knelt amongst the grass and scanned the horizon, but the group of Huronian cavalry which had been in front of him for the past few days were nowhere to be seen.

Did they spot me and gone to ground?

He was tired, hungry and weakening. It was only the strength of his mind which kept him persisting. Were the enemy group aware of his presence, there was no way he could take on ten of them, let alone twenty. Dragging the saddle to him, he unsheathed the musket and blunderbuss. He cocked them and lay the weapons on the ground beside him. He lay down, one weapon either side, and allowed sleep to claim him. Darkness, broken dreams, flitting views of the hot sun and the tickle of grass against his skin kept him company during the daylight hours. A wet sponge pushed on his cheek. He groaned and tried to push the arm away.

Who wakes someone up with a wet bloody sponge? Gods knows where it's been!

The wet sponge pushed his face again, this time harder. He ascended through the depths of slumber, and his eyes flickered open. He had a mind to berate the person using the wet sponge on him, but all that greeted him was the warhorse's snout an inch from his face. Streaks of deep purple painted a section of the western sky, but all else was darkness. He patted the animal, rubbed his face, yawned, and sat up.

"Time to move," he mumbled. He knelt over his

deceased soldier. "Tomorrow morning, I lay you to rest in the King's Own Cemetery, brother."

The night's journey, no less boring than the last, passed with gruesome sluggishness. Twice he dismounted and led the horse by the reins, allowing the animal some reprieve from carrying the body weight of two men.

The destrier plodded onward, head hung low. He patted the powerful shoulder.

"You're tired, too, aren't you boy?" he whispered. "Not long now."

Riding boots were not designed for long distance marching, but Rone ignored the aches in his feet, ankles, and knees. He cursed the burning sections of his toes, where blisters were forming, but refused to remount his horse. Sweat beaded his forehead, exhaustion racked him, and pain assaulted his mind. Rone gritted his teeth and continued. He wore his musket slung across his back, barrel pointing to the star-filled sky. Just in case he happened upon the mysterious enemy patrol.

Stopping, he retrieved a water bladder from a saddle pouch and drank deep. Pouring a small amount into a cupped hand, he held it beneath the warhorse's muzzle, waiting until the animal had licked it clean. Hot spots all over his feet burst into life as he continued the walk towards his home city, the destrier beside him. Sweat dripped into his eyes. He snarled against the sting and wiped a sleeve across his forehead.

Wafting across the night air issued the putrid stink of his dead comrade. Rone stopped again, opened the flap of a saddle pouch, and pulled clear what was left of the poultice. He wiped more beneath his nose and did the same for his horse. The pleasant smell helped, but it was no longer enough to defeat the stench completely.

Rone drew air in between his teeth. He trudged on. The blisters had gathered reinforcements while he'd been applying the poultice, and they attacked with renewed vigour. He felt one blister burst and closed his eyes with relief, albeit short lived.

An explosion boomed in the distance, and his heart leapt into his throat. The noise ripped the night's solace apart. A second explosion followed, and then a cluster roared to life. It was only when the night's peace was restored that he realised it was cannon or mortar fire.

The Huronian Army has arrived at Lisfort to besiege the city. I hope that's Wendurlund cannons firing.

A flicker of light to the southwest caught the corner of his eye, and he scanned the blackness in that direction. A moment later, another battery roared to life, their powder-filled voices echoing across the landscape.

That's a lot of cannons.

"I hope they can hold the wall," he muttered.

The horse snorted in reply and plodded on.

Another long flicker of light silhouetted the tiny shape of Lisfort against the horizon, then the staccato responsible for the brief light show rumbled across the plains. If the city was southwest of his position, he was at least heading in the right direction. The King's Own Cemetery lay somewhere directly ahead.

Rone strode on, ignoring the burning agony radiating across the bottom of his feet. With each boot fall, it felt like hot coals pressing against the skin exploded into flames. Another blister burst, and he breathed out a sigh.

He patted the horse's flank. "Nearly there, lad."

Rone remounted the destrier for a while to give his legs and feet a rest. The cannon-shot was louder with each hour that slid by. The second time he stepped into the saddle, he cast a glance over his shoulder to the east. The sky in that direction was gunmetal grey and lightening by the minute.

"Never thought the damn dawn would come," Rone whispered.

When swirls of pink and orange cast their presence across the sky, Rone walked into the King's Own Cemetery. The newer graves were located on the far western side, but the shovels were kept in the centre, inside a large brick room.

Leaving his warhorse behind him, he turned the handle and pushed open the door. Hinges creaked, and he stepped into the darkness. Although the eastern sky continued to warn of the sun's advance, the light was still too dull to light the room properly. The heady aroma of fresh earth filled his nostrils. The shovels were lined in neat rows against the far wall. His brow creased. They hadn't been cleaned since they'd last been used.

That can't have been more than a few days ago. He knelt by the closest shovel and touched the soft dirt adorning the implement's surface. With a sinking power tugging at his stomach, he stood, grasped the shovel, rested it on one shoulder and strode out of the building. He led the destrier to the west past smart rows of old headstones, belonging to warriors of the King's Own who'd fallen long ago. Some of the graves were hundreds of years old.

They negotiated the wide, paved path leading west. The headstones grew more modern, the letters engraved into the stone much sharper and distinguishable than those etched onto the plot markers closer to the centre of the huge cemetery. The path continued on for half a mile, but the western graves came to an abrupt halt. The smell of freshly tilled earth pervaded the air. Rone dropped the reins and squatted beside the closest.

One of my soldiers. He moved to the next. *And another.* He looked along the line of the newer graves. *All my soldiers.* He counted them, stopping beside each to offer a short prayer. *Forty-two. Gods above. What happened out there?*

When he reached the nearest vacant plot, he sighed.

"Here, lad," Rone called to the warhorse. The animal plodded to him and stopped only when it nuzzled his chest. He stroked the animal's neck.

"I know, my boy. Once this one last thing is done, we can rest."

The officer pulled free his bladder of water and laid it close by. He'd need to quench his thirst often.

He slammed the shovel head into the ground and with a wince, pushed it deep with a boot. The blisters would not relent, their protests sending sharp pain across his foot. He threw the clump of dirt to one side, far enough away that it would not fall back into the grave later. Another shovelful followed the first. He repeated the movement in a continuous cycle, the muscles of his shoulders and arms burning. Half his sub-unit had fallen. He clenched his jaw, ignoring the sting of sweat dripping into his eyes. The blisters had multiplied, seemingly sending reinforcements from his feet to his hands. But he ignored their pain as well. The grave was taking shape. When his hands bled, he stopped for a drink.

When Rone's breathing returned to normal and the ache in his back subsided, he approached the grave, jumped into its depths, and continued work. A horse snorted nearby.

"I know, lad," he managed between breaths. "I'm working as fast as I can. Patience."

It was only when there was a second snort from

another direction that he realised he was no longer alone. He stopped work, gasping for breath, sweat streaming down his face.

They sat upon their warhorses in the near distance watching him. Formed in a semi-circle was the group of Huronian Cavalry he'd desperately attempted to avoid.

"Oh shit."

* * *

Sergeant Graff ran along the rampart of the eastern wall, shoving past soldiers, weaving through throngs and shouting to make way. He glanced intermittently out at the Huronian Army in the distance. They'd set up their cannons, although only several fired in order to obtain ranges, elevations and desired targets.

On the cobbled street far below and paralleling his direction of travel, trotted a horse bearing an artillery gunner. A puff of smoke plumed from the mouth of an enemy cannon, closely followed by the deep *boom* of the shot. The black, round blur tore across the sky, skipped off the ground, gouging a large chunk of grass and flicking it into the air. Then the cannon shot smashed halfway up the wall and fell to the earth.

They're almost on target.

He increased his pace, sweat beading his brow. Graff's legs and lungs ached. "Make way, lads!"

Just a little further and he'd be in line with the main battery of enemy artillery. He stopped only when he positioned himself on the section of the wall that lined up with the middle section of the enemy guns. He swivelled and looked down to the cobbled street. He pointed out towards the enemy.

"This is their centre!" he roared.

The artilleryman turned, cupped his mouth and roared a command. Further back, another mounted gunner nodded and galloped from view to pass on the message to the long-distance guns positioned in the centre of the city.

"What's the plan, Sarge?"

He inhaled a deep breath, refilling his lungs with cool, fresh air. Graff wiped his forehead. "We're going to fucking kill them is what we're going to do."

It was a race against time. The Wendurlund artillery needed to get their guns on target before the Huronian could achieve the same.

The dark smear of the enemy army looked to be about a thousand yards away.

"How far away you lads think they are?"

"Eight hundred, Sergeant," said one.

"Thousand," muttered anther.

"Six-fifty."

"Direction's on!" a distance voice shouted.

The same enemy cannon burst to life, this time the cannon shot hit three quarters up the wall.

We're losing this bloody race.

Graff stared down at the gunner far below. He held open palms around the corners of his mouth. "Distance eight fifty."

The gunner turned away, his powerful voice only a distant noise to the soldiers high up on the rampart. "Eight fifty, send it!"

The second gunner further down the street galloped from view.

He knelt, pulled a time piece from his pocket, unlatched it and counted the seconds. A powerful explosion rocked the city behind him, reverberating through the stones of the rampart.

"Forty seconds," he whispered. "Need to speed up, lads." He snapped the time piece closed and pushed it back into a pocket. A large, black blur streaked above their heads, trailing a crackling shriek as it cut the air. Graff jumped to his feet and watched the distant dot. It reached its zenith and plummeted, smashing into the ground short of the enemy army and bouncing high into the air. Barrelling over its intended target, it disappeared from view. He glared at the spot of bare earth where the cannon ball had fist impacted and judged the distance between it and the enemy.

Graff returned his attention to the gunner staring up at him from far below. "Up one hundred!"

The elevation call was passed on and the second gunner galloped from view to pass on the order to the gun line. The second cannon ball sliced through the air much the same as the first and landed perhaps ten yards short of the enemy guns. But the lead ball, larger than a man's head ricocheted from the ground and smashed into an enemy gun, cutting a soldier in half at the waist and sending the barrel of the huge weapon somersaulting through the air.

"You're on! Repeat fire!" screamed Graff.

The gunner standing on the street below passed on the message. "On! All guns repeat fire!"

The distant *boom* brought Graff's attention back to the enemy. The Huronian cannonball arched through the air, smashed against the parapets and shattered chunks of stone from the wall. The cannonball slowed only a little, taking a soldier's head with it. The fragments of stone cut through a group standing close to the point of impact. Some died immediately, others lay writhing upon the rampart, their life blood leaking upon the stone.

Graff passed a hand through his hair, lowered his

helmet upon his head and attached the chinstrap. "They have their range."

A series of explosions behind him shattered the hum of the city. Every gun of the Wendurlund artillery had copied the direction and elevation of the first cannon and were firing upon their enemy. The scores of shot crackled through the sky above Graff's head, on their way to wreak havoc amongst the Huronian adversary.

Every enemy cannon disappeared behind a thick cloud of spent gunpowder, closely followed by a rolling rumble and their cannonballs were sent skyward, arching towards Lisfort.

Fear gripped Graff. He stared at one small group of black dots, which seemed to hang in the air above him, although they grew larger by the moment. He ducked behind the wall. "Stay low, lads!" He grabbed a young soldier, who was frozen in place, his eyes wide as saucers. "Get your arse down, son!"

"Get down!" an officer further down the line shouted.

"Take cover!" another voice yelled.

A chorus of screeches growing in volume drowned out the panicked voices of soldiers. Graff gritted his teeth, closed his eyes and pressed himself against the stones of the rampart. The noise was deafening. A powerful vibration reverberated through his chest and a small chuck of stone cut through his cheek and mouth. Another sliced his nose, missing an eye by a hair's breadth. A heavy weight fell upon him, slamming his face into the ground. Warm liquid, streaming from the object pinning him down soaked through his uniform. He grunted and tried to move. Spitting blood, Graff growled and with all his strength rolled to one side. Two dead soldiers lay upon him, one missing half his head, the other an arm. The last of their life blood found solace in Graff's uniform.

"You alright Sarge?"

Graff tried to speak, but only a mumbled noise issued from his damaged lips. The weight of the corpses disappeared when they were dragged from him. He pushed himself to his feet with a groan, wiped his face, and winced against the pain.

"Thanks, lad," he managed through the agony.

He looked up and down the rampart, taking in the damage and casualties.

The cannonballs had struck the parapets the length of the eastern wall, shattering merlons and cutting down scores of soldiers. Many were still dying, others had been carried clear, their broken bodies lying upon the cobbled street far below. If the soldiers remained on the ramparts, they'd be cut to ribbons. Only a few were required to remain to feed distance and direction to the gunners waiting on the street.

"Get off the ramparts!" blood-stained phlegm exploded from Graff's mouth with each word. He licked his lips and winced against the sting. Some men complied, but others were too badly wounded.

"Carry the wounded off as best you can, but get down, lads. Form up in the town square." He cast a glance at the enemy guns. Tiny figures moved with rapid, fluid movements, ramming shot down barrels, pushing cannons forward into their original position, ready for the next barrage. "Quickly now, lads!"

Officers and senior soldiers, like Graff instructed the soldiers at their section of wall to do the same. The Wendurlund soldiers, shouting, muttering, moaning, or silent, followed the orders. They carried, dragged, or assisted the wounded down the stairs. One soldier, wounded so badly he was no longer conscious, slipped from the hands of his comrade trying to lift him down the steps. He rolled off and hit the cobbled street below with a dull *thump*. The soldier who'd been carrying the unconscious man covered his face with his hands.

"Keep moving, lad!" Graff roared. "No time to grieve. Now, get going!"

An ear-splitting *boom* exploded from the centre of the city, and the next barrage was sent skyward, the numerous cannon shot, cutting through the air above Graff's head with a familiar screech. He knelt upon the rampart strewn with dead bodies and watched the progress of the artillery's fall of shot. The balls hit in much the same location as before and cut through the enemy with devastating effect. But it was not enough to stop the remaining enemy artillery from opening fire.

Graff leaned over the edge of the rampart and waved his hand until he caught the gunner's eye. "You're still on!"

The man nodded, turned his horse, and roared something at his comrade, who galloped away. Graff was unable to hear the words of the gunner over the noise of his withdrawing troops. He dropped to his stomach, covered head with his hands, clenched his eyes shut, and waited for the enemy cannon balls to strike home. Their crackling progress grew in volume until it drowned out everything else. A series of powerful thuds rocked the battlements of the eastern wall. Graff left the ground by a few inches and slammed back to the stones of the castle, his head smashing against what remained of the closest merlon. His eyelids parted a little, and he blinked against the thick dust settling around him. He coughed, pushed his aching body into a kneeling position and wiped blood from his face.

Some of the soldiers at the back of the withdrawal had been forced to take cover upon the stairs leading down to the streets. A few were thrown clear by the power of the enemy artillery shot. A section of one of the stone stairs had sheered away, taking at least half a section of men with it. Their broken bodies lay upon the ground far below, chunks of stone stairs littering the cobbles around them. Graff cursed and returned his focus to the enemy gun line, visible as a dark line through the clearing dust.

He sniffed, wiped his leaking nose and noticed fresh blood upon his hand. Blood dripped from his beard, splattering upon his armour. Graff returned his attention to the remnants of soldiers clambering down from the parapets.

"Keep going! The next barrage ain't far away." Pain in almost every part of his face and head led to his words slurring. Graff steadied himself when the next volley fired by the Wendurlund gun line roared to life. The enemy guns disappeared behind another thick cloud of smoke. He knelt, agony racking his legs and knees. He groaned.

"I'm getting too old for this shit."

Crackling whines sang over his head, the Wendurlund cannon shot barrelling across the sky towards their targets. No sooner had their symphony of violence faded, the growing shriek of incoming enemy rounds drowned out the shouts of soldiers far below. Graff opened his eyes, lifted his head, and peered over the destroyed merlon. The storm of dark dots arced through the air towards him. A frown creased his blood covered brow.

They've changed their elevation. Fear assaulted the pit of his stomach. He knelt up, ignoring the protest of the muscles in his legs.

"Get to cover!" he shouted at the milling soldiers below him. The whistling screech of inbound cannon balls almost drowned his own voice out. He cupped his mouth. "Get down!"

A scarce few heard his words and spread the command. A hail of dark blobs tore the air asunder around Graff's head. They were so close that he felt the wind they created against the skin of his cheek. The enemy rounds smashed into nearby homes, skimmed over rooftops, bounced upon the cobbled street, but as far as he could see, Graff was unaware of any casualties.

He whirled in time to see the fall of shot of the Wendurlund artillery slam into the enemy rank and file, although their elevation had dipped a touch. They'd also decimated the enemy gun line at which they'd been directing their shot. The thickest section of enemy cannons yet to feel the wrath of Wendurlund artillery were positioned two hundred or so yards to the left.

"Up twenty, left two hundred," he roared at the mounted gunner below.

The soldier stood in his stirrups and cupped a hand to his ear.

Graff repeated the command in a loud, slow deliberate manner.

He nodded and passed on the command.

It'd take time for the gunners to swivel the cannons to the new target. The Huronian artillery opened up with their next volley. Silence emanated from the heart of Wendurlund, where the gun line was still being organised. The enemy rounds cut past Graff, dropping towards buildings below in a lazy arc. They shattered houses, punched holes in walls and several cut down a group of soldiers. The Wendurlund artillery spoke then, their resounding *boom* vibrating the ground upon which Graff stood.

The blobs screamed past him, their fading song gifting him with a high-pitched ringing in his skull. So far, they seemed to be on target, but it was too soon to tell for sure. Graff's eyes were drawn to movement much closer to the ground. He leaned upon the ruined wall, squinted, and ignored the blood-stained strands of saliva hanging in tendrils from his beard. Fear reignited its assault within his guts. The Huronian infantry were advancing.

"Gods," he whispered.

They surged across the open field towards Lisfort. The main charge followed groups of soldiers bearing huge ladders at a steady trot. At this distance they resembled teams of ants.

Graff returned his attention to the cannon shot. The cannon balls struck the earth near the feet of the enemy artillery. Dirt and clumps of grass were sent skyward. The massive pieces of round lead shattered cannons, cut men in half and left countless others critically wounded.

"On! Repeat fire!" he roared at the gunner below. Graff inhaled a deep breath, cupped his mouth, and shouted, "Everyone back on the wall! The infantry is charging. Get back up here!"

An officer further down the wall and looking as bad as he felt, ran to him. "We shouldn't have ordered them off the wall, Sergeant."

"Then we'd have had no one left to fight the bastards off when this happened," he gestured at the closing enemy charge.

The distant, dull wall of sound erupting from

thousands of enemy throats washed over the pair. But the enemy cacophony disappeared as Graff's order was taken up by the soldiers far below. Corporals and some officers organised them into some form of structure and then sent them back up the stairs toward the few senior soldiers and officers who'd chosen to stay on the wall. He stared up and down the ramparts.

"It appears, sir, that we are the only two alive of the few who chose to stay and bear the brunt of the enemy barrages."

The warriors leading the Wendurlund Army negotiated the stairs two at a time and were halfway up. But even their shouts were matched by the charging enemy. Graff leaned upon the destroyed merlon near him and peered out upon the closing dark smear which marred the landscape to the east. He spat blood, wiped his mouth and waited.

"We have maybe two minutes before they reach the wall."

The officer looked behind Graff at the line of soldiers streaming up the rock stairs. "Not enough time."

He could see the individual faces of those carrying the ladders. The front rank of the main charge, all red-cloaked Mortals, broke into a sprint, passing the ladders with ease. They closed the distance fast, stopping in a single rank near the base of the wall. Graff frowned. "What in the blazes are they -"

They brought muskets into their shoulders and aimed up at him. He grabbed the officer's arm. "Down, sir." He ducked out of sight, pulling the younger man with him.

The officer chuckled. "Idiots won't hit anything from that range!"

The staccato of distant musket shots sounded

strangely eerie. Hisses, cracks, and dull whines cut the air above them.

"I don't think that's their intention. They want us ducking for cover to give their comrades time to lean the ladders against the wall."

Graff stood, leaned forward, and stared out over the edge of the wall. "The ladders have arrived," he muttered.

The war cries, yells, screeches, and indecipherable, aggressive blabber rolled over the eastern side of Lisfort. But the resounding *boom* of the Wendurlund Artillery cut through the clamour. The cannon-shot swept over their heads, destined for the enemy gun line in the distance. The Huronian Artillery had ceased fire for the time being, he noted.

That's something at least.

Breathless, the first batch of troops approached Graff. "Right, you lot, push these corpses off the rampart."

They hesitated. One of them stepped forward. "Sarge?"

"You heard me!" Graff roared. "Get it done!"

"Sarge, these are our comrades."

The statement was met with muttered agreement.

Another distant crackle of musket shots and hot lead hissed by their heads, forcing them to duck. The first ladder crashed upon the battlement, bounced a little, and then settled against the stone. Another further down the wall following almost as fast.

"We need room to move. When they start pouring over those ladders, we'll be tripping and losing our balance." Graff took a breath and stepped forward, holding out his hands. "Look, I know it sounds harsh, lads, but we need to push our dead clear of the ramparts so we have freedom of movement."

The soldiers accepted his words and started to work, lifting, pushing or rolling their deceased comrades clear of the ramparts. A team of men started pushing upon the ladder.

"Wait!" Graff yelled. He jogged over to them, leaned out over the edge and peered down at the thronging masses below, waiting their turn to start the climb up to the top of the wall. The first man wasn't even halfway.

The muskets opened up again, and he ducked down just before the rounds reached him, their whines almost inaudible over the calamity.

He held up a hand to the group of soldiers. "Stop! Wait until the first man is almost at the top of the ladder, then we push. Got it?"

"Yes, Sergeant."

The rampart was clear, the cobbled street below now littered with the dead of the Wendurlund Army.

He gestured at the closest group, leaning over the battlements hurling down abuse, chunks of stone, knives, and anything other than their personal weapons and armour. "You soldiers! Get ready to push against a ladder."

Graff leapt up onto the wall, rested a hand upon a nearly intact merlon to steady himself. The first Huronian on the closest ladder was nearing the top. The enemy soldier glanced up at him and snarled. Graff grinned and without haste, dragged an index finger across his throat.

He leapt back off the wall and jogged up and down the rampart organising soldiers into teams ready to start pushing against ladders.

"Ready?" he shouted. "One, two, three push!"

Those closest to him heard his command, but the others watched for his hand signals.

The groups grunted and the ladders slid a few inches.

"One, two, three push!"

Another few inches. Each group worked as a cohesive team. Graff wiped his mouth where blood continued to ooze from his damaged lips and nose. He drew his sword.

"Again!"

The ladder slid a few inches but continued for almost a yard before coming to a rest. The first soldier appeared, leapt clear of the ladder. Graff grabbed him by his chest armour and using his momentum against him, pushed him over the rampart towards the waiting cobbles far below. The soldier's war cry morphed into a scream, his arms flailing.

"A bird he is not!" Graff shouted. This was met by a few chuckles. "Right, once more lads. Push!"

The ladder shifted and gathered momentum, skidding sideways along the battlements. Before it disappeared from view, a Huronian soldier leapt from the doomed ladder and clambered onto the battlements, brandishing a sword. The man charged straight at him. Graff brought his sword up, parried the thrust, punched the man in the face with his spare hand, then kicked him back over the battlements from whence he'd come. The ladder smashed into the next further down the wall, causing that to begin its sideways journey as well, then the pair struck a third and a fourth. The soldiers who'd been clambering towards the top of the wall, held on to the ladders for grim death, but it did them no good. Some let go, free falling towards the mass of Huronian soldiers below.

Graff leapt onto the battlements to watch the ladders speed towards the ground. The massive things thundered to earth, crushing men and sending up clouds of dust. A thick, dark silver mist appeared on the horizon, and the enemy artillery disappeared from view. The *boom* of cannons washed over him, and he jumped clear. The dark dots arced into the sky on their original path. The gunners had lowered their elevation and were firing once more upon the eastern wall.

"Get down!" he roared. "Take cover!"

He threw himself to the stones as did many of those around him. But others, too slow to follow suit, disappeared, swept clear of the battlements by chunks of debris sheered off by the massive rounds. One cannonball cut a man in two, another shattered a soldier's leg clean off. Graff coughed and rose to his feet. The enemy muskets opened fire forcing him to duck back down, the musket balls whining through the air near his head.

A dull *thud* vibrated through his feet and a ladder, looking no worse for wear for its recent demise, slammed against the wall.

Graff ignored the pain coursing through his body, wiped blood from his mouth, and drew a deep breath. "Gather yourselves and prepare to push!"

He peered over the edge of the wall. Where before Huronian soldiers were teetering up the ladder, unsure of their footing, this time red-cloaked warriors ran up the ladder, swords sheathed across their backs.

Fear cut through his pain. "The Mortals," he muttered.

"Hurry up!" he shouted. "Prepare to push the ladder."

The first red-cloaked man was more than halfway

up the ladder and showed no sign of slowing. Those following him were negotiating the rungs just as fast.

"Push!"

The ladder shifted a few inches. "Gather yourselves and push!"

Another fraction of movement. "Ready! Again!"

The ladder slid a small margin, but it wasn't enough. The first Mortal jumped into view, unsheathed his sword and cut a bloody swathe through the soldiers of Wendurlund. He killed seven warriors before he was dispatched. Graff ran towards the battle, where a small group of Mortals were fighting as a cohesive fighting unit, pushing the men of Wendurlund back. More Mortals leapt into view, joining the fight. He pushed his way into the thick of the fight, killing one enemy, kicking the knee out from another, and stabbing a third through the throat.

Another vibration beneath his feet and Graff swivelled. A second ladder appeared further down the wall behind them. He pushed his way through the throng until he reached the edge of the wall. He leaned out over a shattered merlon. Mortals were streaming up that ladder as well. Graff grabbed the arm of the closest soldier.

"You!"

The man, breathless, sweat beading his forehead and streaming down his cheeks stared at him with wide eyes. "Sarge?"

"Run back to the barracks and pass on a message to the commander. Tell him we need immediate reinforcements."

The soldier pushed his way clear and sprinted away.

"And, lad?"

The young man stopped and turned back to him.
"Tell the commander the eastern wall will fall within the hour unless he gets here with more swords."

X

Garx's boots hit the ground together. He patted the horse's neck and approached the exhausted Death Rider. It'd been a long time since he'd needed the Wendurlund language. He was fluent at one time, but he was forced to concentrate on the words.

He stopped a short distance from the grave digger. "I am Garx. How goes it?"

The other nodded and wiped his forehead with a wet sleeve. "Rone. And not so well."

"At least you're honest."

Rone clambered out of the grave. "Let's get it over with then, shall we?"

Garx remained silent, although the constant thunder of cannon fire in the distance did not.

"Just make it quick."

The Huronian officer chuckled. "We are not here to kill you, Death Rider."

Rone shrugged. "Then what else are you here for?"

He gestured at his soldiers behind him, sat astride their warhorses observing the exchange in silence. None of them would know what it was they were saying. "We have been cast out of the Huronian Army by our king. We are no longer welcome in Huron and will be hunted unto death."

Rone dug his spade into the pile of dirt and released the handle, a bloody imprint of his hand staining the wood. "What did you do to earn that?"

"We failed in a task set by King Fillip."

He need not know just yet that it was another King's Own unit we were fighting.

"He sounds like a madman."

He nodded but did not acknowledge Rone's words.

"So we are here to help you."

"I can bury my soldier by myself," Rone grunted. His face softened a little. "Although my thanks for the offer."

"We shall wait then."

When the grave was complete, Rone accepted a second offer of help. Rone and a few of Garx's soldiers lifted the corpse into the grave, then filled it in.

He returned to his horse, rummaged in the closest saddlebag and brought out a clean bandage. Garx gestured for the King's Own warrior to hold out his right hand. Blood was dripping from the fingers. Squeezing a bladder of water over his hand, the King's Own man flinched.

"Hold still," said Garx, binding his hand.

When he was finished, he passed the water bladder to Rone and watched the man, who up until days before had been a mortal enemy, drink his fill.

"Now we talk," said Garx.

Rone wiped his mouth with the back of his hand. "About?"

"What we do next."

"We eat."

Garx laughed. *I'm beginning to like this soldier.* "Fair enough. We eat, and then we plan."

Rone nodded. "Then we plan," he agreed. A fierce glint entered the Death Rider's eyes, giving Garx a moment of pause. "And then we fight the Huronian Army."

He gestured at Rone's weary looking destrier stood nearby. "Do you have any food spare?"

"None, I'm afraid."

"We have plenty. You can share some of ours. Your horse needs some food, water, and rest, too, by the looks."

Rone moved to the warhorse and patted the powerful neck. "He does."

***

When the small group departed the King's Own graveyard, the sun was at its zenith. Rone, mounted in the midst of the cavalry unit allowed the exhaustion to roll over him. He leaned forward and patted the horse, knowing the animal too must be feeling bone tired. It stumbled as if highlighting the point but regained its balance just as fast.

Although he remained calm and ensured his face was impassive, Rone did not like being surrounded by Huronian soldiers. It felt alien to him. He'd spent near ten years training hard to protect his king from just such warriors. Now he rode amongst them. A soft prickle teased the skin of his back reminding him that enemy were directly behind him and could skewer him at their leisure.

What if the story about being thrown out of their army and hunted for traitors is a lie?

He clenched his bandaged hand and in some dark way enjoyed the dull, painful throb emanating from his palm.

What if they have made me a prisoner and I don't even know it?

Rone opened his fingers and stared at the bandage now stained a faint pink. He'd heard how the Huronians treated their prisoners. The skeletal humanoid that was Prince Henry was testament to that. He grunted at the memory of the charge he and his sub unit had conducted against the Huronian Army that day.

You'd know it if you were a prisoner, Rone. Think with logic not fear.

He stretched his back and relaxed.

My hands aren't bound, I'm not gagged, nor have I been beaten. He raised his face, the sun's heat caressing his cheeks. *And unless I'm mistaken, I'm not dead.*

The dull, persistent ruckus issuing from Lisfort continued to pervade the afternoon. They'd moved a little further away from where the battle raged, unseen, some miles away.

"I'm stopping here," said Rone. He brought his horse to a halt, dismounted and unsaddled the beast. He stroked the sweat soaked fur. Rone unclasped the bridle and pulled it clear, allowing the steel bit to fall free of the warhorse's mouth. The animal immediately started grazing.

"Here's as good as anywhere," agreed Garx. The foreign officer said a short sentence in his native tongue, and the group also dismounted.

The men who'd once been his enemy shared their rations with him. When he'd taken his fill of food and water, Rone offered water to his horse. The destrier went through a full water bladder, but the Huronian cavalryman to whom the supply belonged simply shrugged and grinned. He gestured in the direction of the Therondale River and muttered something in his language.

Rone nodded. "More where that came from, I understand." He offered the spent bladder back to the man. "My thanks."

The warhorse continued grazing, filling its empty belly. "Keep it up, my lad, you'll need your strength in the days to come." He patted the powerful rump. Garx approached him and gestured to an open piece of land nearby.

"Yes, let's make a plan on our next course of action."

"No," Garx replied. "I think you should sleep, Rone. You need it. I can see it in the bags beneath your eyes."

"I'm fine."

The foreign officer pointed at the same open piece of ground. "No, my friend, you sleep now. Half my men will rest as well. After sundown, we talk."

He wanted to refuse, but at the mention of sleep, the exhaustion made a second assault on his body, breaching his willpower and depositing lead weights in his limbs and thick mud throughout his skull. He nodded. "Wake me when you're ready."

Sometime in the evening, Rone's eyelids fluttered open, he drew in a deep breath and stretched. He felt movement nearby, a deep groan and a thump. A heavy weight pushed against his flank and his brain, still recovering from slumber, took a moment to process that his warhorse had flopped to the ground beside him, stretched out and fallen asleep. What sounded like the distant rumble of thunder rolled across the landscape. He swore he smelt the faint aroma of spent gunpowder wafting to his nostrils. But it must have been some trick of the mind.

He stroked the animal's flank. His eyelids touched, and the dusk skyline disappeared from view. Sleep came for him again, assaulting his mind. He didn't resist, allowing himself to descend into the thick, warm, dark depths of rest.

Something prodded his arm. Rone rolled over, groaned and rested his head on a hand. A voice spoke his name and a boot nudged his back. He yawned and then slumber retreated at full pace and his eyes snapped open. He sat up and squinted against the morning sun. Smoke drifted across the clearing accompanied by the smell of frying bacon. The far-off thunder still assaulted the sky. Although it wasn't thunder.

Of course it isn't you fool! It's time to move. My people are fighting for their lives.

He burst to his feet, heart thumping. War spirit flooded his body. A hand clasped his shoulder and Garx stopped beside him.

"Good morning, Rone. I see you are full of life."

He grunted. "Let's plan our first course of action and get on with it."

"Soon, my friend. First, we eat. Then we plan." He turned and walked towards the nearby campfire. "Then we fight," he said over his shoulder.

Rone followed him and noticed the Huronian cavalrymen had dug a large indent into the ground in which they'd built the fire. This served to hide the fire from view, only the highest flickers of flame coming close to the level of the ground surrounding the man made cut out. They'd also cleared the ground around the fire of grass to stop the likelihood of the flames spreading. The grass-filled open plains would burn so easily.

His warhorse was grazing nearby amongst a few of the Huronian mounts. The beast lifted his head and stared at Rone. The animal, chewing on a clump of grass, snorted and then returned to his food. Rone focused on the smell of cooking bacon and his stomach tightened.

Garx passed him a thin, wooden platter heaped with bacon and some boiled vegetables. "Here."

He nodded his thanks and sat with the others. The soldiers ate in silence, apart from a couple talking in hushed tones. Rone understood snippets of their language, but given their body language, he knew their topic of conversation was not sinister in nature. The orange vegetable was soft to touch and from memory, was a Huronian root called Makamet. It was soft, sweet, yet carried a hint of bitterness. Rone hadn't eaten it in years. He lifted a piece of crisp bacon to his lips, ignoring the heat.

When they'd eaten their fill, they sat in a tight group away from the fire. Garx translated for Rone and when he voiced an idea, Garx also relayed the message to his soldiers in their native tongue. It would take a little time, but their aim was to use their small force to cause maximum disruption and casualties amongst the Huronian Army.

* * *

Sheer force of numbers dealt The Mortals a foul hand. Their skill at arms was magnificent, but outnumbered and encumbered by the ladders wide enough for one man only to advance onto the rampart was their downfall. Eventually they were defeated, and the ladders flung clear of the wall. Graff leaned against the battlements, mouth open and rasping, ragged breaths filling his desperate lungs. His face stung where an enemy blade had snicked his cheek. Had he not blocked in time, it would have taken his eye.

And half my damn head as well, probably.

He hawked and spat a glob of blood over the wall at the milling enemy far below. The red-cloaked Mortals were still aplenty down there. But for now, they'd ceased their efforts. Another few mass charges like that, and the wall would fall.

Wendurlund artillery thundered behind him and cannonballs screamed overhead towards the decimated enemy battery units. Where once they'd seemed indomitable, their cannons lay mostly destroyed. Although a few continued firing, sending their rounds deep into Lisfort.

"At least our lads have taken out their artillery," panted a young man nearby.

Graff straightened, gaining some control over his breathing. "Hardly, lad. We haven't even seen their mortar lines yet. The mortars can rain hell fire down upon us like something you've never seen."

"If that's the case then why haven't they used them already, Sarge?"

Graff wiped his sword upon the red cloak of a dead enemy and then sheathed the blade. "They'll wait until they take the wall, and when the fighting is conducted house to house and street to street, they'll bring in the mortars to force us out into the open."

The young man remained silent, although over the next minute or two his flushed face took on a whiter pallor, his confident eyes now glinting with fear. "They'll never take the wall." the soldier replied, a slight waver entering his voice.

"Oh, mark my words, lad, they'll take the wall." He gestured at the expanse before them. An expanse now marred with the presence of tens of thousands of enemy soldiers. "How could they not? We can hold them for a time, though."

"What's the point of fighting if we're simply going to lose?" another man spoke up on the other side of Graff.

He chuckled. "Who said anything about losing?"

"You did, just then Sarge!"

"I said they'd take the wall. I said nothing about defeat. Our *withdrawal* from the wall is only the first step, lad."

"Why not just walk off the wall now then and save our losses?"

"We're buying time. More than that I know not. But as you know from our mission brief before this hell storm started, we are to hold the wall as long as possible."

The friendly cannon shot smashed through another few enemy guns, ending their assault.

Graff strode to the edge of the rampart and leaned out. He waved his hand to gain the attention of the mounted gunner standing amongst a crumple of dead bodies. "Elevation's good! Come left one hundred!"

The gunner nodded and passed the bearings on. A powerful shudder vibrated through the rampart almost spilling Graff into thin air. He stepped back from the edge and turned. A battered ladder, chips and chunks gouged from the thick wood, slammed against the wall closely by another four.

"Here they come again!" A soldier bellowed.

Graff clamped a hand to his sword hilt and drew the weapon. His shoulder ached and his arm burned, but that was a small complaint. He stepped onto the outer edge of the battlement and glanced down. The Mortals were streaming up the ladders again like angry ants.

He took a deep breath. "Ready yourselves!"

Graff pushed his way through a throng of his soldiers and approached the closest ladder. The first red cloak burst into view, leapt clear of the ladder and snatched his sword from its scabbard. He grabbed a hold of the man's mail shirt and dragged him over the edge of the battlement. Copying the move, one of his soldiers sent another Mortal tumbling to his death in a similar manner.

"Make way!" a voice roared.

An officer led a group of men carrying a steaming cauldron. They wore gloves and leather aprons to protect them from the hot contents should it accidentally spill. The small team approached a point in the wall where a merlon had been smashed from existence, stepped to the edge of the battlements and upended boiling oil. The steaming liquid streamed from the cauldron.

Distant war cries morphed into high-pitched screams of agony. An archer, with flaming arrow attached to his bow, sent the projectile straight down after the oil. The screeches intensified and spread.

Graff returned his attention to the nearest ladder, stabbed a red cloak through the throat and pushed his way towards the departing officer and his team. They'd be heading back to bring more boiling oil.

"Sir!"

The officer glanced over his shoulder. Graff caught up and walked alongside him. "Sir, can you bring the next batch of oil to one of the ladders?"

"Sergeant, I know what you're going to say next. But the oil, and mind there's not that much left, is better being poured upon those wretches down below. It ruins their morale, not to mention kills them." The man smirked.

"Understood, but if we pour it on the ladders then have your bowman ignite the wood, it'll give those bastard wretches nothing to use to get up here."

The officer grunted but did not reply.

Graff halted. "Sir, we can only hold off another two perhaps three waves of these Mortals. If we don't burn the ladders, the wall will be lost by sundown."

The officer stopped, fixed him with a baleful glare, and nodded. "I'll see what I can do, Sergeant."

Graff strode to his original position and paused. He'd been so fixated upon his section of the wall, he'd neglected to appreciate the other sergeants, officers, and the ranks in between who were commanding squads of soldiers in defence of their city. Ladders lined the length of the eastern wall. Red cloaks and general infantrymen streamed into view, one after the other. Many of them were killed before they could set boot upon stone, but small groups, particularly the red cloaks, had gained a purchase and forced their way into fighting positions.

The combined voice of the Wendurlund artillery spoke as one, the noise drowning out the raucous of battle for a fleeting moment. The shot cut through the air above the rampart with crackling screeches. Graff darted to the edge of the wall, leaned against a merlon, and tracked the group of tiny cannonballs slicing the sky towards their target. They bounced off the ground, cutting deep gouges from the earth and smashed into cannons and soldiers alike.

He ran to the opposite edge of the rampart and glared down at the mess of dead bodies littering the cobbled street below. He caught the eye of the mounted cannoneer.

"On!" he shouted. "Repeat fire!"

The man nodded and passed the message along.

The soldiers defending the section of wall under his command were making a good account of themselves. They were tired, some were injured and there may not have been as many standing as there had been mere hours before, but they were holding their enemies at bay.

For now, anyway.

His lungs burned less so, and the muscles of his arms and legs were rested. Unlike the soldiers closest the action who were breathless, fighting for their lives. Anger's warmth pierced him, and he advanced through the throng, shouldering aside his soldiers to join the battle at the base of the closest ladder. One young man, red-faced, saliva hanging from his mouth in strands, gasping for breath, blocked a sword thrust with a clumsy stroke. Graff clenched a fist-full of the soldier's mail shirt and pulled him away from the fight, sidestepped him, and placed himself where the young man had been standing moments before.

He batted aside the enemy's next attack and smashed the pommel of his sword against the Huronian's face. Blood exploded from his nose, and he doubled over, dropped his sword and cupped his hands to his nose. Graff delivered a powerful kick, sending the injured enemy soldier backward and over the wall, disappearing from view with a shriek.

Graff sent his sword whistling through the air, the blade severing a man's head from his neck. He stepped over the body, stabbed another adversary and ducked below the wicked sweep of an axe that would have shattered his skull. He shoulder-barged the axe bearer, a bear of a man, and bounced clear of him like he was a child. He slipped on fresh blood and fell to the rampart beside the headless corpse he'd so recently dispatched.

The giant stood above Graff, one boot either side of his hips and lifted the axe high above his head. A snarl stretched his lips apart, displaying missing and yellowed teeth beyond. He brought up his sword and stabbed it into the man's groin, feeling the metal bite deep. Bright blood streamed from the wound and down the blade, wetting his hand. The huge axe-bearer roared in fury and pain. He brought the axe down. Graff shifted to one side, but the boot of his enemy stopped him from moving any further. The heavy weapon bounced off stone beside Graff's head with a deafening ring and sending several sparks flying.

Graff ripped the sword free and stabbed again, this time the sharp metal finding a home in axe-man's belly. The massive enemy fell to his knees and brought his weapon down for a second time. Graff attempted to pull his sword free, but his hand, slick with blood, slipped from the hilt. He lifted his arms and gripped the axe haft with both hands, stopping the blade inches from his nose. The curved blade glistened with fresh blood, a clump of hair stuck to one side, and the bottom edge of the steel was chipped. Graff looked beyond the weapon hovering above his head and focused upon the face of the dying enemy. Hatred, anger, and determination glinted from his narrowed eyes. But pain resided there as well.

"Well, what are you waiting for?" Graff roared. "You going to kill me or not?"

Axe man growled and muttered a string of foreign words. Warm liquid soaked through Graff's mail shirt and down his leggings. For a moment, he thought he'd pissed himself, but realisation dawned on him as the light of life departed the eyes of his giant enemy. His grip faltered, and Graff pulled the axe clear of the man's hand, throwing it clear. He pushed the dying titan away, the man collapsing onto his side and lying still, blood leaking out upon the stones beneath him.

Graff left him to his dying and regained his feet, the lower half of his armour stained with blood. It looked like he'd been wading through a river of the stuff.

He stooped, pulled clear his sword, ducked under a sweep that would have claimed his head, and kicked a man's knee out from under him.

"Push them back!" Graff shouted. He swung his sword two handed, ensuring it did not slip from his grip. The sharp steel cleaved through the neck of an enemy. The man dropped his club, eyes wide and held his hands against the deep wound, from which spurted bright red blood. Graff took a step back and kicked the mortally wounded warrior back over the wall from whence he'd come.

"Move forward!" he roared over his shoulder.

His soldiers rallied behind him, and the Huronian warriors, red cloaks and general infantrymen alike, fell back. Those on the ladders started yelling for those below to climb back down. Panic swept their ranks, and they were soon overwhelmed and sent on their way to meet whatever maker in which they believed.

The sound of battle was almost inaudible, aside from the occasional chorus of artillery opening fire. A flock of tiny birds sat on a branch nearby twittering amongst themselves. Wind passed through the forest canopy in a soft whisper, competing with the distant shouts, screams and clamour. Garx waited in the middle of the road. His sword was sheathed, and he kept his hands by his sides. The supply wagon rumbled towards him, the driver had already seen him and called the heavy horse to slow his pace.

Garx grinned a lifted a hand. "Ho there!"

The wagon rolled to a halt, and the driver applied the wheel brake. "You're a long way from the battle, friend." He looked Garx up and down. "Cavalry, hey? Where's your horse?"

"Lost him a few days back. Colic."

"Ah, sorry to hear that. Not a nice way for them to go." He leaned forward and patted his own horse. "Not nice at all." He frowned. "Still, the battle's that way." He jerked a thumb over his shoulder.

"Oh, I'm well aware. I'm on my way there now. How fares the fight?"

The driver shrugged. "They're making slow progress. The Wendurlund soldiers holding the wall are fighting well. Their artillery is some of the finest I've seen. Better than I thought they would be, to be honest." He paused and scratched the heavy beard covering his chin. "Still, once we start using the mortars, we'll take the walls within a day." He cast a glance around him and lowered his voice. "I'm not sure why his majesty has not ordered the mortars forward before now."

"That's because he's a bloody madman and doesn't have a clue what he's doing."

The driver's eyes widened and his mouth dropped opened. "What?" he hissed. "You can't say that! Not if you want to keep your head, my friend."

"I'll say what I like about King Fillip, he's a raving lunatic." Garx dropped his hand to his sword hilt and drew the weapon. "And I'm not your friend."

"That so?"

"Step down from there. I'll take your wagon from here."

The driver's hand disappeared into a hidden pocket in his shirt and reappeared clenching a pistol. He pulled the hammer back and pointed the weapon at Garx. "I think not, *friend*."

He hesitated, staring at the dark barrel.

"Now get out of my way!"

Garx stepped forward, clenched a tighter grip on his sword and snarled. "Not going to happen I'm afraid. Either get down from there or die."

"Only one man dyin' today."

The pistol spoke with a loud bang, gun smoke hiding the driver from view. A loud buzz snapped past Garx's head, the small, round piece of lead close enough he felt the wind against his skin.

Thank the gods he missed.

The heavy horse, frightened by the sudden noise, reared, eyes wide. When the animal's front hooves slammed back to earth, the horse sprang into action, trotting towards Garx.

He jumped out of the way, landing on his shoulder and rolling to his feet, taking cover behind a nearby tree. He sheathed his sword. The horse swept past, closely followed by the wagon, creaking and groaning. Garx darted forward, clenched a grip on the back of the wagon and stepped up onto the rear tray. The wagon was empty. He ducked under the cream canvas flap of the canopy stretched over the rear tray in an arch the length of the vehicle.

Running in a crouch, he almost lost his balance when a wheel rolled into a pothole in the road. He righted himself and stopped at the front of the wagon. A sheet of canvas hanging from the roof, hid him from the driver. The man's voice called to the horse in soft tones, reassuring the animal, but ensuring he maintained the pace. Garx knelt and withdrew a knife. He reached out with care and pushed the canvas aside as quiet as possible. The driver sat on a bench directly in front of him. The forest whizzed by around them. But one wrong hoof fall, or a fracture in the axle, would send them careening off the road and into a tree. Sweat glistened upon the flanks of the heavy horse and still the driver pushed the animal on.

It won't keep this pace up for long.

Garx steadied himself, and then lunged. One arm snaked around the driver's face and pulled his head back, the other hand plunged the knife into his neck. The man tried to resist, attempted to break free of Garx's iron grip, cried out, and gathered his legs beneath him, but Garx held him firm. When the struggles weakened, Garx released his hold and pushed the dying driver over the edge. His body hit the ground sweeping by with a dull *thud.*

Garx stood, pushed the canvas sheet aside, stepped through and sat upon the driver's bench. Warm liquid imbued the fabric of his trousers and touched his skin beyond. He ignored it and picked up the reins, which had fallen onto the hitching bar below. He pulled on the reins, released the pressure, and pulled back for a second time. He clicked at the animal.

"Whoa down there, boy. Steady." He pulled back for a third time. "Steady there."

The animal, winded and exhausted, slowed to a walk and eventually stopped altogether. Garx engaged the wheel brake and jumped down. He strode to the animal and smoothed down the fur of its face with an open palm. "Relax, my lad, nothing to worry about now."

The thunder of many hooves upon the road grew in volume, but Garx continued speaking in a hushed voice to the resting horse. The group of cavalry came into view on either side of the wagon and halted nearby, Rone leading them.

The Death Rider grinned. "You led us on a merry

chase!"

He shrugged, thought about the words he wanted to speak and switched to the Wendurlund language. "Didn't think the stupid bastard would actually pull the trigger."

Rone chuckled and leaned forward, resting an arm on the pommel of his saddle. "Those things are useless. I'd be surprised if they hit anything even at point blank range. Sure do make a bang though."

"They sure do." He patted the animal's flank. "Don't they, boy?"

The horse took a deep breath and snorted, speckles of wet snot setting upon Garx's face. "Charming." He wiped his beard with the back of a hand. "Shall we get organised?"

Rone nodded, the grin disappearing.

Garx switched back to the Huronian tongue. "Let's go! Get rid of that driver's body. You know what to do."

* * *

Garx had ordered his soldiers to hide the wagon at the edge of the road. The heavy horse had been disconnected and joined the cavalry herd. There'd been some bickering amongst the animals as the newcomer learned his rank in the pecking order, but within the hour they were settled, grazing in the large temporary paddock deeper in the forest set out by a group of soldiers. The boundary was created with string and patrolled by five cavalrymen. Most of the horses kept within the limits of the paddock, but there were a couple who liked to jump and explore, hence the guards patrolling the paddock perimetre.

Garx sat, back against a tree, chewing on a piece of

grass and staring idly at the patches of sky visible beyond the canopy. There was an eagle up there soaring high above. He caught glimpses of it between branches and boughs. It disappeared behind clumps of leaves. Visible for a fleeting moment and then gone again. Such a powerful, graceful animal and when required a merciless killer. A boot crunched upon a twig behind him and a hand touched his shoulder. He lurched, startled from his thoughts. He spat the glob of grass out and noticed Rone crouched beside him.

The man moves like a ghost!

"There's a wagon heading down the road towards us."

"Heading to Lisfort?"

Rone nodded and stood.

Garx rose to his feet and followed the King's Own warrior. The road was perhaps one hundred yards to their front. Rone'd been lying in wait, watching for any supply wagons. They brushed past a few saplings and stepped over thick roots protruding through the leaf litter. The road appeared through the forest, and Garx stopped, crouching beside a thick bush.

Rone pointed to their left. "Coming from that direction."

He remained silent, ears taking in the natural noises of the forest. Insects buzzed overhead, others clicked and chattered to each other in high-pitched *pops*. Tiny birds scudded around the canopy twittering to one another while lizards and beetles scurried through the leaf litter.

"You hear that?"

"What the birds and bloody ear-piercing insects?"

Rone chuckled, teeth flashing beneath his beard. "Wait for it," he whispered.

The muscle of Garx's thigh burned. He shifted his weight onto his opposite leg. It was only then he noticed several of his soldiers kneeling or squatting in the forest behind logs or shrubs on the opposite edge of the road. One of them nodded at him.

He returned his focus to the road. "Nope, all I'm getting is insects assaulting my ears."

"Patience." Then Rone glanced at him, humour glinting in his eyes. "Are you sure you're not becoming deaf?"

A *clop-clop,* ever so faint drifted to him. Then the soft, wooden creak of the wagon swaying upon its axles. The gentle rumble of the wheel turning upon the road.

His brow relaxed. "I hear it." He shifted his weight again. "Want me to stand in the road again and bring him to a halt."

Rone smirked. "Didn't work too well last time, Garx. Didn't really matter when the wagon was heading away from the battle. But if this driver makes a break, he's heading towards the fight. If he gets way, he'll spread the word, and we'll have a hunting force on us before we can sneeze."

"True. So, what do you want me to do?"

Rone patted his shoulder. "You sit here and relax." The Death Rider grinned and moved away in a crouch towards the growing wagon sounds.

Garx grunted and shifted closer to the bush. Through the narrow gaps in the shrub, the wagon came into view around a distant bend. This vehicle moved much slower than its predecessor, hinting at the load the animal hauled. His stomach rumbled.

Hope there's some fresh food on board.

The driver sat relaxed upon the bench just behind the horse. He held the long reins in one hand, while the other relaxed upon a knee. The man was not suspicious or nervous in the slightest. Closer the wagon came, near enough the whites of the driver's eyes shone from beneath his short-brimmed hat.

Garx shuffled back from the road with slow, deliberate movements, ensuring he remained behind the thick bush. Soon, the wagon would pass them, the opportunity lost.

What in hells is Rone doing?

He glanced across the road, but his soldiers had gone to ground. Invisible. Garx returned his attention to the wagon. The driver clicked at the horse and offered a few soft words of encouragement. Movement in Garx's peripheral vision caught his attention. Rone sprinted out of cover, leapt onto the driver's bench and delivered a powerful kick to the man's midriff, which lifted him clear of the bench. He sailed through the air and landed on the far side of the wagon. One of Garx's men dashed out of cover and finished the man struggling to his feet with a powerful sword thrust.

Rone pulled back on the reins, slowing the animal to a halt and applied the wheel brake. He looked at Garx and winked.

Smart arse.

The driver's body was dragged from the road and stripped of his clothes. The horse was coaxed to tow the wagon off the road and out of sight. Rone parked it alongside the first wagon. Then the soldiers opened the rear canvas flap and inspected the contents of the supplies.

Garx stood, leaning against the wooden tailgate peering in at the pair of soldiers rummaging through boxes and ripping open hessian sacks.

"Any food?"

The soldiers paused and looked at their commander, grins splitting their faces. "It's all food, sir. Fresh bloody food."

"Thank the gods. Crack open a set of rations and let's eat our fill before we head on our way. It may be the last meal we eat in a while."

One of the soldiers threw a box towards the tailgate with a grunt. "Might be it's the last meal we ever eat, sir."

He lifted the box down and dumped it on the ground. "Where we're going, quite possibly."

* * *

Garx was the last to step up onto the tray of the wagon. He sat, eight soldiers at his back. He nodded at Rone standing outside looking up at him.

The King's Own warrior lifted a few boxes of supplies into place on the very rear of the tray, hiding the soldiers from view and making it look like the wagon was fully loaded with supplies. The view out the rear of the wagon disappeared behind crates, boxes and baskets of root vegetables not prone to fast perishing. Then he heard the canvas flap pulled down and tied in place.

Rone would then move onto the next wagon and secure a similar group of Huronian soldiers. For all the army would know, two supply wagons were making entrance into the encampment.

A cavalryman, wearing the bloodied clothes of the dead driver, sat on the driver's bench at the front. His click and gentle urges pierced the evening air. The wagon jolted a little, and it rumbled forward. A similar noise followed them and Garx knew the second wagon was underway.

"Damn that food was good," a gruff voice said. Then a soldier, presumably the speaker, broke wind behind Garx.

Garx sniffed the air. "It was. Strange though. I don't remember eating a fucking half-rotten ferret."

A few chuckles greeted his words. The original speaker hushed them with a hiss. "You all hear that?"

They fell silent, no noise breaching the darkness other than the wagon's creak or the horse's occasional snort.

"What?" Garx whispered.

"Listen carefully."

Garx closed his eyes, and then the same soldier broke wind, the sound like thunder in the enclosed space. "Ah, that's better, lads!"

"In the name of the gods!" one man roared.

A soldier dry-retched and groaned.

"You shit yourself, didn't you?" another asked.

Garx smiled and withheld a chuckle. Then the stench reached him. He closed his mouth and winced.

When the volume of the cannons and clamour of battle increased, the soldiers quietened, their demeanour more serious. The wagon lurched over a rock in the road, and the wheel slammed back onto flat ground on the other side of the obstacle, sending a jar straight up Garx's spine. He stretched his back, adjusted his sword to avoid the pommel driving into his hip and waited. The small group of soldiers remained silent, their good humour tucked away for the time being. They ignored the distant crackling scream of incoming enemy cannon shot, said not a word when the dull *thud* of the massive lead balls slammed into the ground. Listened to the shouts and cries of panic when the chaos of the enemy guns was fully realised. Then the next series of *booms* and another chorus of crackles, rapidly growing closer. All the while, in the background, the relentless wave of noise as the Huronian Army struggled to gain a foothold upon the walls.

Garx could now hear the clash of steel on steel or clap of steel on wood when an attack was thwarted by a shield. Soon, they would stop and it would be time to get to work. Or it would be time to die trying. One or the other.

A hand touched his shoulder. "Luck, sir," the man muttered.

"You too."

XI

Word spread throughout the highlands like wild-fire. Hushed whispers shared by villagers around crackling fires. A warlord had united the highlands and defeated one of the cruellest clans in living memory. He'd brought Firestorm to heal permanently. Maybe hurt them so bad they may never recover.

Tiny clans all over the highlands learned of the altercation and memorised Vyder's name. No longer was the Shadolian Highlands a land dotted with many individual tribes. They were now a nation. And the smaller clans wanted to see Vyder with their own eyes.

Vyder sat by the campfire, staring into the flames, vaguely aware of the coming dawn. All around him slept men and women from the various tribes who'd joined him. They hailed from the mainstay of the larger highland clans and had been with him for the long term. But much smaller ones had joined them, eager to travel south and join battle as a unified Highland Army. To prove just how powerful the highlanders really were.

Hyglak flicked a twig into the fire. "We'll reach the port this time tomorrow. Then we sail into fate's arms."

"No, my friend. Then we sail into history. Our story will be remembered for a thousand generations by both Wendurlund and Huronian alike."

"Fate is gentler than history."

Vyder nodded. "Aye, she is that."

Hyglak stretched his back and groaned. "How many do we have with us now?"

The assassin touched the black brooch around his neck given him by Agoth so long ago. "About seven thousand at last count. Made up from near a hundred clans. Some clans have contributed no more than five or six warriors."

"There is a tiny group, Clan Thunderstrike, who have no more than fifty souls in their entire clan. For them five or six would be a fair portion of their fighting force."

"Oh, you'll get no complaint from me, Hyglak. I appreciate every contribution, no matter how small. If the Huronian Army is not stopped at Lisfort, they'll be infecting Shadolia before we know it."

Something small and wet touched his leg, breaking Vyder's thoughts. Saigh sniffed his leg again. She looked up at him and wagged her tail.

"Good morning my lass, I see you are awake." He stroked her broad head. "And did you sleep well?"

Saigh licked her jowls, groaned and rolled on her back, tail still thumping upon the ground. "Aye of course you did." He patted her belly, and the tail thumping increased in speed and power.

Hyglak shifted into a kneeling position and stared out over Vyder's head. "More are arriving, my lord."

Vyder twisted. A small, dark smear, nigh-invisible in the dim light moved down the path towards the outer edge of the encampment. Another small highland clan come to join the Great Highland Army as it was now known.

You are becoming quite popular, little brother.
I see you are awake, Gorgoroth.
We should go to greet these little humans.
Aye.

He repeated Gorgoroth's suggestion.

"A fine idea, my lord."

The pair stood. Saigh did likewise, she leaned into Vyder's leg, a soft growl rumbling in her throat. She stared at the distant newcomers, occasionally sniffing the air. Some people roused, packing away their bedrolls or preparing breakfast. Others tended to their horses, cleaned and oiled weapons while a group sat talking quietly amongst each other. When Vyder and Hyglak passed, they called soft greetings so as not to disturb others still sleeping around them.

They reached the outer edge of the highland camp. Vyder raised a hand. "A fair morning to you," he called.

"And to you," the woman leading them replied. She was tall, perhaps thirty summers of age with flaming red hair and piercing green eyes. She wore deerskin clothes, a round shield strapped to her back and sword sheathed at her hip. A spear was clutched in her right hand. About forty men and women followed her. The strip of tartan cloth worn diagonally across her chest was adorned with a colour pattern with which Vyder was unfamiliar.

She noticed Vyder staring at the tartan. "We hail from Clan Wolfmoon."

"I've heard of your clan." He gestured at the clan colours. "But I've never before seen your tartan. If I'm not mistaken you come from a small number of islands north of Shadolia?"

"You'd be correct. The Katakornias is the group of islands from which we originate." She placed the butt of her spear upon the ground and leaned upon the haft. "Judging by your oddly coloured eyes, you'd be Vyder?"

"Aye. Welcome to the Highland Army. This is Hyglak, one of my officers."

Hyglak nodded.

She stepped forward and offered her hand. "I'm Hilka, and this is a quarter of my fighting force." She gestured at the warriors behind her. "Our swords are yours. We wish to be part of the Great Highland Army."

"You have my thanks, Hilka. Have you eaten?"

"We haven't yet broken our fast, no."

"Then you are welcome to join us."

And then there were forty more. It appears my forest, or the Waning Wood as you call it, will be safe after all.

Vyder turned from Hilka and led them back towards the encampment.

Don't be so sure, Gorgoroth. We may be too late for all we know. Don't misjudge the Huronians either, they are a force to be reckoned with.

Are they human, little brother?

Of course they are.

Then they can be killed. The smile was evident in Gorgoroth's voice.

* * *

An hour after the sun had broken the horizon and commenced its ascent towards afternoon's summit, the Highland Army broke camp and marched south. Vyder sat upon Storm, Henry and Ahitika beside him on their own destriers.

"Father will be proud of what you have done, Vyder," Henry said.

"You will take the credit, Henry. I will tell him as much as well."

If he still lives when we arrive.

King George would not be king of Wendurlund for ever and it was important to Vyder that the successor would be a friend to Shadolia.

Ahitika grinned. "Yes, you take credit, I take Huronian scalps." She patted the varied lengths of hair tied to her belt. "Three more Huronian scalps and my initiation is at an end. I will be a fully-fledged Kalote warrior."

The thunder of a horse's hooves broke their chatter and Rafe reined in beside him.

The berserker stood in the saddles and looked over his shoulder. "A fine sight, my lord!"

Vyder did likewise. The road upon which they marched was only wide enough for four horses to walk abreast. The Highland Army wound along the path as far as the eye could see. At the rear were the smaller clans. Many of them did not own horses, so proceeded on foot. But he'd heard no complaints from them. Vyder expected none, either. The Highlanders were a warrior race, bred to a more robust quality than their southern neighbours.

A solitary, distant bagpipe droned a sad lament about the end of days. The tune picked up pace and volume when Thros was introduced and how the goddess saved the world from certain doom. Vyder sat in silence, listening to the song, his thoughts dampened and body relaxed. He stared at the horizon where a group of clouds hung suspended. A second bagpipe joined the first, and then another added its voice. Soon a small army of pipes were in perfect tune, blasting songs old and new across the marching army. Many warriors added their voices. Some simply enjoyed the musical stories woven by the haunting instruments.

"Anything from Bulvye?" Rafe's voice jarred Vyder back to the present.

He blinked and focused upon the dark-haired chieftain. "Nothing yet, no."

He'd sent Bulvye ahead of the army almost a week ago in order to advise Clan Steelforge of the approaching Highland Army and to prepare longships in order to transport them across the Shadolian Sea.

A furious glint entered the berserker's eyes. "Mayhaps he has met with ill fate." He stood in the stirrups again and shielded his eyes from the sun, staring to their front as if he'd be able to see his friend. "Should I go after him, my lord?"

"It would be pointless, Rafe. We'll be at the port in another few hours, anyway."

Rafe dropped back into his saddle. "Aye, lord, you are correct." He nodded. "We'll kill all of Steelforge if he has met with death."

And I thought you were mad, Gorgoroth.

The nature spirit's laughter boomed in his mind.

"I'm sure he's fine, Rafe, and Thros willing, he'll have a fleet of Steelforge longships ready to take us over to Wendurlund."

Her name is Thoron.

Well, the highlanders call her Thros, so I'll call her Thros if it's all the same to you, Gorgoroth.

Rafe grunted, turned his horse, and galloped back towards his clan a half mile behind the front.

"Good talk," said Vyder.

"I like him," Hyglak jerked a thumb over his shoulder at the retreating berserker. "Madder than a cut snake, of course, but he's handy to have around in a scrap."

"Definitely."

A chuckle caught his ear. Henry and Ahitika were talking quietly to one another, riding so close together their legs brushed. The young prince leaned into her and whispered something at which she threw back her head and laughed.

Vyder smiled and returned his attention to the horizon in front of them. The clouds had moved slightly, but they appeared to be closer. Or was it his imagination?

He called a halt on several occasions to rest the horses and give those at the rear time to rest their feet and legs. When the sun reached its peak, he called a longer rest stop to give them time to prepare a midday meal. He left Storm to graze and walked through pockets of the army, stopping here and there to talk, to show his face, and remind them that their warlord was not disconnected from them. Vyder wanted them to know although he led them, he was still a highlander at heart.

When it seemed most people had finished their meal, he returned to the front, mounted Storm and called for those in the huge column following to do the same. Within five minutes the Great Highland Army was once again on the move, marching southward towards the port.

Three hours after the completion of their midday meal, they mounted a small hill leading down to the port. Vyder leaned back a little in the saddle so as Storm was able to easier maintain his balance. The bright blue of the Shadolian Sea swept out into the distance before them. Lining the port was a navy of longships. There must have been near seventy of them, rocking and weaving in lazy movements, slaves to the gentle, sheltered sea beneath them. Twenty or so were moored at the port's berth. The remainder of longships anchored out at sea, waiting their turn to navigate into the port in order to load their share of warriors.

"Gods above," Hyglak breathed.

Waiting near the berthed ships stood a massive group of who Vyder could only assume were Steelforge clansmen. From this distance it was difficult to see because they looked more like ants than people. A few tiny dark figures clambered across the decks of various ships, tugging on ropes, carrying supplies below deck, or climbing up the pole mast to check on the sail. One man mounted a horse and thundered up the hill towards them, a thin cloud of dust trailing him.

Saigh ran forward a few steps, staring at the oncoming horseman and barked, her tail a blur.

"Yes, it's Bulvye isn't it, lass?" Vyder called to the war hound.

She looked back at him, whined and then refocused upon Bulvye. She offered a high-pitched bark.

Bulvye swept by Saigh, leaned down, passed a hand along her back and reined in beside Vyder. "Steelforge were open to your offer, lord."

"So I see. Well done, my friend."

"Their chieftain has spread his sailors thin. There are only ten men per ship, so he's expecting that our people can help where and when required."

"Makes sense. Once we're down there, I'll call a meeting with the officers so they can disseminate the instructions to the army."

Bulvye nodded. "Aye, lord. There'll be one hundred warriors per ship." He checked Saigh was not beneath the hooves of his horse and turned the animal around to face the same direction as the rest of the army.

Vyder nudged Storm forward, and the army followed like some giant caterpillar. The bag pipes petered away to silence.

"Hyglak, gather the officers and bring them to the front."

"Aye, lord."

Inside a few short minutes Vyder's officers surrounded him. On one side, in between he and Henry, rode Rafe. "It is good to see you, Bulvye!" Rafe grinned, leaned over in his saddle and slapped the man on the shoulder. "I worried for your life. I feared I would have to put Clan Steelforge to my sword." The berserker laughed at his own words, but Vyder knew the man wasn't joking.

Bulvye shrugged. "It was easier than I thought."

On Vyder's left was positioned Hyglak and on the far side, upon a huge highland warhorse sat the flame-haired Bordrog. Just to the assassin's front was Holrik.

Vyder explained the situation and that the highlanders would be required to assist the Steelforge sailors if necessary.

"If they require us to row, bind your hands!" Bordrog said. "Make sure you pass the word, we'll be useless at the other end if we can't even hold a weapon because our hands are blistered and bleeding."

Rafe scoffed. "It'll do your soft skin good to grow tough." He held up his own hands. "Do these look like they need binding?"

Bordrog rolled his eyes. "Don't come complaining to me when you're holding back tears, and the skin of your palms are peeling off the flesh."

"Bah! Won't happen." The berserker chuckled.

The jaw of the red-haired chieftain bulged. "Maybe not, but spread the word to your section of the army anyway, Rafe."

"Aye, I will." Rafe sniffed. "It's pointless, though," he muttered.

Bordrog swung in his saddle. Vyder held up his hands. "Knock it off, you two. Rafe, pass Bordrog's advice on. It is good thinking."

Rafe nodded and grunted. "I will, lord," he said finally.

Vyder took a deep breath. "I'll speak with the Steelforge chieftain, but I'm of the thinking that the mounted highlanders should be loaded with their horses first. It'll be less waiting around for the animals."

"And the horses?" asked Bulvye, flashing a grin.

The group chuckled.

"Well, well, if it isn't Vyder Ironstone." It was Snarri. The Steelforge chieftain pointed at him. "And I see you're wearing a tartan again." His brow creased. "Although I'm not familiar with the colours."

Vyder smiled and dismounted. He clasped hands with the warrior. He gestured to the tartan. "It is the colours of many of the clans who've joined us. More are joining us all the time, so it doesn't represent all of our tribes. But most of them."

Snarri looked beyond Vyder, his eyes sweeping along the huge column snaking up the path and disappearing over the distant hill. He whistled. "The Great Highland Army, eh? It lives up to its name. Bulvye said the Huronians have invaded Wendurlund and put Lisfort to the sword."

"Aye."

"If that's true, then the Wendurlunds deserve nothing more than the justice they're being dealt at the moment." Snarri held up a hand. "But I do understand the concern that the Huronians will target us next if Lisfort falls."

Vyder looked at Ahitika nearby. "Or the people of Kalote. Either way, Shadolia will eventually be their target."

"Aye, I agree, Vyder. The Huronian king is a madman worth stomping on while we have the chance."

Hyglak nudged his horse forward. "With respect, but he is to be addressed as lord."

Snarri grinned and shrugged. "Then lord it is."

"*Lord?* You're still nothing more than a half-blood

pretend highlander," one of the nearby Steelforge clansmen shouted.

Vyder looked beyond Snarri and stepped past him. Snarri had been astute enough to know that Vyder was a different man than the highlander who set off all those weeks before.

The Steelforge clansman, a tall warrior, pushed forward of the throng, defiance shining in his eyes. Vyder didn't slow. He drew his sword.

"And what are you going to do, *lord?*" he grinned, crossed his arms, and waited.

Vyder swung the sword in a blistering side cut, the sharp steel whistling through the air. The blade took the man's head clean off. The headless corpse dropped to the ground like a ragdoll, his head striking the wood with a dull *thud*.

"What in the gods?" a nearby Steelforge clansman shouted. He rushed forward, knelt by his comrade, and unsheathed the man's hand axe, pushing the wooden haft into the dead hand so that the deceased highlander might have a weapon on hand when he made his journey across The Frost River.

Vyder bent down and cleaned the bloodied sword upon the fallen man's shirt, then sheathed the weapon. Stooping again, he snatched the hand axe from the dead fingers and gripped a fistful of hair from the decapitated head. He lifted both high for all to see.

"Both of these belong to me now!" he roared.

Blood dribbled from the severed neck down the underside of Vyder's forearm.

Pushing the haft of the hand axe into his belt, he grabbed the dead man's shirt and dragged him towards the water's edge. "Make way!" he shouted at the throng of Steelforge highlanders. Rafe, Hyglak, and the other officers were by his side. He knew if any Steelforge highlander attempted to block his progress, or attack him, his men would kill them without question.

"This man will have no ceremony!" The headless body painted the wood of the port with a trail of blood. "He shall know no peace." The cluster of Steelforge sailors stepped aside, making a corridor down which Vyder pulled the corpse. First, he threw the head out into the sea, then kicked the body over the edge, where it met the water with a splash before sinking from view.

Vyder turned back to the group of Steelforge sailors and pulled the hand axe free of his belt, the smooth, wooden haft felt good in his hand. "Does anyone else wish to question my authority to lead this army?" he gestured at the massive column of highlanders wending away from the port, making their way down towards the water's edge.

"No, lord," one man muttered.

"What was that?" yelled Rafe. "I couldn't hear you."

"He said, 'No, lord!'" shouted Snarri. "And if any other Steelforge highlander disrespects the warlord or the clans under his command, I shall take your head myself!"

* * *

The first twenty longships were loaded with smooth efficiency, the handful of sailors aboard each giving instructions to the newcomers. Vyder seated himself in front of an oar and as Bordrog suggested, used a long piece of thin leather he found draped over the oar to wrap his hands. The leather was soft, and the dry stains of sweat and blood gave an indication it was well worn. Other men and women did likewise. Within minutes, each oar sported two people.

One Steelforge clansman stood at the far end of the oar-room. "Wait for my instruction! When I say to push through, you highlanders seated on the right feed your oars through the slots and push against the jetty. You will be pushing us away from the port and out to sea. When I say to pull, you on the right start rowing forward, you on the left reverse row. Understood?" The highlander strode along the narrow walkway separating the two oar banks. "This is important. Are you sure you all understand? Any mistakes and we'll end up in the port and sinking."

He was met with an army of nodding heads.

"Good! Then the command all forward will be given. Can you guess what that means?"

"We all row forward?" one woman said.

The Steelforge warrior shrugged. "Pretty simple isn't it?"

"Anchor comin' up!" a distant voice shouted.

The Steelforge sailor walked back the way he'd come. "Prepare yourselves!"

A wooden *clunk* echoed through the hull.

"Anchor's up!"

"Push through!"

Vyder grabbed the oar and push it through the oar slot. He slid it no more than a few feet before it connected with the wooden uprights of the Shadolian port and its progress stopped. He gritted his teeth and pushed against the resistance. The oar slid further through the slot, and the longship moved inch by inch away from the jetty.

"Push harder!" the sailor roared.

Those seated on the right side of the bank of oars

leaned into their work, the longship's sideways movement gaining speed. Sweat beaded Vyder's brow, his arm's burned and ached.

Take a rest, brother.

Gorgoroth stood, gripped the oar and pushed with inhuman effort, propelling the longship fast away from the port. The standing Steelforge warrior stumbled and almost lost his balance. He watched Vyder with a new respect.

"Well done, my lord."

Vyder sat down and coughed to alleviate his itching throat. His hands and feet tingled.

Thank you, Gorgoroth.

Always welcome.

"And pull!"

The oars dipped into the sea together, and the longship surged through the water. The highlander on the upper deck controlling the steer-board, turned them to the south. Soon twenty longships in close formation cut through the sea towards Wendurlund. Behind them, another twenty moved towards the port at a snail's pace, preparing to berth and accept more members of the Great Highland Army.

And do your animals still live, Gorgoroth?

Thoron! What a pleasant surprise. I know not. Time will tell.

Sweat streamed down Vyder's face and his muscles screamed, but he was working in a rhythm with the others seated in the oar-room. The resistance against the water started to ease and his shoulders recovered.

"I could do this all day!" one highlander laughed.

The Steelforge man, still standing at the front of the oar-room was frozen in place, his brow creased.

The next stroke Vyder performed felt as if the sea

wasn't there at all. It was then he heard the strong wind above decks, blustering across the longship.

Then allow me get you home, my friend, so that you might save them.

"Drop the sail," a distant voice called from above. "Thros be praised! The wind is behind us, drop the sail!"

* * *

Tork's hand slammed upon the table, his open palm hitting the polished wood with a *crack*. "We are useless caged in Lisfort. We should be out there!" he shouted. "Fighting the Huronian Army."

"Tame yourself, Commander Tork! This is the third time you've asked this of the king and thrice he has returned the same answer," Jad roared, a thick vein threatening to burst from the skin of his neck. Jad's face was flushed, his dark eyes flashing with fury. "And do *not* presume to raise your voice to me!"

The muffled *boom* of Wendurlund artillery vibrated through the War Room bringing both men to silence.

Jad sighed and dropped his quill into the pot of ink near his hand. "The king has decreed the King's Own is to remain inside the city to assuage any assault should the enemy breach the walls."

"I already know this," Tork clenched a fist, his knuckles turning white. "I've known this for the past two days."

The adviser pushed the parchment away from him and shrugged. "Then you have your answer, Commander."

Tork's eyelids met, and the room disappeared from view. He relaxed his hand and inhaled a deep breath of cool air. "Jad, we will lose this fight if we're not careful.

The soldiers holding the walls are doing a fine job, but they can't hold out forever. They'll be overwhelmed by sheer weight of numbers." His eyes peeled apart, and the room came back into view. "Come on, Jad, you know this. Surely?"

"There are more than twenty thousand enemy soldiers out there. What do you expect two thousand King's Own warriors to do?"

Tork leaned back in his chair. "More than you think. We are an unconventional force by our very nature. We are highly mobile and can strike fast and hard where it's least expected. My soldiers can do nothing cooped up in Lisfort. Nor can we do much on horseback when...*when* the eastern wall falls."

Jad spread his hands. "I'm only passing on the wishes of his grace, Tork."

"The wishes of his grace will mean nothing when Lisfort is burning to the ground and her people slaughtered or put to the chains of slavery."

Tork pushed his chair away from the table and stood. "I understand that, Jad. But the wishes of one man, king or no, may be the end of our empire. Sometimes what King George doesn't know about won't harm him. It's easier to seek forgiveness and all that."

Jad shrugged. "You've been given your answer. Be satisfied with it."

He turned away and strode towards the door.

"You must remain inside the city's walls by royal decree, Tork!" Jad called after him.

He ignored the king's adviser, pulled the door open and stepped through. The pair of King's Own guards standing either side of the entrance came to attention with a simultaneous *thud*.

"Tork, your unit will not leave Lisfort!" Jad

shouted. "Do you understand me?"

He allowed the guards to close the door behind him. He smirked. "Watch me."

***

The wooden floor rattled with each bump in the road, the wagon's axles groaning and squeaking. Apart from the occasional gentle words of the driver, the men were silent, each lost in his own thoughts. Garx sat cross-legged concentrating on the rhythmic song of the cannons. After each deafening volley, the distant sound of battles upon the walls of Lisfort returned. Without any view of the battlefield, it was difficult to know exactly what was taking place. All he knew was that the Huronian Army had gained a foothold upon the eastern wall and were fighting hard. If they could push beyond the wall, they'd be able to open the Eastern Gate and allow entrance for the rest of the Huronian Army.

If that happened, Lisfort would fall in a day, or if the madman king used his forces to his advantage, in a matter of hours. That couldn't be allowed to happen. Garx stretched his legs out, the dull ache in his thighs subsiding. If the Huronian Army was victorious, Garx and his soldiers would be put to death, not to mention the soldiers under his command, who had chosen to journey home to retrieve their families and spirit them away to safety.

"Think we'll make any difference?" one man asked from further back in the wagon.

"We're about to find out," another answered.

Garx cleared his throat. "One way or another the mad king must be stopped. We'll die if he wins, anyway. So, we may as well attempt to thwart him while we can."

"But, sir, why not simply run far from here? We'd be safe."

Someone swore. "You turnin' coward, Harton?"

"No!" Harton said. "Just a simple question is all."

"And what do you think will happen if Lisfort falls to the mad king?" Garx asked. "You think they'll pack up their army and simply march home?"

Silence met him in the darkness.

He crossed his legs again. "No, of course they won't. They'll bring Lisfort into subjugation. Then they'll take over all Wendurlund and we'll be safe nowhere ever again. Except perhaps Shadolia." Garx leaned back. "So, we *could* run for now and be safe for a time. But we'd always be looking over our shoulder. You want to live like that?"

"No, sir," Harton muttered.

"So, we have a choice then. Do nothing and leave the Army of Wendurlund to deal with the assault on their own. Or, few as we are, try to help where we can."

His words were met with muttered agreement.

The driver called a greeting, his voice muffled a little by the canvas canopy.

"Here we go," a man whispered just behind Garx.

"What you hauling?" a gruff voice asked from outside.

The men piled in the wagon were silent. Garx was unaware he'd been holding his breath until his chest started aching.

"Rations for his majesty's army," the driver said in a cheery voice.

"Food! Sounds good to me," the gruff voice wavered on the edge of a chuckle. "What happened to your shirt? That blood?"

"No, my wife was experimenting with ochre and

spilled a heap on our clean clothes. Haven't been able to get the damn stain out. This is the least stained shirt I own."

A long pause followed. "Is that so?"

"On my life."

"Jump down, my lad, show me what you're hauling."

The driver's bench creaked and a *thud* resounded. "Fine. You don't believe me?"

The question went unanswered.

Oh, this isn't good.

Garx rest a hand upon his knife, his fingers encircling the deer horn hilt.

To their credit, the soldiers sitting behind Garx remained silent, although the soft whisper of a knife unsheathed from a rabbit hide scabbard teased his ears. The rear canvas flap was untied and loosened. The driver whistled a tune as he worked. Cracks of sunlight appeared between the tiny gaps between the ration boxes.

"There you go. See?"

The wagon rocked a little. "Looks good to me," the guard's voice was much louder than it'd been, leading Garx to think the man had climbed up into the back of the wagon. One of the boxes slid clear, and Garx ducked down. "What have we here?"

He withdrew his knife slowly.

"That's preserved beef," the driver said.

"My favourite." The box slid back into place casting the interior of the wagon into darkness once more.

"Really? Too salty for me."

"You grow accustomed to it, waggoneer. You don't train in the field as often as us, I suppose."

A smirk touched the edges of Garx's mouth. The Huronian Cavalry, an elite unit, deployed with far more regularity than the foot sloggers.

"True. That's something for which I'm thankful."

The wagon moved again, and the driver's bench creaked for a second time.

"Well, on you go. Let's get these troops fed, shall we?"

"My thanks!" the driver called. He clicked, the leather reins snapped, and they lurched forward.

Garx let out a breath and sheathed his knife.

"On you go!" the guard bellowed behind them, probably allowing the second wagon to pass through.

"Gods that was close," a whisper broke the silence.

"I may need to change my drawers," another soldier muttered.

"Keep it down," said Garx.

The chatter died to silence.

"Over this way, driver!" someone yelled in the distance.

They changed direction, and the road became even more pot-hole riddled. A ration box slid clear and landed on Garx. He cursed and pushed it away, rubbing his arm.

"Gods, who cut this road, a brain hurt blind man?" someone hissed.

"I don't think we're on a road," another said, his voice juddering with each vibration.

Garx rolled his eyes. "What makes you think that?"

His arse left the wooden floor, and then slammed back onto the hard surface again. Garx winced and adjusted his position. A grunt exploded from behind him.

"Bloody hell, feels like a giant just pounded my arse cheeks!" a soldier grumbled.

"Shut up, Barkod, no one wants to hear what you got up to on the weekend."

Suppressed laughter came from all sides.

"Shut it!" hissed Garx.

Apart from a soft chuckle, silence returned once again.

"Alright driver, pull er up beside the others. Good to see you! Come and share a drink with us, then we'll help you unload."

"Sounds good!" the driver called.

The wagon ground to a halt, and the squeak of the wheel brake pierced Garx's ears. The soldiers remained quiet and seated, listening idly as the horse was unhitched from the wagon and led away to join the other animals, which were probably kept in a makeshift paddock somewhere in the nearby vicinity.

"We moving, sir?"

"No," Garx whispered.

"Beggin' your pardon, sir, but when are we makin' a move? My arse has gone numb."

"Then you shoulda stayed home on the weekend, Barkod," a soldier whispered.

"Shut it!" Barkod retorted, with a chuckle.

"We wait for nightfall. Then we move. Make yourself comfortable."

* * *

Rone sat upon the grass in the middle of the makeshift paddock. Two of the Huronian cavalry horses stood close by, dozing. The others were grazing in the distance. He cleaned his blunderbuss of blackened powder, ensured the hammer was oiled and moved with ease. He pushed a lightly oiled rag down the barrel, then loaded the weapon and placed it away. Withdrawing his musket, he unloaded it and commenced the cleaning process. When he'd finished, he inspected it for damage or malfunctioning components and when he was satisfied, he loaded the weapon. Sheathing it in the leather holster attached to the saddle at his feet.

Cleaning weapons was always somehow cathartic to Rone, almost as if he was in some kind of meditative trance. Using a small amount of oil on a cloth, he rubbed the spear's tip until it shone. When he was satisfied, he tested the edge with a thumb for sharpness. Shifting closer to his saddle, he delved into one of the smaller pouches and came away with a sharpening stone. A few strokes on each edge returned the spear head to a lethal sharpness that would cut through almost anything. Placing both the stone and weapon away, he stood and stretched.

Hot air blew against his cheek and he turned to face the horse sniffing his skin. The dark, intelligent eyes watched him, ears flicked forward waiting for a command. The animal knew something was about to happen, knew that before long he and those of his herd would be called to work once more. Rone stroked the soft nose.

"Eat while you can, my friend."

He ran a hand along the shining flank. Other than a few words, Rone couldn't speak the Huronian language fluently, so he'd been unable to travel with Garx and his team of cavalrymen. Someone had to look after the horses left behind, so it was better for him to sit out the infiltration. When the time came, it would be up to him to make the horses ready so that he and his new comrades could make an escape.

If their mission was successful, they'd have dealt a

deadly blow to the Huronian Army, but it'd be at the expense of their identity. When night fell, he'd gather the horses together and tie them to the long hitching line in the centre of the temporary paddock, ready for the signal that would mean the small group of cavalrymen were withdrawing to his position. But for now, most of the animals ate their fill.

When the sun sank in the west throwing a pink-streaked orange blanket across the sky, he led each horse to the hitching rope placed in the centre of the rudimentary paddock. He saddled each one, going through the same process with each. He pulled on the pommel, ensuring the girth was tight and that when the destrier's owner stepped into the stirrup, the saddle wouldn't slip sideways. He moved from one beast to the next, checking all the tack in the same way. The last war horse to accompany him was his own. Lifting the leather saddle onto the back of his destrier, he tightened the girth, tested it, tightened it a little more and then waited.

"What will be the signal?" Rone had asked of Garx.

"Oh, you'll know," the officer had replied, a smile touching the edges of his mouth. "By the gods, you'll know."

* * *

Night came, but it felt like a damn eternity had passed. The sound of battle had quietened, and the cannons from within Lisfort were mute. Although their hungry maws would be fed again with the dawn, no doubt. Garx moved into a crouch and felt his calf spasm. He sucked a breath in through clenched teeth and attempted to stretch out his leg. It seemed to help spirit away the pain. The crunch of boots across the forest floor towards them gave him pause. He knelt back down and pain shot through his calf, but he ignored it.

"Lads!" a voice whispered from outside the wagon. "Hey, lads!"

"We're here," Garx replied through clenched teeth.

"I convinced the others we'd unload the wagons in the morning."

Garx swivelled to face the rear of the wagon, and the group of soldiers behind him hidden within the blackness. "Time to move."

With the help of the soldier who had driven them into the midst of the enemy camp, they unpacked the ration boxes and one by one, leapt down. Some of them lay stretched out upon the ground, others rubbed aching legs or backs.

Garx ignored the aches in his body. "Right, get yourselves together." He took a few minutes to stretch out his calf.

The group of soldiers, reinforced by those in the second wagon, gathered around.

"We need to get out of these uniforms," said Garx.

"They have a number of dead placed in groups over there, sir," the former driver pointed away into the forest.

An army of campfires were visible beyond the forest where the Huronian military had setup for the night. In the far distance, groans, cries and screams of pain rent the night, no doubt where medics and surgeons were working to remedy the injuries of those wounded in battle.

"What uniforms do the dead wear?"

The driver grinned. "It appears we've been transferred to the artillery, sir."

Garx smiled. "Artillery it is. Lead the way."

The driver saluted. "Sir." He strode away, the group following him.

Within an hour all of the members of Garx's unit had replaced their cavalry uniforms with those of the dead artillery soldiers. They buried the cavalry uniforms under a blanket of long dead leaves and made their way back to the wagon to eat their evening meal and prepare for the coming day. It was going to be challenging, not to mention dangerous.

* * *

Garx awoke before dawn. He relieved himself against a tree, then strolled back to his soldiers. Many of them still slept. A few of them stirred. He stretched his back and rubbed a growing ache out of his left leg. His stomach was no longer willing to be ignored, and he levered the lids off several of the ration boxes in search of something palatable. While they hadn't commenced their jobs as would be gunners in the Huronian Artillery, he could afford to be picky in his choice of meal.

Using his fingers, Garx ate the cold meal straight out of the ration box.

"What you got there, sir?" one soldier whispered, squatting beside him.

"Preserved bacon and boiled eggs," he managed between mouthfuls.

The man didn't look impressed and went in search of something else.

Garx shrugged. "Suit yourself."

When he'd finished eating, he downed a long pull of fresh water. He stood, enjoying the feeling of a full stomach and walked around those still deep in slumber, waking them with a gentle kick, tap, whisper, or shake of the shoulder. When his soldiers were sitting in a group eating and muttering between themselves, the eastern sky displayed a few spears of pink tinge.

He knelt beside one young man and tapped him on the back. "What's wrong, lad?"

"Not hungry, sir."

He recognised the voice from the darkness of the wagon. "You have to eat, Harton."

"I really don't feel like it."

"You might not, lad, but your body needs it. We may not eat a decent meal again for some time, so make the most of it."

Harton sighed and delved into a ration box.

"Good man." Garx stood and swept an eye over his soldiers. They were all eating. One of them talked in hushed tones while those close by chuckled.

"What in the name of the gods is happening over here!" someone yelled.

Garx whirled and spotted a man of medium height striding towards them. He was well-built and dressed in the dark garb of the Huronian Artillery. Dark stains coloured his face.

"Breakfast!" he replied walking to intercept the newcomer's advance.

"And who said you could break your fast?"

"That little runt of an officer. I've forgotten his name." Garx held up an open palm. "I mean no offence."

"You mean Brogat?"

"Brogat, yes that's the man."

The newcomer halted before Garx and nodded. "Very well. You artillery or bombardiers?"

He hadn't taken much notice of the Huronian Artillery during his time in the army. He'd been too preoccupied with the endless missions and tasks given to the Huronian cavalry.

What the hell's the difference?

He didn't want to refrain from answering for too long so simply chose one. "Bombardiers."

"Well, you'll know that now it's your time to shine. We've done our bit and paid for it as well." He gestured towards a destroyed cannon nearby. "So good luck to you bombardiers and I hope you give those bastards sheer bloody hell!"

"Of course we will!" Garx grinned. He hoped it looked convincing.

The newcomer nodded again, glanced over Garx's shoulder at the men staring back at him, turned on his heel and walked away.

"Sir?" someone hissed.

Garx looked back at the group of seated cavalrymen. "What?"

"What was he talking about?"

He shrugged. "No idea." He strode back to them. "I guess we'll find out soon."

XII

Graff sat against the wall, or what remained of it, one leg bent up, his forearm resting on his knee. He stretched his other leg out and rubbed at the muscles of his thigh. He was bone weary. His arms ached, his legs were heavy and salt from dried sweat made the skin of his face itchy.

Half of the soldiers who'd been tasked with holding the eastern wall had now fallen. With dusk setting, the enemy had withdrawn from their efforts.

And taken their damn ladders with them, thank the gods.

Come the dawn, though, they'd be back. Of that he was sure.

"How long can we hold, Sarge?" a young man asked from nearby.

Graff looked at the soldier lying flat on his back, hands resting on his chest. Long dried blood spattered his armour and his sword lay upon the ground beside him.

He sucked a breath in through his teeth and turned his attention to the darkening sky. "Maybe another day. Perhaps two at best. But no more."

"We're weakening them, though," the young warrior said in a tone of voice that gave way to the fact he was attempting to convince himself.

He shrugged. Graff'd been soldiering long before the lad sprawled out nearby had been born. What the boy spoke was the truth, to a point. "Just not fast enough," he added. "Unless something changes, we can hold for another day or two."

The smell of burnt wood and charred flesh still hung in the air, as did the ear-piercing screams of Huronian soldiers when the boiling oil had been poured onto the ladders and then set alight. Brutal, but effective. Graff tried to shake the inhuman noise from his mind, but the screeching of dying men continued to bounce around his skull.

"The mess is open!" a voice yelled from far below.

"Half you lot head on down to eat. The rest of us will stand guard. We'll swap once you've finished."

"I'm not hungry, Sarge," a man muttered. "I'll stay up here."

"Reckon I'll vomit if I smell roast meat," a second man said.

Graff pushed himself to his feet and winced. He used all his inner strength to stop crying out when his left leg cramped. "Go and eat!" he roared. "You might not feel hungry now, but you'll thank me for it tomorrow. Get some food in your guts, even if you don't feel hungry!"

Some of the soldiers around him grumbled or tutted, but they did as they were told. He turned away from the lines of warriors descending from the wall down various lines of steps, which were still intact and leaned against the wall. Where there had once been merlons and crenels, there was now raw, jagged rock. Parts of the rampart itself in some cases had been cut away by cannon shot.

"One more day," he muttered. "Then they'll be inside the city."

"And we'll be fighting from house to house and street to street," a voice finished.

He noticed an officer standing beside him.

"We won't be, sir."

"Oh?" one eyebrow arched. "And why not, Sergeant? You planning to go somewhere?"

"No, sir. We'll be dead."

The eyebrow descended, and the officer's eyes widened a little. "Yes, well, I'm off to eat."

"Help yourself, sir." He watched the man's departing back. "Might be it's your last supper," he muttered.

*   *   *

Several horses snorted, and one pawed at the cobbled street, impatient and eager to be underway.

"Open the gate," Commander Tork said.

The guards glanced at one another. One took an interest in his own feet. The other held Tork's stare. "We can't, sir. We were warned that the King's Own might try this. The king has ordered that —"

"Open...the...gate."

"But, sir, we'll be whipped within an inch of our lives and be out of a job, not to mention homeless."

Tork nudged Might forward. The war horse complied. His large, shod hooves clopped upon the road until the seventeen hand animal stood directly in front of the guards. One guard took a step back.

"There's an enemy out there that will very likely breach the walls soon. When they do, you'll die screaming on the end of a sword." A slight smile touched his lips. "Although on the upside, you won't have to worry about being homeless. Tell your superior you were overpowered and opened the gate under duress."

The guard sighed and nodded. "Alright, sir. I'm not happy about it, but I'll do it."

"I shall take the blame if anything is said. Well," he smiled, "if we return, that is. Open the gate as quietly as you can."

The drop bar was craned clear of the massive doors. Then, inch by inch, the Northern Gate creaked open. When it was wide enough to allow three horses to ride abreast, the guards ceased from opening the gate any further.

He pushed Might onward, and the destrier walked through and out into the darkness, closely followed by Roland, Tork's bugler. Tork was careful to maintain the pace at a steady walk. At a gallop, or even a trot, one thousand horses would be heard by the Huronians on the eastern side of the city. Noise tended to travel further after the sun retired.

When the group of King's Own were clear of the city, the gate was closed, and the drop bar craned gently back into place. Tork turned his soldiers to the east, following the city's wall around towards where the battle had raged for the past few days. King George would not be happy, to say the least.

If I survive, I'll probably be whipped within an inch of my life and cast from my home.

He sniffed and relaxed in the saddle.

Oh well, too late to turn back now. When the enemy is at the gates, one does not hide inside and hope for the best.

The stars blotted the dark sky like an infinite black, glistening blanket. The formation of mounted warriors hugged the wall. Tork drew them to a halt in the blackness out of sight of the enemy. Come dawn, they'd hit the enemy like a battering ram.

* * *

The eastern sky was gun-metal grey, the sun's advance still more than an hour away. Yet onward they came, their war cries piercing the once still, cool morning air. He guessed it'd take the Huronian foot sloggers a good five minutes to reach the eastern wall. By the time they'd placed their ladders, commenced climbing, and reached the wall to join battle, the sun should be kissing the horizon.

I can only hope, anyway. I don't fancy fighting in the dark.

"Look lively, lads!" Graff shouted.

The closest soldier, sprawled out on his side snoring was unlucky enough to receive a sharp tap with Graff's boot. "Up, lads!"

Other soldiers whose turn it'd been to stand watch were also shouting warnings. Exhausted warriors were ripped from slumber. Sharp, fear-filled reality settled into place where carefree sleep had once resided. Swords were drawn, some given one last sharpen. Spears were readied, clubs leaned against what remained of the wall and tired, aching muscles stretched.

"Ready yourselves!"

They'd changed their tactics a little. The ladders were pushed clear of the wall immediately, giving the Wendurlund troops precious time while wearing out their Huronian adversary. The soldiers holding Lisfort's eastern wall no longer possessed the energy to push clear ladders teaming with climbing enemy warriors.

Graff and the remaining sergeants and officers much preferred their men withhold their waning energy for combat. The overwhelming barrage of war cries pervading the eastern side of the city gave evidence as to how close the enemy were to commencing the day's fighting. A ladder came soaring through the darkness, slammed against the stone, bounced once and then settled.

"Push it clear, lads!" Graff roared.

A team of men gathered on one side of the ladder

and pushed it away. The thing slid sideways, gathering momentum and smashed into another which had just been placed against the wall. Both went shearing clear of the wall and disappeared into the darkness below. Ladders up and down the wall all met a similar fate, aside from one, which had managed to wedge in a large crack in the wall. Despite their attempts to lift it clear, the Wendurlund troops could not budge it. With each passing minute, and with more enemy warriors beginning the long climb, the ladder became heavier, until the soldiers stopped their attempts to lift or push the ladder. Preparing instead to fight their fast approaching adversary. The head of the first Huronian was shattered like a melon with a sickening strike from a club. He fell away, limp. The next died with his neck half-severed. The third and fourth met with the wrong end of a razor-sharp spear head. But the fifth, a bull of a man wielding a double headed battle axe, smashed Wendurlund soldiers clear and jumped onto the rampart. His comrades oozed over the ladder and followed him in quick succession like ants.

Graff watched the fight further down the wall and couldn't help but admire the axe-wielding brute. He appeared unstoppable. A loud *thump* and vibration moving up through his feet brought his attention back to his section of wall. The ladder had reappeared in its original position.

"Send it back where it came from!" Graff shouted.

Again, the ladder was pushed sliding from the wall. The eastern sky was seared with shades of pink and orange, dim light now gracing the land with its presence. He stepped onto the jagged, raw edge of what had once been a crenellation and peered down the sheer drop of the wall just forward of his boots.

Lucky heights don't bother me.

The Huronian army, visible as a dark smear upon the ground below, continued to bellow their war cries. Intermittent musket shots rang out, but they were nowhere near Graff. Besides, a musket ball drilling a hole through his skull might not be such a bad thing given events to come, if the wall was breached. The ladder was lifted back into an upright position, and then flung forward, towards where Graff stood. He jumped back onto the rampart.

"Prepare yourselves! The ladder's back!"

It bounced onto the wall, and soldiers immediately teamed around it, attempting to push it clear, but it wasn't budging. Graff darted forward, leaned out over the wall. The Mortals were back. The red cloaked demons were already halfway up the ladder and ascending at a run.

"The Mortals are coming!"

"Gods save us," one man muttered.

A young soldier nearby licked his lips, eyes wide, sweat shone upon his forehead.

"Remember their name!" Graff roared. "They are called The Mortals. It means they can be killed!"

The first red-cloaked Huronian burst into view and was upon the wall readying to jump onto the rampart, sword in hand, when Graff's blade cleaved his head clear of his neck. The corpse dropped from view.

"You see?" Graff shouted.

The second Mortal leapt clear of the ladder and met Graff's boot, sending him out into thin air. Graff's sword skewered the guts of the third.

"They can die!" he panted. "Nothing to be scared of."

Shouting war cries of their own, the warriors under

Graff's command surged forward to stand shoulder to shoulder with him.

***

Dawn announced its presence with a smear of pink across the horizon. A glow of light in the centre of the eastern skyline told of the sun's advance. Tork pushed Might on and trotted clear of the King's Own formation, halted and turned back to face them. He stood in his stirrups, held his arms above his head and made slow, deliberate hand signals.

I am the centre. Single file. No war cry. At the trot.

Tork slammed his helmet's visor down into place with a metallic *clap*. His soldiers followed suit. He guided Might around to face away from his troops and urged the war horse into a trot. Roland accelerated alongside him, bugle in his hand.

He didn't need to cast a glance over his shoulder to know his soldiers were following in a tight formation. They negotiated further around the slow curving wall, and the noise of battle increased in volume with each hoof fall. Tork stood in his stirrups and signalled *canter*. Might's stride lengthened, and the ground beneath slid by at speed. Remaining standing in the stirrups, he noticed bright hues of orange had joined the pink, and the first hint of the blazing ball kissed the horizon, sending shards of light spearing through the sky.

The battle hove into view around a bend in the city's wall. Tork drew his arm back and snapped it forward. *Full charge!*

Might's gait chewed up the ground, blankets of grass blurring by beneath Tork's feet. He swivelled in the saddle to ensure Roland was with him. The bugler was on his left flank. His soldiers snaked out behind him in single file, thundering across the terrain, a light cloud of dust rising into the air. The enemy infantry assaulting the eastern wall of Lisfort hadn't seen the unit of King's Own. They were focused on taking the wall, the noise they were making drowning out the powerful drumming the thousand war horses galloping to their rear created.

Tork guided Might within a stone's throw of the enemy soldiers. When he was sure those behind him at the front of the single file formation were in line with the enemy, he turned to Roland and rotated his visor up, clear of his face. "Rolling blunderbuss! Right flank!"

Roland lifted the instrument to his lips. The piercing call of the bugle cut through the battle's clamour. Blunderbusses roared their fury one after the other. The King's Own warriors only opened fire once they'd reached the enemy troops laying siege to Lisfort. The continuing staccato of blunderbuss sent relentless lead pellets amongst the Huronian adversary. Men fell in their scores and as the blunderbusses persisted, the attention of the Huronian Army was turned to their rear. Tork stood in his stirrups to see over the heads of those who followed immediately behind him. The very last King's Own soldier galloped into view, pulled his blunderbuss into his shoulder and squeezed the trigger, then swerved away from the enemy soldiers, to re-join his unit.

"Swine array!"

The bugle sang the command, and the long, snake-like single file formation changed shape as if by magic. Those at the front slowed to a trot, the middle proceeded at a canter, and the very rear continued in a gallop. In less than a minute the swine array had circled around and was facing the Huronian infantry. They advanced at a walk, allowing the war horses to recover their breath.

Tork, who'd remained standing, stared at the distant Huronian Army proper still deployed far from Lisfort. No response to the presence of the King's Own had yet been employed. He'd expected a cavalry charge at the very least.

"Sir, they're charging!" the bugler's voice forced him to face the front again.

What looked to be near five thousand infantry ran towards them, possibly in the hopes of surrounding and destroying Tork's outnumbered unit.

"Split four!"

Roland gave the command, and the swine array formation turned instantly into four neat formations, each row twenty soldiers across and ten deep.

"Halt! Reload!"

There was no use wasting energy when the enemy were doing just that to close the distance. When the charging enemy, roaring their war cries and insults were halfway to the King's Own unit, the blunderbusses were reloaded and holstered. Warriors sat upon their destriers in silence, watching the approaching threat.

"Muskets! Hold fire!"

Men pulled clear their muskets from the leather holsters just forward of each soldier's right knee and laid the weapon across saddle pommels. Index fingers were placed outside the trigger guards, and the wait continued. The enemy mass was now almost upon the grossly outnumbered King's Own unit. In stark contrast to the Huronian charge, the only noise issuing from the King's Own formations were the occasional snort or nicker of a horse, a stamp of a hoof here, the swish of a tail there. Tork appraised his warriors and pride swelled. They held firm, fear finding no resting place.

He turned his attention to Roland. "Fighting withdrawal!"

The piercing bugle call cut through the wall of noise issuing from the Huronian charge. Muskets opened fire from the front rank of each formation. The rank broke left and right, galloping clear to re-join at the rear of the formation to commence reloading. The new front rank opened fire and copied the move, clearing out of the way so the next rank could bring their weapons to bear upon the charging enemy. Every five seconds, eighty rounds were sent hissing through the air to embed in soft, Huronian flesh.

Within two minutes, more than one thousand enemy soldiers were dead or dying without the loss of a single King's Own soldier. Running out of ground between his unit and the closing enemy charge, Tork's hand was forced. "Withdraw! Gallop! Swine Array!"

The four separate formations conducted an about turn, accelerated into a gallop and merged into a single swine array formation, leaving a trail of dust where they had once stood. The exhausted Huronian soldiers stopped to regain their breath.

Cool wind streaked through Tork's open visor and teased his sweat plastered head. He guided the charging swine array around to face the isolated group of enemy infantry. Far from the wall of Lisfort and the safety of their comrades, and too far from the main Huronian force, they'd be easy pickings for the King's Own.

"Arrow-head!"

Tork, Roland following directly behind him, formed the tip of the arrow-head, diagonal left and right flanks snaking out behind him.

"Battle at will!"

Tork reached forward, lifted clear his blunderbuss and pulled it into his shoulder. Clenching his thighs tight to Might's body, he ensured he didn't slide clear of the saddle. He stared down the metal sights at the closest Huronian soldier hunkered down behind his shield, wide eyes peering at him above the flat piece of metal. Tork squeezed the trigger. The cloud of gunpowder spewing from the wide barrel and thundering *boom* occurred simultaneously, leaving his ears ringing. Then he slammed into the enemy ranks, Might hardly slowing. The warhorse bit one man's face clear of his skull, trampled another, barged a third out the way to fall beneath Roland's destrier.

A rolling thunder and crackle of blunderbusses and muskets echoed out behind him.

"OBRAGARDA!"

The rest of the arrow-head formation struck the Huronian force like a sledge hammer. Tork dropped his blunderbuss into the leather holster and withdrew his spear. He stabbed it into a soldier's neck and ripped it clear of the terrible wound before Might galloped by the dying man and momentum could sweep the weapon out of Tork's hands.

Leaning forward in the saddle, he thrust the spear, the weapon burying deep into a warrior's gut. Tork twisted the haft and dragged it clear, the smooth wood almost ripped clear of his grasp. A long-handled axe swept straight for him. The heavy weapon bounced from his helmet with a metallic explosion that snapped back his head and left his ears ringing. The dent the axe head left pressed against the skin of his forehead.

Clamping the spear between his thigh and the saddle, Tork pulled clear his musket, aimed it one handed into the mass of enemy soldiers teaming in front of him and pulled the trigger. He dropped the spent weapon back into the leather holster and took the spear back up, stabbing it down at a wounded soldier on his knees. The spear slid through the soldier's leather armour and pierced the skin of his shoulder and embedded deep into his chest, parallel with his spine.

Gritting his teeth, Tork stood in the saddle and used both hands in an attempt to drag free the spear, but the wooden haft was carried clear of his grasp. Might continued in a headlong gallop. Clenching his legs tight about Might's body, he leaned to one side in the saddle, allowing the enemy sword to cut through thin air beside his shoulder. Retrieving his blunderbuss, he reversed the weapon and used the butt stock as a club. The thick, polished wood shattered a soldier's face, bounced from a steel helmet, smashed the wind from one man, fractured an arm, and sent teeth sky bound. Then Might pushed clear of the Huronian force. Tork tilted forward in the saddle, clamping a hand to the pommel to right his balance. He heard the *thud* of Might's double-barrelled kick connecting with a Huronian skull.

He grasped his visor and pushed it upward, but it was stuck. Using two hands, he pushed the visor up and away from his eyes. With a stubborn screech, the visor shifted, opening his field of vision from the narrow horizontal slot he'd been enjoying up to that point. The dent left by the axe had ruined the hinges of his visor. Turning in the saddle, relief washed over him. Roland was still galloping nearby, although a deep gash in his forehead had allowed a river of blood to wash down his face.

"Swine array!"

The bugle's high-pitched tune sang its song, and the arrow head formation morphed in shape, leaving the beleaguered enemy force fast departing behind them. Tork led the formation around in a wide arc.

"Canter!"

The command was given, and the horses were allowed a little reprieve. The formation continued to come about towards the isolated group of Huronian infantry in the near distance. Tork estimated at least another thousand or so had met their maker. Close to half their number had been systematically taken out of the fight in short order by the King's Own unit. Overconfident of their abilities, and realising the King's Own hadn't yet finished with them, the enemy group turned and fled towards Lisfort and the safety of their comrades.

"Trot!"

Again, the horses slowed.

"Walk!"

Breathing slowed and tired muscles regained strength.

"Sir, cavalry to our rear!" shouted a man from the back of the swine array formation.

"Halt! About turn!"

The rear rank became the front, and Tork galloped around the swine array, closely followed by Roland, to re-join the front once more. In the distance, trotting towards them came a large force of Huronian cavalry.

This fight won't be so easy.

* * *

Graff kicked the soldier from him and dashed forward, shoulder barging him over the wall and into thin air, where he fell to his death. The advance up the ladders and onto the wall had slowed since the appearance of the King's Own on the open plain below.

The next Huronian didn't appear for some moments, but when he did finally negotiate the last few rungs of the ladder and attempted to scramble onto the wall, a spear stabbed through his throat. He slid from view, gurgling, arms flailing.

The eastern wall was now teaming with soldiers of the Wendurlund Army, cheering and shouting in support of the galloping formation of King's Own. They'd dealt serious damage to the enemy mass at the base of the wall, but with many thousands of foot soldiers now in pursuit, even with their speed and agility, Graff feared the mounted warriors would be soon overrun.

How wrong he'd been. He found himself shouting and cheering with the soldiers around him and watched in awe as the outnumbered King's Own went through the chasing enemy throng like a dose of salts. The blob of enemy infantry, isolated and alone far out on the flat plain fled for their lives. They ran towards the wall and their comrades. When the King's Own formation turned back to prepare for another charge at the enemy soldiers, the Huronians had started climbing the ladders in earnest.

No longer were they fighting to take the wall, they were attempting to overrun the rampart to escape the advance of the deadly King's Own.

"Gods, here they come again!" Graff roared. "Prepare yourselves!"

The enemy soldiers streamed up the ladders and made purchase on several sections of the wall. Fear caused them to fight with angry, wild, carefree abandon and it made them dangerous. Almost each enemy troop fought like some crazed berserker from Shadolian myth. Where one fell, three more replaced him.

Graff ducked a sword stroke, stabbed a soldier in the midriff and stepped away to prepare for the next assault. His boot landed in a pool of blood, and he slipped upon the slick stone, almost losing his footing. On each side of him battled men under his command. They fought well, accounting for at least two, or perhaps three enemy dead per soldier. But it wasn't enough to win the day.

He blocked a spear thrust, grabbed the wooden haft before the weapon could be withdrawn and pulled the enemy soldier to him. Graff's sword slid into the man's chest, grating against rib bones. He pulled the spear free of the dying man's grip and hurled it back at the enemy host spewing over the ladders and onto the rampart. It took a man in the shoulder. Pain lined his face, and he fell from view. In a slight gap between the advance of the Huronian Army, a giant force of enemy cavalry advanced towards the unit of King's Own. He would dearly liked to have watched that battle, but his men were fighting for the wall. They battled for their city and their families, but it was still not enough.

The day is lost.

***

Garx pushed one of the mortars, aided by a small team of his soldiers. On either side of him, small groups of the former Huronian cavalry, now dressed in the uniforms of bombardiers, strained against the weight of their mortars. The weapon was placed upon a set of miniature wagon wheels for easy manoeuvrability upon the battlefield. One of the wheels butted against a rock, and the forward momentum stopped.

"Easy to move, my smelly arse!" roared one of

Garx's troops.

"Shut it!" Garx panted. "And push!"

The group heaved as one, and the wheel edged over the rock with the speed of a snail. Then they were underway again. The thunder of hooves overcame the squeak of the axle, indicating the mortar commander was inbound.

"You lads, speed it up! The rest of the mortar crews are already in position!" shouted the officer galloping past.

"Good for them," one man growled.

The mortar itself was nothing special. The barrel was short. Were it resting upon the ground, the entire weapon would only reach an average man's hip. But the maw of the barrel was huge, the mortar rounds requiring two soldiers to lift them into place. They eventually trundled the mortars into position, in line with the other bombardier teams.

"Took your bloody time!" someone yelled from down the line.

"You don't, I hear," one of Garx's soldiers roared.

"Oh? Says who?"

"Your wife!"

Laughter washed over the area.

Garx darted forward and grabbed the soldier by the arm. "That's enough," he hissed. He turned. The man his soldier had insulted was storming towards them. "You!" he yelled, pointing at the red-faced bombardier. "Forget it and return to your post. Now! I'll take care of this."

Garx leaned closer to his soldier, his face murderous, teeth bared. "Do you know how hard I had to work to stop from laughing?"

"Sorry, sir."

"Good work, lad, keep it up." He slapped the soldier on the back of the head, his face still lined with mock fury.

"Shut your mouths before I have you all whipped!" the officer roared. "Change elevation to five notches. Target is the city of Lisfort!"

"What does five notches mean?"

He and his soldiers observed the other crews and how they adjusted their mortars.

"You down the end there!" the officer withdrew his sabre and pointed it at them. "Stop dawdling and get to work! Adjust your elevation!"

"Right, something to do with this wooden pin, here." Garx took hold of the peg and pulled it clear. The mortar barrel swivelled upward, and he pushed the pin back into place before it could rotate any further. He made a show of kneeling behind the mortar, closing one eye and lining it up with the distant city. "Looks good."

"Does it, sir?"

He shrugged. "We'll find out soon," he whispered.

"Load!"

Powder was poured down the barrel, but Garx realised too late that the more experienced bombardiers were measuring the powder in a small bucket, prior to pouring it down the barrel. Pairs of soldiers lifted the massive, lead mortar rounds into the barrel.

"Ram!"

Two or three soldiers were required to use the thick ramrod. Five or six rams was enough to pack the ball into the pillow of powder beneath.

"And fire!"

Garx pulled a thick mitten on and snatched a red-hot poker from a fire nearby. He held the glowing tip to the fuse, which sputtered to life with a soft hiss. He shoved the poker back into the coals. An earth-shattering *boom* exploded from the mortar and the round scudded through the sky and disappeared from view. He didn't need to be an expert to know the heavy lead ball had overshot its target by a large distance. A series of much tamer *booms* echoed down the firing line, and the rounds soared through the sky heading straight for Lisfort.

The mortars either side of Garx, crewed by his soldiers roared to life, their noise causing the ground to vibrate. The elevation peg on one mortar tumbled free, and the barrel swung on its axis. The huge ball shot through the air in the opposite direction of the target, whilst gun smoke from the second blotted everything from view.

"Just what in the hells is going on down that end of the firing line?" the officer shouted.

Garx tried to reply, but all that left his mouth was a series of coughs.

"One round went *behind* us! Another overshot Lisfort. What were you aiming at? The fucking moon?"

"Apologies, sir!" Garx said. "Won't happen again."

"No, it bloody won't. Same elevation, apart from you lot down the far end. Fix it up! Powder!"

Garx knelt behind the mortar, not that he could see anything through the cloud of gunpowder still pervading the area. "Bring her down!" he said loud enough the officer would have heard. Although he did not change the elevation. "Right, that's good. Get her loaded."

More powder fed the hungry mortars, shot was rammed into the bed of powder. Fresh fuses were pushed into the recess and hot pokers were held in place until soft, sibilant hisses indicated the mortars were about to speak once more.

And speak they did, all save those of Garx and his soldiers, those mortars screamed, vibrating the ground with their powerful voices. All three rounds rocketed into the air, overshooting Lisfort by a good margin.

"You bombardiers at the end of the firing line, cease fire!"

"Apologies, sir," Garx said. "But we don't have measuring buckets. We're guessing."

"Runner. More powder canisters!"

"Yes, sir!"

Garx rubbed his eyes, attempting to alleviate the grit of burnt gunpowder from settling there. "And, sir?"

"What!"

"We're out of powder."

"What do you mean?"

"Does he want us to draw a picture?" a soldier whispered from close by.

"Shut it!" Garx said.

The cloud of gunpowder cleared, and Garx was able to make out the mounted officer trotting towards them. The man brought his mount to a halt nearby.

"How much bloody powder did you use? You're lucky not to have blown yourselves up!" he held his forehead in his hand. "Fine, send a few of your men to retrieve more powder. The rest of you continue to fire on Lisfort at your will!"

"Yes, sir!"

Garx waited for the officer to turn away and make his way further down the line in the opposite direction. Then he grabbed the closest soldier and dragged him closer. It was Harton. The soldier's face was painted black with spent gunpowder.

"Harton, you and I are going to find where the

powder storage is —"

"And bring more back, sir?"

"No," Garx said. He pointed at the poker buried in the glowing coals close by. "I'm going to blow the fucker up."

He strode through the thinning cloud of gun smoke, blinking the sting from his eyes. He cleared the haze, the poker clenched in his gloved hand. He took a deep breath of fresh air and let it out in a rush. If life had taught Garx one thing, it was that to move with confidence and a purpose made one invisible. It was a good five-minute walk to the powder wagons, so there was a chance they might be intercepted before they reached their target. Advancing with meek steps and a posture worthy of the defeated drew attention. He glanced behind him. Harton followed, staring at the ground, his wide eyes darting around in search of some enemy that had not yet presented itself.

"Head up, lad! Back straight, look ahead, stop trying to mimic a stunned fish."

"Yes, sir. Sorry, sir. I'm no hero."

"Harton, a hero is only ever a person who learned to harness their fear. You can't be a hero without fear, or even terror lining your guts first."

That helped. The young lad pulled his shoulders back, and his wide eyes narrowed.

"Good lad."

The mortar line roared to life behind them and more rounds were sent spearing through the sky to wreak havoc amongst the city of Lisfort. He spotted a supply wagon in the distance. The canvas canopy had been stripped from it, leaving the curved bare wooden ribs visible. On the floor of the wagon were stacked barrels of gunpowder three high. Two soldiers sat by the rear wheel, talking.

"That's as far as you need to come, Harton. Stop behind this tree and don't advance any further. You hear?"

"Sir!"

Garx left his soldier behind. The mortar officer, too preoccupied with his firing line, hadn't noticed that Harton had stopped, or even that Garx carried an implement that could blow the powder wagon to kingdom come. Heat continued to bleed from the poker, and the metal's tip, once bright red, was turning a dull orange.

He walked past the pair of soldiers deep in conversation and stepped up onto the rear of the wagon. The axles squeaked under his weight, drawing attention from the two men nearby.

"Oi!" one shouted. "You can't bring that thing here." He pointed at the smoking poker, the orange glow fast fleeing the tip. "You'll bloody kill us all!"

Garx jumped back down and walked to the pair. "Oh shit, forgot I had this with me," he waved the piece of steel in front of him. "I just need a barrel of powder."

The closest soldier stooped and picked up a cow hide parchment and quill. He lowered the feathered end of the quill in Garx's direction. "Fine, but place that bloody poker on the ground first."

Garx grinned and continued advancing. "But of course."

He lunged and buried the poker in the soldier's neck, the hot steel skewering his throat in one clean, sizzling stab. He withdrew the makeshift weapon, allowing the mortally wounded man to drop to his knees, clutching the terrible, cauterised wound at his throat. The second man withdrew a pistol, levelled it, and fired.

Agony exploded in his guts, and Garx stumbled backward. He lost his balance, fell on his arse and spat blood. The soldier reloaded the pistol with rushed, nervous movements. He held a hand to his abdomen and winced as fresh pain lanced his body. His fingers came away painted with fresh, bright red blood.

A dull, staccato of *thuds* closed upon Garx and for a moment he thought it might have been the mortars firing once more. But movement caught his attention. Harton sprinted past him and shoulder barged the soldier making ready to fire a second shot. The young cavalryman followed his adversary to the ground and opened the soldier's throat with a knife.

All strength fled Garx, and he fell to the ground, staring up at the clear sky. A small cloud drifted above at a lazy speed. The pain in his midriff was easing, but then numbness was spreading throughout his body, so it was little wonder. A shadow blocked out the sun and Harton stood above him, blood dripping from his hands.

"Sir!" the young lad's voice was muffled. "Sir, you have to get up."

Garx attempted to sit, but fresh agony exploded, and he groaned. The mitt was ripped clear of his hand as was the poker. The young cavalryman stepped beyond him and climbed onto the wagon. Garx held up a hand to try and stop his soldier. He should be the one to die, not Harton. The lad had so much of life left to live. Detaching the lid of the closest barrel, Harton threw it clear. Taking the poker in a reverse grip, Harton held the smoking tip above the exposed powder.

He tried to speak, attempted to tell Harton to stand down, but all that left his mouth was a stream of blood. Ignoring the pain spearing his body, Garx forced himself into a kneeling position, gathered his legs beneath him and stumbled to his feet. Blood dripped from his chin, soaking his armour. He held an open hand at Harton and shook his head.

"What in the gods are you doing?" a distant voice boomed. "Stop!"

Harton glanced up, caught Garx's eye and grinned. "So long, sir. It was a pleasure."

"Hang on, lad!" he said. He spat blood and groaned as new agony attempted to double him over. Climbing onto the rear of the wagon, he pushed with his legs, forcing himself onto his stomach on the wooden floor. He cried out, blood oozing from his lips. "Help me up," he said, the words bubbling upon his lips.

Harton grasped him under the arms and assisted him to his feet.

He grabbed the poker, and Harton resisted. The skin of his hand sizzled, and the stench of burnt flesh filled his nostrils. The pain was intense but was nothing compared with the gut shot slowly taking away his life.

"Give it here," whispered Garx.

Harton released his grip.

"Get you gone, boy! This is my task and mine alone."

"But, sir."

"Go. Now!"

The young cavalryman cursed and leapt down. He ran towards the distant mortar line.

A wracking cough took hold of him, each one forcing blood spraying from his mouth. "And Harton!" he shouted, wiping his mouth with the back of his hand.

The lad stopped, turned.

"Fight hard, boy!"

Harton touched a clenched fist to his chest. Then he ran.

"Fight hard," he muttered.

"Oi! You! Stop this instant or we'll shoot!"

He ignored the voice, as he did the musket blasts. One round took him through the calf.

He looked at the small group of guards, his lips stretched wide in a death's head grin. "I'll see you in hell."

The guard commander raised his pistol. Garx rammed the smoking poker deep into the gun powder barrel.

* * *

Graff slashed, stabbed, blocked, kicked and punched. His soldiers fought just as hard, their ferocity unmatched by their adversary. The Huronian Army continued to push onto the rampart, though. He kicked one man's knee out from under him, and the disabled opponent disappeared beneath the feet of his comrades.

A series of deep *booms* echoed out over the plains, and the rounds, much larger than the previous cannon balls, streaked high above the heads of those battling for the wall. Graff only caught a glimpse of them out the corner of his eye. The massive balls of lead were heading into the deep heart of Lisfort, where they would, no doubt, smash apart buildings and cause fresh chaos.

The next warrior leapt at Graff, forcing the sergeant back. The rampart was only ten yards wide, so he was aware to maintain his balance and not stumble too far towards the rear edge. To do so would see him fall to his death. Clenching a fistful of the Huronian's chain mail shirt, he dragged the man close, clamped his teeth onto his ear, and bit down until he felt the gristle give way. The man's high-pitched scream exploded in

Graff's ear. He threw his enemy away and spat clear the appendage. Stepping forward, he rammed his sword into the man's guts, withdrew the blade, and met the next attack on the forefoot.

What sounded like a god striking a bass drum rolled over Lisfort. The stones beneath Graff's feet vibrated with such force he lost his balance. He'd heard stories told about earth quakes, but he'd never experienced one. His back hit the rampart's hard surface and his breath left him in a rush. The sword went skidding from the safety of his fingers. Opening his mouth, he breathed in, but no air filled his chest. He noticed almost all the warriors had lost their feet, as well.

Rolling onto his knees, he stood and darted the few yards to his fallen weapon, scooping it up. Desperation flooded him, and he attempted to inhale again. This time fresh, cool air quenched him. He stabbed one warrior attempting to clamber to his feet, hacked a head clear, kicked another from the wall. He stared over the mass of soldiers still finding their feet and noticed a thick pall of spent gun-powder sweeping the distant Huronian army blotting the infinite camp from view.

He grinned, brought down his sword in a merciless arc, and another head was swept clear of a neck. "It appears their comrades blew themselves up! On your feet, lads!"

Many of the soldiers under his command were already standing and taking the fight to their adversary anew. A high-pitched sound cut through the sky and a series of loud blasts rent the air. The Huronian soldiers so close to taking the wall backed away. Some even climbed onto the ladders and descended towards the safety of the ground below, shouting and pleading with those beneath to do the same. A war cry erupted soon after. He knew it well and relief washed over him.

The King's Own sprinted onto the rampart. There must have been near a thousand of them. They slung their blunderbusses, withdrew their muskets, and fired again. The bugle spoke, muskets were slung, and spears appeared in the hands of the elite warriors. And they charged.

"Rally!" Graff yelled. He didn't take the time to notice if his soldiers had obeyed, but ran at the Huronian soldiers in front of him. Where there had been arrogant confidence, now only fear shone in their eyes. They backed away to the safety of their ladders.

Amazing how one small unit could have such an impact on a force outnumbering the defenders. Less than ten minutes and the Wendurlund Army were the only ones standing upon the wall. Another noise, gentle at first, gathered in volume. The incessant wailing soon drowned out the screams of the wounded and groans of the dying. The new sound was coming from the north.

He gestured at the soldiers around him "You lads stay here! Defend the wall if those bastards return. I'm going to check on what's approaching from the north."

He sheathed his sword and jogged along the wall, brushing past clusters of troops, leaping over bodies. He almost lost his footing in a pool of coagulating blood.

"Make way!" he shouted.

"Shit, sorry Sarge."

On he ran, ignoring the ache in his lungs. His thighs burned and with each boot fall his ankles shot pain up his shins. He burst clear of the furthest flank of the Wendurlund defence and pushed on. Graff followed the slow curve of the wall that would, in time, lead to the Northern Wall. The wailing was louder, piercing his ears. He slowed, the pants of air clearing his mouth turning to a chuckle and then a laugh.

I haven't heard that sound in years!

A thunder of boot falls slowed behind him.

"What's that gods awful sound, Sarge?"

Graff's arms dropped to his sides, hands slapping his thighs. He looked up at the sky, and his laughter boomed.

Graff turned to the panting trooper nearby and clapped a hand onto the young man's shoulder.

"I take it you've never heard bagpipes before?"

He pointed to the north, the soldier's gaze following. The trooper's eyes bulged, and he took a step backward.

Silhouetted against the northern horizon stood a mass of people in an extended line. There must have been five thousand of them. Some were mounted, many were not, but they were all armed. In front of the host was a mounted warrior. By his side was a war hound that looked to be half the height of the destrier. Nearby, a Kalote woman sat without saddle upon her horse. Mounted beside her was a soldier. And not just any soldier. Graff grinned.

I'd know that armour anywhere.

"Prince Henry's back!" shouted Graff. "And he's brought a bloody highland army with him!"

✳ ✳ ✳

To be continued...

<u>Novels by Keith McArdle</u>

<u>The Unforeseen Series</u>

The Reckoning: The Day Australia Fell
The Unforeseen Series Book One

Australia has been invaded.

While the outnumbered Australian Defence Force fights on the ground, in the air and at sea, this quickly becomes a war involving ordinary people.

Ben, an IT consultant has never fought a day in his life. Will he survive?

Grant, a security guard at Sydney's International Airport, finds himself captured and living in the filth and squalor of one of the concentration camps dotted around Australia. Knowing death awaits him if he stays, he plans a daring escape.

This is a dark day in Australia's history. This is terror, loneliness, starvation and adrenaline all mixed together in a sour cocktail. This is the day Australia fell.

Aftermath

The Unforeseen Series Book Two

Mick and his family have returned home to the farm following Indonesia's withdrawal. But thousands of battle-hardened enemy soldiers remain hidden in the forests and hills, ready to strike when they are least expected. This fight will take Mick to the limit, and protecting his family will require all his strength and determination.

Jimmy and Spud lead a platoon through the Australian scrub on relentless guerrilla strikes. But when they find themselves outnumbered and outgunned, it might have all been for nothing.

A new Australia will rise again ... or will it?

Havoc

The Unforeseen Series Book Three

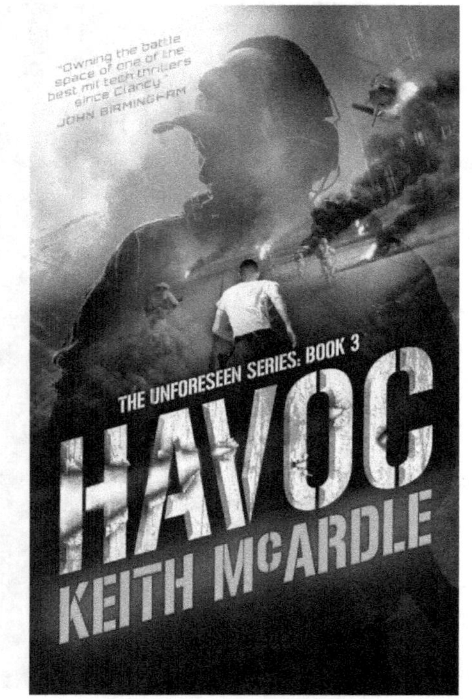

Australia has survived invasion.

Now the people of Brisbane must face a new, fearsome threat. At the same time, Ethan and his small team of specialist soldiers are tasked with a mission deep within the heart of Indonesia. When the mission goes horribly wrong, they have to fight their way out of a situation that may be their end.

Hiding is no longer an option.

<u>Stand Alone Novels</u>

Tour To Midgard

Tasked with a mission in Iraq, an Australian SAS patrol deploy deep behind enemy lines. But when they activate a time portal, the soldiers find themselves in 10th century Viking Denmark, a place far more dangerous and lawless than modern Iraq. The soldiers have no way back. Join the SAS patrol on this action adventure and journey into the depths of a hostile land, far from the support of the Allied front line. Step into another world…another time.

Short Stories by Keith McArdle

Assassin

Vyder Ironstone is an assassin with a troubled past. At the order of his king, Vyder must undertake his most dangerous mission yet. A mission from which he may never return. If he is successful, it might just be enough to alleviate war tearing the kingdom apart. The prospect of failure is not worth considering.

Against The Odds

Three veteran hunters are on the trail of a supernatural creature. It is a simple tracking mission, promising easy money. But things go horribly wrong and the mercenaries realise too late that they are facing one of the deadliest creatures known to man. Embroiled in a desperate fight for survival, their doom may well await them.

Ground Zero

Generations after a bloody nuclear civil war, the United States is not as we know it. The inhabitants of the Northern states live as normal, but the South, after being decimated during the Second Civil War, are a changed people. Nuclear fallout has stolen any vestige of humanity. When the aircraft carrying the President of the Northern United States takes an erroneous detour, it is shot down somewhere over the south.

Now Brek and his small team of Delta Force soldiers must infiltrate enemy territory to save the president. But outnumbered and with time rapidly running out, they will be hard pressed to fight off the onslaught about to surround them. Can they survive?

My Street Team. You guys and girls rock! Thank you so much for your support, advice and encouragement these past few years. It makes the journey that much easier.

Finally my Grimdarkling family, you know who you are, but you may not know how much you mean to me. I don't use the word 'family' lightly either. Your encouragement, humour and sometimes blunt advice has been a breath of fresh air.

Now...onwards!

ACKNOWLEDGMENTS

They say it takes a village to raise a child. A novel is similar. My name might appear on the cover, and although I wrote the novel, there is a small army behind the scenes who are responsible for making the end product as presentable as possible.

Thanks to my amazing wife, Simone, who didn't once ever doubt my passion for this craft. She has been my biggest supporter and advocate. Simone has always been there through thick and thin, pushing me on when I needed it. She's watched my six from day one and never once hesitated in voicing her support. I'm one very lucky man. I love you to bits, babe.

To the true friends, and there are too many to list here, your support means so much to me and helps steel my resolve to ensure characters like Vyder still walk the land.

Pen Astridge, my cover artist, is a true graphic design master. In my opinion, her skill is unrivalled and I hope she chooses to continue to work in the graphic design industry for many years to come. Thanks for another amazing cover, Pen.

Nothing is ever too much for my editor, Tim Marquitz. He takes everything in his stride and gets the job done with speed and efficiency. Although his writing hand must be sore from using his red pen so much. Thanks for running your eagle eye over my work, Tim.

Once again, Dean Samed of Neotsock, thanks for providing the photograph of Karlos Moir.